Serendipity Green

Serendipity Green

by

Rob Levandoski

THE PERMANENT PRESS
SAG HARBOR, NY 11963

Library of Congress Cataloging-in-Publication Data

Levandoski, Rob
     Serendipity Green / by Rob Levandoski
        p. cm.
     ISBN   1-57962-063-9
     I. Title.
     PS3562.E8637S47 2000
     813'.54--dc21   99-39277
                                      CIP

First printing: April, 2000

THE PERMANENT PRESS
4170 Noyac Road
Sag Harbor, NY 11963

To Manoucher Parvin, for his friendship, the little Ghiradelli chocolates, and for lending me Pirooz.

PART I

"How happens it that in the United States, where the inhabitants arrived but as yesterday upon the soil which they now occupy, and brought neither customs nor traditions with them there; where they met each other for the first time with no previous acquaintance; where, in short, the instinctive love of country can hardly exist—how happens it that everyone takes as zealous an interest in the affairs of his township, his county, and the whole State, as if they were his own?"

Alexis de Tocqueville
Democracy In America, 1835

1

Green.
Yellow.
Red.

The cars on South Mill stop. The cars on Tocqueville go.

It is only fifteen past six, but this being February, and this being Ohio, the sky is already the purple-black of frost-bitten toes. An unimpeded prairie wind is driving the snow horizontally.

One of the cars stopping for the new traffic light at South Mill and Tocqueville is an American-made Japanese luxury sedan. It is the kind of car you'd expect someone like D. William Aitchbone to be driving: Sensibly pretentious. Benignly authoritarian. A muted pewter paintjob worthy of the car's hefty sticker price.

Unlike the other denizens of Tuttwyler, Ohio, squashed bumper-to-bumper at that new traffic light, fat flakes of horizontal snow befouling the windshields of their minivans and sport utility vehicles like squirts of gooseshit, D. William Aitchbone is not the least bit impatient. He likes the new traffic light. Likes it fine. Likes the growth and prosperity it symbolizes.

The more cars that traffic light traps the better. Stuck flies on the spider web of progress.

Fourteen years earlier, when he was fresh out of Cleveland Marshall College of Law, there hadn't been a light at South Mill and Tocqueville; nor at North Mill and East Walnut; nor at Church and West Wooseman. Tuttwyler then was a village of just twenty-two hundred, a musty old quilt of a village draped over criss-crossing state routes that went ostensibly nowhere. Then eight years ago the long-awaited eastern leg of I-491 was completed, making Cleveland and its spreading suburban miasma a doable commute. Developers descended on the farmers living east, west, north and south of the village, making them offers

9

they'd simply be nuts to wrinkle their noses at. Barns were bulldozed. Fence-rows plucked. Topsoil rich with a century's worth of cow manure was scraped and piled as high as ancient Indian burial mounds, so it could be trucked off, vomited into polyethylene bags, and then sold at garden centers for anything but dirt-cheap prices. After the farms were erased, hundreds and hundreds and hundreds of houses were built. Hundreds and hundreds and hundreds of expensive houses with to-die-for foyers, cavernous carpet-gobbling greatrooms, sunny gourmet kitchens, and too many bathrooms. Hundred and hundreds and hundreds of houses with big-nut-to-crack mortgages. Mortgages that required two incomes. Mortgages that required fatigued and sexless marriages. Mortgages that sooner or later required legal separations, restraining orders, divorces, custody fights, new wills, complicated codicils to old wills, and—bless the weak hearts of these mortgage holders—probate when they fell over dead from exhaustion, prenuptial agreements when they cautiously fell in love again. Yes. Big-nut-to-crack mortgages that required the ongoing services of a lawyer like D. William Aitchbone.

So D. William Aitchbone likes the new traffic light at South Mill and Tocqueville. Likes it fine. Stuck flies on the spider web of his personal progress.

But D. William Aitchbone does not live in one of the new subdivisions. No big-nut-to-crack mortgagor he. He is Old Tuttwyler. Original Tuttwyler. He lives in one of the coveted nineteenth-century Victorians in the original part of the village, just a hundred yards from where he now sits in his American-made Japanese luxury sedan, patiently drumming his fingers to a New Age CD, Yobisch Podka's lively *Insipientia.*

Red.

Yellow.

Green.

The cars on Tocqueville stop. The cars on South Mill go.

D. William Aitchbone drives through the intersection. He's spent the day in New Waterbury, the seat of Wyssock

County, expediting the end of one heavily mortgaged marriage after another. Through the horizontal snow goose-shitting his windshield he now sees his own precious house. It is a magnificent three-story Queen Anne, built in 1883 by his great uncle, John W. Aitchbone, the first of the Aitchbones to wisely give up tilling fields in favor of tilling the Ohio Revised Code. The house, as square and white as a new bar of soap, has dozens of dark green shutters, a wraparound porch with lacy scroll-sawn spandrels connecting the posts, a confusion of gables dripping with decoration, and a bell-roofed turret that rises up the side of the house like the proud old phallus it is.

He drives past his driveway. No dinner with Karen and kids tonight. Nosireebob. Tonight is too important for that unnatural ritual. Tonight—just an hour and thirteen minutes from now, in fact—is the year's first meeting of the Squaw Days Committee.

South Mill is Tuttwyler's most impressive street. One of the most impressive streets in the state. It is newly paved with historically accurate burnt-orange bricks. Wide slate sidewalks rise and fall over the roots of grand oaks and maples. And the Victorians! Sweet Jesus the Victorians! Impressive Queen Annes. Impressive steep-roofed Gothics. Impressive flat-roofed Italianates. Impressive Second Empires with cake-like mansard roofs. Equally impressive are the antebellum Greek Revivals, with their squat trian-gular pediments, intricate cornices, broad doors and stoic pilasters. And just as impressive as the Victorians and Greek Revivals are the square-jawed Prairie School houses. One of them, the one that D. William Aitchbone is passing now, was designed by Frank Lloyd Wright himself. There is also a sprinkling of early twentieth-century Tudors and colonials and capes, even a few arts-and-crafts bungalows built in the teens and twenties. Regardless of their age and style, all of the houses on this impressive street are painted the same clean soapy white as D. William Aitchbone's Queen Anne. And all have dark green shutters.

All but one house.

This house, a narrow two-story frame built on a shoe-string during the Great Depression, is not painted white. It is not painted at all. Just the sight of its raw, gray-brown clapboards, its filmy, shutterless windows, its sagging, leaf-filled gutters, its moss-covered shingles, its tilting porch and untrimmed beard of shrubs, sends a river of burning black bile into D. William Aitchbone's temperamental bowels. "Lazy bastard," he hisses through his thin lips. The lazy bastard is, of course, Howie Dornick, the owner of that paintless, shutterless, unimpressive two-story frame.

D. William Aitchbone reaches the village square and circles it, pulling into a parking slot in front of Paula Varny's Just Giraffes stuffed animal shop. He trots through the horizontal snow, stuffed leather attaché in hand, to the Daydream Beanery for a double cappuccino, lowfat zucchini muffin and a final strategy session with himself. The dressed-all-in-black counter girl, nose ring dangling above her blackcherry lips, punches his Coffee Club card; one more punch and his next cappuccino is free.

Despite the numbing dulcimer music sprinkling from the speaker box above his head, D. William Aitchbone's strategy session with himself goes well. At 7:25 he starts toward the library on the opposite side of the square. Except for the Daydream Beanery and the Pizza Teepee, all of the shops on the square are closed for the day, drifting snow barricading their sunken doorways. As he walks past the square's grand gazebo, he frowns at the huge red bows and plastic pine garlands still dangling from its roof. "What's that lazy bastard waiting for, Easter?" he hisses through even thinner lips, the lazy bastard once again being Howie Dornick, owner of the unpainted two-story frame on South Mill and the village's maintenance *engineer*.

When D. William Aitchbone reaches the library he does not head for the glass double-doors at the front of the old ginger-brown brick building, but follows the shrub-lined walk that leads to the back. He crunches down a set of concrete steps sprinkled with blue ice-melting pellets, to a windowless gray metal door. Stenciled across the door, in efficient, two-inch-high black enamel letters, are the words COMMUNITY ROOM. He takes the cold knob in his hand and twists it. He eases the door open, just a quiet inch. He presses his ear into that quiet inch. Inside, the other members of the Squaw Days Committee are just beginning to wonder if their busy new chairman will make it on time. "Maybe he slid off the road," Delores Poltruski worries to Katherine Hardihood.

"The D. William Aitchbones of the world never slide off the road," Katherine Hardihood says.

What better cue than that? D. William Aitchbone flings the door wide and blows in, like the winter wind that he is, brushing the snow from the shoulders of his epauletted, belted Burberry, the expensive trenchcoat he always wanted and bought for himself just before Christmas at the new mall at the I-491 interchange. "Not late am I?"

"I was afraid you slid off the road," Delores Poltruski says to him.

The new chairman of the Squaw Days Committee hangs up his Burberry and takes his seat at the head of the table. "Almost did a couple of times," he says, cleansing the committee with his perfected courtroom smile. "Everybody here then?"

Everybody is.

In addition to Katherine Hardihood and Delores Poltruski, Mayor Woodrow Wilson Sadlebyrne is there. He is Tuttwyler's first Democratic mayor since before the Civil War. Had former Mayor Donald Grinspoon not tried for an eighth term—and hadn't fallen off the stage at the Meet The Candidates night at G.A. Hemphill Elementary School, reminding everyone he was a less-than-nimble seventy-nine—Woodrow Wilson Sadlebyrne would still be a harm-less ward councilman and cable TV installer.

"Evening, Woody."

"Evening, Bill."

Former Mayor Grinspoon is there, trembling fingers making his Styrofoam cup of black coffee squeak.

"Glad you could make it, Donald."

Dick Mueller is there. He is post commander of the VFW and owner of Mueller Auto Parts.

"How's the new addition coming, Dick?"

"Floor's going down Thursday," Dick Mueller reports proudly. Everyone at the table knows he is not talking about the floor at the VFW hall, or the floor of his auto parts store. He is talking about the floor of the new Sunday School wing at St. Mark's Lutheran Church, where he is treasurer of the building fund.

"Tile or carpet?" Delores Poltruski asks him, already knowing the answer.

"Tile," Dick Mueller answers too quickly.

Everyone at the table knows why Delores Poltruski feels it necessary to ask a question for which she already knows the answer, and why Dick Mueller has answered her so earnestly. Dick and Delores are trying to hide their love affair. They have been copulating not-so-secretly once a week since 1986, the year after his wife of thirty years died of cervical cancer, and two years after her husband of thirty-five years drowned in Hornpayne, Ontario, while on his annual fishing trip with his Knights of Columbus buddies. Not only are their relentless efforts to conceal their affair in vain, they also are unnecessary. Everyone at the table knows. And no one gives a damn—understanding that if Delores wasn't such a good Catholic, and Dick wasn't such an important Lutheran, they surely would be married by now, copulating legally, if not quite as often.

"Tile is always a good choice," Delores Poltruski says.

In addition to her work on the Squaw Days Committee, Delores Poltruski sells real estate and sits on the school board. Some in Tuttwyler consider this a conflict of interest, inasmuch as the houses she so enthusiastically sells requires the school board to put a new tax levy on the ballot every year or two. D. William Aitchbone is not so narrow-minded. He doesn't like the higher taxes, of course, and regularly votes against them, but he does like all the new kids crowding into the schools, a small but profitable percentage of them sure to require some sort of legal representation before they graduate.

There are two people on the Squaw Days Committee from the new housing developments north, south, east and west of the village. One is Paula Varney, owner of Just Giraffes. Paula Varney hardly sells enough stuffed giraffes to pay the shop's light bill, let alone the rent. But making money isn't the objective. The objective is something for Paula Varney to do now that her twin sons Sean and Jarrod are away at Kenyon College, one studying anthropology, the other modern dance. Her husband Dave's enormous salary as comptroller for Zedonk Industries Inc. easily covers Just Giraffe's light bill and rent, just as it easily covers two tuitions and the mortgage on their five-bedroom *faux*-Georgian in the new Mallard Lakes Estates, built on the rolling hills of Bud Paddaway's old two-hundred-cow dairy farm.

"I see Zedonk's stock has bounced back a bit after that takeover rumor," D. William Aitchbone says to Paula Varney, his courtroom smile in full flower.

The smile she returns is little more than a twitch. "That takeover was just a rumor, Bill."

The other committee member from the new developments is Kevin Hassock. Kevin Hassock does not want to be at this meeting. He does not want to be on the Squaw Days Committee. He wants to spend this evening and every evening full-tilt in his black leather recliner, flipping between ESPN and ESPN-2, in the sunken family room of his *faux*-French country house in Woodchuck Ridge, where old Norm Umplebee used to raise a lot of corn and soybeans. But Kevin Hassock's employer, DWP America Ltd., likes its young executives to get involved in their communities, even if they are likely to be transferred or downsized within twenty-four months. "How you like these Ohio winters of ours?" D. William Aitchbone asks him.

"They keep you awake, that's for sure," Kevin Hassock answers in his native North Carolinian. He does not know that his unhappy wife just that morning called D. William Aitchbone's office for an appointment.

So everyone is there. D. William Aitchbone had spent much of his hour and five minutes at the Daydream Beanery assessing how to handle each of them.

Some have to be handled with respect.

Donald Grinspoon certainly has to be. The former mayor is a fellow Republican, and a successful businessman to boot—successful, that is, until the mall opened at the I-491 interchange. Grinspoon's Department Store had been a fixture on the village square since 1893. It had survived the Great Depression and Tuttwyler Mills' decision in 1975 to close the snack cake line. It even survived the explosion of shopping plazas on West Wooseman. But the new mall was another matter and Grinspoon's was forced to close just two weeks before the same November election that ended Donald Grinspoon's twenty-six year stint as mayor. Most of the village's political insiders, D. William Aitchbone among them, had expected him to retreat to the family condo in Key Largo after those back-to-back defeats. But Donald Grinspoon is a genetically optimistic man. He not only remained in his big impressive Victorian Gothic on South Mill Street, he also held onto his chairmanship of the Squaw Days Committee. And he still would be chairman if his wife of fifty-two years, Penelope (nee Tuttwyler) Grinspoon, finally hadn't surrendered to the hat trick of emphysema, osteoporosis and Alzheimer's creeping respectively through her lungs, bones, and brain since Reagan's first term. Now Donald Grinspoon's days are filled with long visits to the Sparrow Hill Nursing Home forty miles north in Strongsville. And although he is happy to stay on the Squaw Days Committee as long as the others will have him, he has turned the chairmanship over to younger blood. In particular, the younger blood of his personal lawyer and political protégé, one D. William Aitchbone. So a certain amount respect for Donald Grinspoon is in order.

A certain amount of respect also is in order for the new mayor, Woodrow Wilson Sadlebyrne. Public respect anyway. Woody Sadlebyrne not only is Tuttwyler's first Democratic mayor since the Civil War, he also is Tuttwyler's youngest mayor ever, just twenty-eight on election day, just twenty-nine now. Woody has big plans for the village. But Woody also has a big problem—a big problem named D. William Aitchbone, president of the village council, vice-chairman of the Wyssock County Republican Party, and now, chairman of the Squaw Days Committee. D. William Aitchbone also is the man certain to unseat him in the next mayoral election. Everybody understands the inevitability of that. Even Woody Sadlebyrne himself surely understands the inevitability of that.

Other members of the committee simply can be tolerated.

Dick Mueller and Delores Poltruski fall into that category. Paula Varney, too. As the months whittle toward August they will have plenty to say at these meetings, but in the end nothing at all to say about the big changes D. William Aitchbone has in mind.

One member of the committee can be ignored completely.

That member, of course, is Kevin Hassock. He is there because his résumé requires it. He will appreciate the new chairman's inattention.

That leaves Katherine Hardihood. She must be handled with oven mitts.

"Well," D. William Aitchbone says, "what do you say we get started."

2

"I suppose the first thing we need to do," begins D. William Aitchbone, "is to make sure everybody is happy with their subcommittee assignments."

This is the customary way to begin the year's first meeting of the Squaw Days Committee; not just the actual discussion of subcommittee assignments, but the words "make sure everybody is happy." Those are the exact words Donald Grinspoon used every year since the first Squaw Days was planned, thirteen years ago. Now it is D. William Aitchbone's turn to use those words, to simultaneously pay homage to his predecessor while stealing away his power and prestige. "Dick, you'll coordinate the parade again, won't you? And the memorial services?"

Dick Mueller nods. Of course he will coordinate the parade and the memorial services. And, and always, Delores Poltruski will coordinate the craft show and the food tents. And Paula Varney, as president of the Chamber of Commerce, will coordinate merchant contributions and the big sidewalk sale. And former Mayor Grinspoon will continue to coordinate his three favorite events: the pie-eating contest, the tobacco-spitting competition, and the closing night fireworks. And present Mayor Woodrow Wilson Sadlebyrne will coordinate participation by the various village service departments: the police for traffic control, fire engines for the parade, paramedics standing by, clean-up by the village's maintenance engineer when it's all over for another year.

"And Kevin, I know this is your first year on the committee, but could you coordinate the carnival rides?"

The dread of responsibility races through Kevin Hassock like embalming fluid through a corpse. Runaway tilt-a-whirls. Blood on the parking lot. Unbathed carnies from New Jersey and Alabama drugging and buggering junior high school kids. Lawsuits up the wazoo. "I'd be happy to," Kevin Hassock says.

"Just make sure they bring the big Ferris wheel," D. William Aitchbone says. "They always try to sneak the little one in."

"Gotcha," says Kevin Hassock.

Finally, Katherine Hardihood again will coordinate the historical display at the library, the band concert at the gazebo, and, most importantly, the Re-Enactment.

"And I'll coordinate the coordination," D. William Aitchbone says. It is another old Donald Grinspoon line. Everyone laughs, just as they had always laughed when Donald Grinspoon said it. Another homage to the old man's authority and respect.

D. William Aitchbone now listens intently as each of them, for a few minutes permitted to feel important, go over their checklists:

Dick Mueller says the parade units, as usual, will line up at the old snack cake plant, proceed up East Wooseman to the square, go once around, then proceed out South Mill to the cemetery for the memorial services. Both the high school and junior high bands have agreed to march again, he says, and the Chirpy Chipmunks unicycle troupe from Akron also has expressed interest in returning, though he hasn't talked to them since October. "But I will real soon," he pledges.

Delores Poltruski says that the food tents again will be set up on the north side of the square, and the craft booths on the east side, "making a nice convenient *L*," she says. She warns of one potential problem. "Howie Dornick still hasn't cut that dead limb out of the box elder. The Knights of Columbus are afraid if there's any wind at all, that limb could come down right through the sloppy joe tent."

"We'll get the limb cut," Donald Grinspoon assures her, forgetting he is no longer mayor.

The new mayor handles this awkward moment graciously. "We might just take the whole tree down," Woodrow Wilson Sadlebyrne says. "There really aren't that many limbs left anyway."

"It's the only box elder left on the square," Katherine Hardihood reminds everyone.

The unanticipated dead-limb-debate delights D. William Aitchbone. "If you've noticed, Howie Dornick still hasn't removed the Christmas decorations from the gazebo either," he says. "So whether it's just the one limb or the entire tree, Woody, you need to get Howie popping."

"I'll talk to him in the morning," Woodrow Wilson Sadlebyrne promises.

"You might mention his house again," D. William Aitchbone says.

"Oh yes, please," Paula Varney says. "Mention his house."

"His house is a disgrace," Dick Mueller says.

"And right on the parade route," Delores Poltruski says.

"That's exactly what I'm saying," says Dick Mueller, his head going up and down like a rocking chair. "People from all over the Ohio line up on South Mill for the parade. Television crews, too."

"I'll talk to Howie about painting his house," Woodrow Wilson Sadlebyrne assures everyone.

D. William Aitchbone now makes sure there is just the right amount of bristle in his voice. "We need more than talk, Woody."

Woodrow Wilson Sadlebyrne does not appreciate the bristle. He weakly bristles back. "I'll handle it, Bill."

D. William Aitchbone fakes a nod of contrition and moves on to the next subcommittee report. "So, Donald, what you got planned for the pie-eating contest this year? Blueberry? Cherry?"

Former Mayor Donald Grinspoon brightens. "Nothing makes a mess like blueberry."

Paula Varney rests her plump palm on the old man's knuckles. "That reminds me, Donald. Tom Winkler at Denny's says he'll give us the pies at cost again."

Now it's Katherine Hardihood's turn to bristle. "I'm not sure what sticking your face in a blueberry pie has to do with remembering what happened to Princess Pogawedka."

D. William Aitchbone lets Katherine Hardihood's dig slide. The subcommittee reports go on. Donald Grinspoon has a second cup of coffee. Three or four times Dick

Mueller slips and called Delores Poltruski "Dee Dee." Before the meeting ends D. William Aitchbone gives Kevin Hassock the phone number for the Happy Landings Ride Company; he also gives him a folder containing the already-signed contacts, permits, and insurance documents. "Looks easy enough," Kevin Hassock says, greatly relieved that most of his work is already done.

"Pretty cut and dried, really," says D. William Aitchbone. "Just remember: Big Ferris wheel."

The year's first meeting of the Squaw Days Committee ends. Members disappear like movie ghosts into the horizontal February snow. D. William Aitchbone catches up with Mayor Woodrow Wilson Sadlebyrne half way across the square. "Woody! Wait a sec!"

The mayor stiffens and stops and turns into the goose-shitting snow.

"Sorry if I got a little gruff before," D. William Aitchbone says.

The mayor bats the flakes away from his eyes. He doesn't want to have this conversation. He wants to go home and have a bowl of raisin bran. He wants to watch Letterman. "I'll talk to Howie in the morning."

D. William Aitchbone puts his hand on the mayor's shoulder and swivels him about. They walk. "We've been talking to him for years, Woody. Talking to Howie Dornick is like trying to fart a rainbow."

"I think I can get Howie to cut down one box elder limb by August."

"Who cares about the box elder limb? The house, Woody. I want his goddamn house painted."

"Everybody wants his house painted. But you can't order someone to paint their house."

"Not in so many words you can't."

Woodrow Wilson Sadlebyrne stops and turns his face back into the snow and lets the flakes land where they may. "You want me to threaten him with his job? He's Civil Service. And don't forget he's also the son of Artie Brown."

"The *illegitimate* son of Artie Brown," D. William Aitchbone points out.

"Well, he's legitimately protected by Civil Service."

They walk on, to the top of the square. D. William Aitchbone's American-made Japanese luxury sedan is parked across the street, four or five spaces down from Woodrow Wilson Sadlebyrne's red Ford Tempo. "I just want Squaw Days to go well, Woody. It's my first year as chairman. Just like it's your first year as mayor. We both want things to go well, right?"

"That we do."

D. William Aitchbone grins and extends his hand. "See you at the council meeting. I've got some interesting new ideas about plugging that budget shortfall." He crosses the street and brushes the snow off his windshield. As he brushes, he shakes his head at the expensive giraffes in the window of Paula Varney's something-to-do shop. One giraffe is dressed in a top hat and tails. Another wears a scarf and Russian fur hat. Most of the other giraffes are naked except for the pastel silk ribbons around their endless necks. "Who in their right mind would pay that kind of money for a stuffed animal?" he asks himself.

Paula Varney is not the only something-to-do shop-keeper on the square. Something-to-do is the objective of most of the shops on the square these days. These days the real retail action is along the ever-expanding strip on West Wooseman, where Wal-mart and Kmart do battle 24 hours a day; where McDonald's and Burger King and Denny's and Pizza Hut and Taco Bell do battle; where the two quick-stop oil-change shops and the two fully automated car washes do battle; where four Chinese take-outs and three sub shops do battle; where two national supermarket chains, three national convenience-store chains and four national gas-mart chains do battle; where a national hardware chain battles with a national home improvement chain; where five national banks and their handy 24-hour ATMs do battle; where three car dealerships do battle; where a national drug store chain with "always-low" prices battles a national drugstore chain offering "everyday prices"; where local paychecks are surrendered to faraway corporate stockholders; where criminals all the way from Cleveland gather to steal CD players from cars, if not the cars themselves.

The strip on West Wooseman leaves precious little important commerce for the old brick buildings surrounding the square. And so there is Paula Varney's Just Giraffes stuffed animal shop where H. W. Colby's Hardware used to be; an art gallery and framing shop where Borden Brother's Shoes used to be; one antique shop where Porter's Western Auto used to be, another where Morton's IGA used to be; a travel agency where Klinger's Paint used to be; the Pizza Tepee with its wooden Indian holding a large Italian pie, each pepperoni slice intricately carved, where Sylvia's Family Restaurant used to be; the Daydream Beanery with its muffins and cappuccino and brain-numbing dulcimer music, where Grinspoon's Department Store used to be.

So all the real businesses and the real business people are gone from the square, either forced to close or forced to relocate to one of the asphalt-moated plazas on West Wooseman, on the flat fertile soil that used to be the Van Welter family farm and the Grabenstetter family farm and the Warner family farm and the McBiffy family farm.

When Karen Aitchbone feels her husband slip into bed, she whispers what she whispers at least three nights a week. "How'd your meeting go, honey bun?"

D. William Aitchbone kisses his wife's cold ear. "That woman has got more brass than a marching band."

She knows who he's talking about. He's talking about Katherine Hardihood.

3

Katherine Hardihood is the last to leave the library community room. She is the last to leave because she has the key. She has the key because she is head librarian of the Tuttwyler branch. She has been head librarian for twenty-one years now. She also is one of the original members of the Squaw Days Committee, along with Donald Grinspoon, Delores Poltruski, and unfortunately, D. William Aitchbone.

A year shy of fifty, Katherine Hardihood has not a single physical feature a man might find appetizing. She is a throwback—and she knows it—to the time when all unappetizing women—if their brains could carry it—served their communities as either schoolteachers or librarians. But no one in Tuttwyler feels particularly sorry for Katherine Hardihood. It is obvious to all that she loves her solitary librarian's life.

She pulls the plug on the Mr. Coffee and turns the thermostat down to sixty. Before clicking off the lights, she pulls a white knit hat over her straight, chopped-at-the-jaw librarian's hair. She loops a matching scarf around her spindly librarian's neck. She spider-walks her dry librarian's fingers into a pair of white mittens, then pulls on a noisy caramel-brown polyester coat. It falls all the way to her blue Eskimo boots, which she had worn throughout the meeting to keep her flat librarian's feet warm. She closes the door behind her, twice shaking the knob to make sure it's locked. She ascends into the horizontal snow, her enormous librarian's glasses protecting her square librarian's head like the visor on a welder's helmet.

Despite I-491, Tuttwyler is still far enough from Cleveland for Katherine Hardihood to walk home alone in the dark, though she does hold the community room key ready in her be-mittened hand. She knows just what to do if she's attacked: She'll take that key and pop the rapist's eye like a raw oyster, and scream at the top of her librarian's lungs, *fire, fire, fire.* She's read somewhere that yelling *help* chases good Samaritans away, while yelling *fire* brings them in droves. So she'll yell *fire, fire, fire.*

She walks down East Wooseman to North Grant. The old three-story Odd Fellows building, now an antique mall, keeps the wind and snow away from her for an entire block. The In & Out convenience store is still open and she considers going in for a pint of lime sherbet, but through the front window she sees Dick Mueller and Delores Poltruski browsing the snack aisle. She will give them their space. Who in their right mind eats sherbet on a night like this, anyway? She crosses the snow covered parking lot and heads up Oak Street.

Oak is a modest street, lined not with oaks but with evergreens and sycamore. Most of the houses on Oak were built just after World War II, affordable starter homes for newly returned GIs and their high school sweetheart brides. They are tiny, two-bedroom ranches with one bathroom, no dining room, and a kitchen hardly wide enough for a table. Despite their modest profiles, these houses are painted the same soapy white as the impressive giants on South Mill. And all have dark green shutters.

Katherine Hardihood's tiny ranch is exactly half way down Oak Street. Still three houses away she can see her orange cat, Rhubarb, sitting on the window table, as straight and still as a bowling trophy. "There's my little mister," she sings out. She exchanges the community room key for her house key and goes in. The dark-yellow stench of ammonia fills her narrow librarian's nose. "Jiminy Cricket, Rhubarb, not again!"

What Rhubarb has done again is piss the curio cabinet. Backed up and pissed it like an African lion marking the baobab tree where he hangs his kill.

Katherine Hardihood goes immediately for the rag and Pine Sol she keeps under the sink. Still in her noisy coat, knit hat and mittens, she wipes down the cabinet, then goes twice around her miniature living room with a spraycan of Glade. She picks up Rhubarb and cradles him on his back like a human baby. She buries her face in his soft belly, his full tomcat balls just a half-inch from her hollow librarian's cheek. "You're worse than Bill Aitchbone, do you know that?" she says in that high gooey voice people reserve for babies and pets. "Do you know that? Do you? Hmmm?"

As she talks to Rhubarb she can see Dick Mueller pull into his driveway. A few seconds later Delores Poltruski pulls in. Snacks in hand they go inside. A bad night for sherbet, maybe, but a good night for love.

Katherine Hardihood does not mind that Dick and Delores are copulating right across the street from her. She does not mind that people up and down Oak Street are copulating. She does not mind that people all over Old Tuttwyler and New Tuttwyler, and all over the world are copulating. She loves her uncomplicated, uncopulative life. She loves her little house and her big pissing tomcat. Most of all she loves the library.

Katherine Hardihood never knew Rhubarb's first human name, if indeed he ever had one. She found him three hot Junes ago, already full-grown, licking the melted chocolate off a Milky Way wrapper in the parking lot of the In & Out. It was obvious from his intense licking, and the enormous size of his head in relationship to the rest of his scrawny frame, that he was a starving street cat. So she took him home and fed him milk and tunafish and bowl after bowl of Meow Mix. And she cuddled him and snuggled him and talked and sang to him, and went for the Pine Sol whenever he pissed the curio cabinet she inherited from her Aunt Edith. She named the cat Melvil, after Melvil Dewey, originator of the Dewey Decimal system.

One August morning, when Melvil was finally fat, and his head again in proper proportion to his body, she let him outside. He disappeared until November, reappearing at her back door during the year's first real snow, as scrawny and big-headed as before. The following summer when she again let Melvil outside, she tied him to twenty feet of clothesline. Fastened to a stake in the middle of the yard, Melvil was free to explore as he wished now, though his world was infinitely smaller, and no matter which direction he went, he always ended up back where he began.

Melvil at first hated the clothesline and his bejeweled pink collar, and his Magellan-like existence. He strained so hard to pull free that he wore the fur off his neck. But after a few outings he surrendered to his mistress' madness and accepted his shrunken world. When he was hungry or thirsty he'd circle to the backdoor where his Meow Mix and water bowls sat. When he wanted to warm up, he'd sit in full sun on the edge of the concrete patio. When he got too warm, he'd make a half-circle to the rhubarb patch, and shade himself under the broad green leaves.

Katherine Hardihood had not planted the rhubarb. It had been planted years ago by the original owner of the house, Phil Davenport, high school buddy of Artie Brown—the same Artie Brown who came home from World War II with one foot and a Congressional Medal of Honor, and in the glow of his celebrity, impregnated Lois Dornick, an appetizing girl still in high school.

Seeing Melvil encamped under the rhubarb leaves made Katherine Hardihood laugh, and made her love him more. Soon she was calling him Rhubarb more than Melvil. Soon Rhubarb was his name.

Sometimes she would anger Rhubarb by clipping off the red stalks that supported his leafy canopy, and then bake them into a pie. Once she had given a piece of her rhubarb pie to Howie Dornick when he was working in front of her house, cleaning out the storm sewer. He ate it in four or five bites and told her it was very good. For a few days afterward she considered baking him an entire rhubarb pie, and taking it to his unpainted house on South Mill. But in the end she didn't. Despite being born of a beautiful high school girl, and sired by a Congressional Medal of Honor winner, Howie Dornick was as unappetizing as she.

Katherine Hardihood loves the library because that's where the *facts* are. She loves facts—any fact that pertains to something or someone other than herself. She loves finding out that tomatoes aren't a vegetable but a fruit; that the button was invented in 1200 AD; that the words *truth, tree* and *endure* share the same Indo-European root, *deru*; that the gestation period for the opossum is just 13 days; that a black man from Cleveland, Garrett A. Morgan, invented those automatic traffic lights that go from red to yellow to green, like the new one at South Mill and Tocqueville.

She knows other facts as well: that fathers don't always return home from the wars they fight; that mothers sometimes die in car accidents; that the aunts who take you in have fat, wonderful laps; that uncles, when their fat-lapped wives are away shopping, are not always as nice as they seem. In short, Katherine Hardihood discovered early in her life that facts about other things keep your mind off the facts about yourself.

Her need for facts about other things drew her to the library. My, the facts in there! Billions of them. Gathered. Numbed. Alphabetized. Indexed. Chronologized. Footnoted. Explained. Defined. Put in plain English. Tantalizingly sprinkled into poetry. Churned into wonderful works of fiction. Scrupulously researched and worried over by others who love facts as much as she does.

It is this love of facts that brought Katherine Hardihood so willingly to the Squaw Days Committee thirteen years before. It is this love of facts that keeps her on the committee now, fighting her relentless guerrilla war against those who do not.

Squaw Days had been Donald Grinspoon's idea—at least the idea of holding some kind of annual festival had been his idea. "The town's drying up like a prune," he told the handful of carefully-selected people gathered in his office one November night. He and fellow Republican Ronald Reagan had just won re-election to their respective jobs. "Tuttwyler Mills has been closed for a decade now, and nobody's shown a lick of interest in taking over the snack cake plant. Two-thirds of the stores on the square are empty. Even some of the houses on South Mill are for sale. We need a shot in the arm."

D. William Aitchbone, then just one year out of law school, had an idea. "We need a Japanese auto plant."

Dick Mueller, serving his first stint as post commander of the VFW, rejected that idea immediately. "No we don't."

D. William Aitchbone persisted. "They're building plants all over the United States now. Why shouldn't we get one? Think of the jobs!"

That brought Dick Mueller straight out of his chair. "Think of Artie Brown, young man! He left his right foot on Guadalcanal."

That ended any further discussion of luring a Japanese auto plant to Tuttwyler.

"There's no way any new plant is coming here anyway," Donald Grinspoon said, "not without the I-491 leg. And we'll all be long in the grave before that gets built."

"Maybe we could get a junior college," Katherine Hardihood suggested.

"Or a prison," Sheriff Norman F. Cole said.

"Or a landfill," D. William Aitchbone said.

"Or a nuclear power plant," Delores Poltruski said.

"I like Katherine's junior college idea," said Phyllis Bastinado, principal at G.A. Hemphill Elementary. Phyllis Bastinado was a huge woman, the approximate weight and shape of a fully inflated farm tractor tire.

That's when Donald Grinspoon demonstrated just why he never lost an election. "Those are all fine ideas. Even the Japanese auto plant is a fine idea, Bill, if you eliminate the Japanese part. But all of those things would take years. We need something now. Something that puts us back on the map right away. Tuttwyler's drying up like a prune."

"Are you sure we can't get the snack cake line back?" asked Dick Mueller. "Your wife's a Tuttwyler."

Donald Grinspoon's eyes filled with tears. "The Tuttwyler's haven't had a say in the company since the

Fifties. If they had, it wouldn't have moved to Tennessee in the first place."

Dick Mueller understood the tears in the mayor's eyes. His wife was in bad shape, too. "What do hillbillies know about making snack cakes?"

Everyone nodded. The company's baked goods never tasted the same since the move, especially their famous chocolate cupcakes, with their script frosting T and whipped cream surprise inside.

"I think we should have a festival," Donald Grinspoon finally said, revealing the real reason for the meeting. "An annual festival that brings in folks from all over the state. From other states, too. A grand festival that will put us back on the map. Something that will make Tuttwyler so damn famous people will visit all year long. Tourism, ladies and gentlemen. That's our ticket to prosperity."

Everyone agreed that an annual festival was grand idea. Everyone but Katherine Hardihood. "What are we going to be festive about?" she asked.

Everyone waited to hear the mayor's answer, certain he already knew what the festival should be about. Why would he have called the meeting otherwise? But Donald Grinspoon did not know what the festival should be about. "I'm not sure," he confessed. "Tuttwyler isn't really famous for anything. All we ever did around here was make snack cakes."

"What about Artie Brown?" said Dick Mueller, patriotically shaking his fist in the air. "Artie Brown Days! That would pull them in."

Only D. William Aitchbone had the nerve to challenge Dick Mueller's blind love of country. "Nobody outside Tuttwyler gives a damn that Artie Brown hobbled on one foot for six miles. "

Dick Mueller's fist was now shaking squarely in D. William Aitchbone's face. "He saved an entire company of Seabees from the goddamn Nips."

"There goes our Japanese auto plant," Katherine Hardihood couldn't resist whispering to Delores Poltruski.

"Artie Brown Days was my first inclination, too," Donald Grinspoon said. "But Bill's right. Artie isn't all that famous outside Tuttwyler."

"We could make him famous," Sheriff Norman F. Cole said.

Again Katherine Hardihood couldn't resist. This time she didn't whisper. "We could have a six-mile hobble. Our own little Boston Marathon."

Even Dick Mueller chuckled at that.

"And we can't forget what else Artie Brown is famous for," D. William Aitchbone said. He was referring, of course, to Artie's 1945 coupling with the appetizing but under-aged Lois Dornick, and, of course, the bastard son that unfortunate union produced.

So there was no more talk of Artie Brown Days.

"Too bad the snack cake line moved," Phyllis Bastinado said, scratching the oat-bag of pink fat hanging from her horse jaws. "We could have Cupcake Days."

Everyone diverted their eyes and nodded.

"We've got to be famous for something," Delores Poltruski said.

That's when Katherine Hardihood discovered why Donald Grinspoon had invited her to the meeting. "Katherine, you've got all those old books and records and things at the library. Find our what we're famous for!"

And so Katherine Hardihood's search for a festival began.

Tuttwyler is the southern-most village in Wyssock County, the southern-most county in a three-million-acre swath of northeastern Ohio called the Western Reserve. Originally this three-million-acre swath was owned by God, who, for a long time, decided it should be covered by ice. After a while God let the ice melt, exposing gentle slopes and low hills, flatlands and swamps, lakes and rivers and creeks. Unfortunately there were no great mountains or waterfalls or caverns to give future tourists something interesting to gaze at.

When the ice was gone, trees grew and animals migrated in. But these were fairly run-of-the mill animals: rabbits and raccoons and the like, nothing exotic for later vacationers to see. The only animals with any potential for tourism—woolly elephants called mammoths—were killed off by the first humans to find the iceless swath. These humans, later to be called Indians by other humans called Europeans, lived on the land for many thousands of years. And they never built any grand fortresses or temples to attract future visitors.

In 1630, James I of England decided he owned this swath. Had he located his throne there, later-day sightseers would have had something grand to gaze at. Instead he granted the swath to the Earl of Warwick, who, along with a gaggle of puritans and witches, was busy creating future tourist destinations on another swath of land called Massachusetts.

Eventually the swath went to the tiny upstart colony of Connecticut, which did nothing to enhance its tourism potential for the next one hundred and seventy years. Neither did the French, nor the Eries and Hurons and Senecas, all of whom mistakenly thought the swath belonged to them. After the famous revolution that created dozens of future tourist destinations, Connecticut finally turned its attention to the swath and promptly sold it to forty-eight developers for, the fact-loving Katherine Hardihood read in one old book, a bargain-basement million-two.

One of those forty-eight developers was a Yale-educated lawyer named Moses Cleaveland. In 1796, Cleaveland led fifty surveyors westward into the swath now called the Western Reserve. It was measured into counties and townships and settlers began trickling in.

Settlers did not trickle into southern Wyssock County until after Ohio became a state in 1803. Those who trickled into the hills along Three Fish Creek were more concerned with planting wheat and corn than creating a future tourist destination. Search as she may through the library's old books and records, Katherine Hardihood found nothing more interesting than the story of how Three Fish Creek got its name.

"Well, Katherine," said Mayor Donald Grinspoon when his hand-picked committee of saviors again gathered in his office, "what are we famous for?"

"Not much," she said, "though it is interesting how Three Fish Creek got its name."

"Really?" Dick Mueller said. "I've always wondered."

"You know, so have I," Delores Poltruski said.

Katherine Hardihood told them what she'd learned: "It was the Tuttwyler brothers themselves. John and Amos had just arrived from Connecticut and were looking for a place to build a grist mill and they were checking out all the creeks to find one strong enough to turn a waterwheel. According to *The Official History of Wyssock County* published by the New Waterbury Historical Society in 1938, John looked at the shallow creek and supposedly said 'It haint much of a stream is it, Amos?' And Amos supposedly said, 'I bet there haint three fish in it.' Then John supposedly said, 'But it runs pretty fast and I bet these hills keeps it filled all summer.' And so the Tuttwyler brothers decided to build their grist mill on the creek they now jokingly called Three Fish Creek."

"I don't see how we make a festival out of that," D. William Aitchbone said.

"I think we better reconsider Artie Brown Days," Dick Mueller said.

Donald Grinspoon ordered Katherine Hardihood to keep digging.

So the next morning she drove all the way to Berea to visit Helen Smith, a retired history professor at Baldwin Wallace College, who knew more about the swath called the Western Reserve than anyone alive. Helen Smith offered her buttered saltines and hot tea and they leafed through ancient, brittle-paged books that smelled for all the world like sweaty pioneers. Among Helen Smith's old books was the 1847 edition of *Henry Howe's Historical Collections of Ohio,* and the next week when Mayor Donald Grinspoon called the saviors together, Katherine Hardihood finally had something to report.

What she had was the story of an Indian woman who was clubbed to death by white settlers on the bank of Three Fish Creek. Her newborn baby was clubbed to death, too.

"Where's the festival in that?" D. William Aitchbone wondered.

Katherine Hardihood slowly picked her way through the facts she'd found in Henry Howe's history: "It seems that several years later the ghost of this Indian woman appeared to a group of settlers burning stumps."

"Now it's getting good," Dick Mueller said.

"Did she come right up out of the smoke?" Delores Poltruski asked.

"I don't know about that," Katherine Hardihood said. "But according to the story, she forgave the whites for killing her and her baby."

Donald Grinspoon was elated. "Oh, that's good."

Katherine Hardihood continued: "And she gave the settlers her blessing, saying, according to the story, of course, that 'I am proud to be the last of my people to die for this sacred land. Now, my white brothers and sisters, it is your land. May you find peace and prosperity upon it. May it bless you in your time as it blessed my people in theirs.'"

"Oh, Katherine! That's damn good!" said Donald Grinspoon.

Katherine Hardihood raised a cautious finger. "Maybe not so good. The whites who clubbed the Indian woman and her baby were John and Amos Tuttwyler."

Donald Grinspoon grabbed the edge of his desk. "Oh."

The implication of that fact did not immediately register with Dick Mueller. "Serves them right for moving the snack cake line."

D. William Aitchbone enlightened him. "The mayor's wife is a Tuttwyler, Dick."

Dick Mueller felt terrible. "Oh, that's right. Sorry."

Donald Grinspoon let go of his desk. He went to the window. He looked at the village square and the empty stores surrounding it. He looked at his own business, Grinspoon's Department Store, which had survived the Great Depression and the closing of Tuttwyler Mills snack cake line in 1975, and was now having its worst November in seven years. Soon even the underwear would have to be marked down. He thought of his wife, and the hat trick of afflictions reshaping her body and mind. "Penny was born a Tuttwyler but she's a Grinspoon now. And we Grinspoons do what we have to do."

And so Squaw Days was born.

And now it is thirteen years later and D. William Aitchbone is chairman of the Squaw Days Committee, and Katherine Hardihood, home from the first meeting of the year, wearing a flannel nightgown and two pairs of socks, is wriggling into bed. From under her pile of pillows—where she also keeps a steak knife, claw hammer and can of mace—she pulls out her TV remote. She flips to WVIZ, Cleveland's public television station. For the eighth time since Christmas they are broadcasting Yobisch Podka's 1991 performance with the Santa Fe Symphony. Yobisch is just halfway through his most popular New Age monstrosity, *Noir and Far*. She quickly flips to Channel 19 and the local news: The Cleveland Indians' equipment truck is leaving for Winter Haven, Florida, for the start of spring training. The driver is waving to the camera. On his cap and on his jacket, and even on the side of the truck's long trailer, is Chief Wahoo, the team's cartoon mascot with skin as red as an Italian tomato, huge eyes shaped like teepees, a Shylock nose, Japanese buckteeth protruding through a Stepinfetchit smile, a happy-go-lucky little Injun, safely locked away in the American League cellar most of his imaginary life. The camera also shows a few seconds of the

CRI, Cleveland's Real Indians, protesting, as they do every spring, the team's racist insensitivity. Prominent among the five or six CRI members shaking homemade signs is their leader, emerald-eyed Ernest Not Irish.

Katherine Hardihood turns off the TV and turns on the radio, the dial glued by years of habit to Cleveland's only big band station. Dinah Shore is singing a song Katherine first heard when she was a little girl, when her parents were still alive and her world was still a safe and beautiful place: *"If you want to do right by your appetite . . . If you're fussy about your food . . . Take a choo-choo today, head New England way . . . And we'll put you in the happiest mood with . . . Shoo fly pie and apple pan dowdy . . . Makes your eyes light up, your tummy say howdy . . . Shoo fly pie and apple pan dowdy . . . I never get enough of that wonderful stuff."*

4

Howie Dornick has a clock radio, but he never uses it to wake up. His brain gets him up. "When I get in bed I just tell myself what time I need to get up, and I do," he often brags at the Eagles Club, where he won the very clock radio he never uses in a Friday night raffle. Howie Dornick is a member of the Eagles, but not the VFW, though he did spend a year in Japan with the Air Force during the early years of the Vietnam War. No one had to tell him that the illegitimate son of Artie Brown wasn't welcome at the Artie Brown Post of the Veterans of Foreign Wars.

Howie Dornick told himself to get up at four-thirty. So at exactly four-thirty his eyes open and he swings out of the bed he's slept in since he was twelve. He quick-steps to the bathroom. He urinates and brushes his teeth and washes his face. It being Friday, he doesn't shower; he showers on Saturdays, Mondays and Wednesdays. He does rub his armpits with Right Guard. He also checks his undershorts to see if he can get another day out of them, which he decides he can. Back in the bedroom he puts on his thermal under-wear and a plaid shirt and his canvas overalls. It is still dark outside, though from the street light in front of his two-story frame he can see that the snow has stopped.

He groans all the way down the steps, his fingers leaving yet another streak of oil on the wallpaper. It has been twenty years since he put that wallpaper up for his mother; gray and white kittens playing in blue petunias, not the pattern Howie would have preferred. In the 1930s even shoestring houses like his were built with fireplaces. On the mantle rests his father's prosthetic foot and a photograph of his mother, taken when she was cafeteria manager at G.A. Hemphill Elementary School.

In the kitchen he puts on his boots, and while waiting for a teakettle of water to boil for his Thermos of instant coffee, he sits at his little table and eats three Tuttwyler snack cakes—one jelly roll and two chocolate cupcakes with the famous script *T* icing. You can take the Tuttwyler Mills snack cake line out of Tuttwyler, but you can't take the snack cakes out of a Tuttwylerite's diet; everyone knows that everyone secretly eats a lot of them.

He walks to the village hall. No one is there yet. No one will be there for hours. He pours himself a coffee and turns up the heat. There is only one piece of paper in his mailbox, a note from Mayor Woodrow Wilson Sadlebyrne asking him to meet him at the gazebo at 9:30. He finishes his coffee and goes outside to shovel the walk. He sprinkles de-icing pellets. He goes back inside for second cup of coffee and then, with a big empty cardboard box under one arm and a ladder under the other, wades through the snow to the gazebo and takes down the plastic pine garland and red plastic bows. Surely that's what the mayor wants to see him about. It is always good to have a job done when you're told for the umpteenth time to get it done. He stores the box and ladder away and drives the village pickup to the fire station to scrape the snow away from the doors.

At 9:30 he meets the mayor at the gazebo.

"See you took the decorations down," Woodrow Wilson Sadlebyrne says.

"That plastic pine garland was a good idea, mayor," says Howie Dornick. "It'll last a good twenty years. I'm not so sure about the ribbons, though."

"Well, I'm glad you got it down."

"Stored away until next November."

"Well, that's good."

Now Howie Dornick learns that the mayor does not want to see him about the gazebo decorations.

"Howie, that dead limb on the box elder has got to come down right away."

"We ought to cut the whole damn tree down."

"Wish we could. But it's the last box elder on the square."

"So what?"

"It's not so much the box elder. It's Katherine Hardihood."

Howie Dornick understands the mayor's dilemma. While Katherine Hardihood is a fine woman—she once

38

brought him a piece of rhubarb pie when he was digging the leaves out of her storm sewer—she also is something of a fanatic. He imagines coming to the square some morning with a chain saw and finding Katherine Hardihood padlocked to the trunk of the box elder, a half-dozen sticks of dynamite strapped to her chest. "I'll put the limb on my spring list," he promises.

"Better put it on this morning's list, Howie."

"OK. But the ground's slicker than shit. You'll have to hold the ladder."

An hour later Howie Dornick, carbon dioxide rolling out his bright red nostrils, inches his way up the box elder with the village's heavy chain saw. Mayor Woodrow Wilson Sadlebyrne is below him, holding steady the village's ice-cold aluminum ladder, as well as his political future. "For God's sake be careful, Howie."

"Just hold her still," Howie Dornick answers. He could just as easily be talking about Katherine Hardihood as the ice-cold aluminum ladder.

Howie Dornick reaches the tree's wide crotch and eases off the ladder. Lying flat against one the tree's still-living limbs, he yanks the cord on the chain saw. The roar fills the square. He leans and sinks the saw's flying blade into the numb, corky wood of the limb in question. Woody shrapnel bounces off Howie Dornick's plastic safety glasses and rains onto the mayor's unprotected face. "Stand back!" Howie Dornick shouts over the roar. The mayor retreats. The limb moans and drops.

Howie Dornick now goes to work on the limb, trimming it into fireplace logs. The mayor helps him load the logs into a wheelbarrow. "There's another matter we need to talk about, Howie," the mayor says as they head toward the village hall.

And so Woodrow Wilson Sadlebyrne broaches the subject of his unpainted house.

"Katherine Hardihood got a bug up her flat behind about that, too, does she?"

"Everybody on the Squaw Days Committee, actually."

They reach the street just as the Don't Walk sign begins flashing. Howie Dornick sets the wheelbarrow down. He is embarrassed now. And angry. And full of self pity. "I know it's bad," he says, meaning both the condition of his house and his own personal sloth, "but paint ain't exactly in my budget."

Woodrow Wilson Sadlebyrne drops his head. "I know the village doesn't pay you much."

"Benefits aren't any good either. I'm still paying off my mother's medical bills and she's been dead for six years."

The sign flashes *WALK*. Howie Dornick lifts the wheelbarrow and starts across the street. The mayor pursues him. "Maybe we can get some paint donated."

"I don't want no charity."

Woodrow Wilson Sadlebyrne knows he must be careful. And he knows that Howie Dornick knows it, too. "We all appreciate your service to the village."

Howie Dornick gives the wheelbarrow an extra push. It's fat rubber wheel bounces over the curb. They head for the rear of the village hall. "What you appreciate, mayor, is my father's service. You know well as me that the only reason I've got this crumb-bum job is because the great Artie Brown saved those Seabees and lost his foot. The same reason my mother got that crumb-bum job fixing lunches at the elementary school."

"Now, Howie."

"True, ain't it?"

"True," the mayor admits.

Howie Dornick appreciates his honesty. "I voted for you, you know."

"Really? I figured all the village employees voted Republican out of self-preservation."

"I'm protected by Civil Service."

They both laugh a little. Their difficult conversation is over. Howie Dornick heads across the parking lot with the wheelbarrow. "Say, mayor," he calls out. "You don't mind if I take this wood home for my fireplace, do you?"

"Not at all, Howie."

Woodrow Wilson Sadelbyrne heads back to his office. He's gotten the box elder limb cut—Katherine Hardihood and Delores Poltruski and the Knights of Columbus will be happy about that— but he's gotten absolutely nowhere with Howie Dornick's unpainted house. D. William Aitchbone will not be happy about that. He chuckles at his defeat. The ground isn't the only thing slicker than shit, he thinks.

At four-thirty Howie Dornick walks home to his unpainted two-story frame on South Mill, pushing the village-owned wheelbarrow filled with logs cut from the box elder on the village square. As he struggles up his icy driveway he tries to picture his house with a fresh coat of soap-white paint. But the picture won't stick in his mind any more than a layer of paint would stick to those warped and weathered clapboards. He likes his unpainted house. Likes it fine. It has always been unpainted, at least as long as he and his mother lived there. A coat of paint on those clapboards would be as unnatural as a wedding ring on his mother's rough cafeteria manager hand.

For his supper Howie Dornick makes three Swiss cheese and bologna sandwiches. He makes the sandwiches on wheat bread. He always eats wheat bread. He flavors the sandwiches with brown mustard. He does not eat his sandwiches at the kitchen table, but takes them into the living room, setting them right on the arm of his La-Z-Boy recliner. He turns on the *Jerry Springer* show. Jerry is interviewing mixed-race girls who don't know that their mixed-race boyfriends are really mixed-race girls like themselves, disguising their sex under baggy sweaters, baggy pants and backwards baseball caps. Howie Dornick cannot keep his eyes from drifting to the mantle, to the photograph of his mother and to Artie Brown's prosthetic foot.

His mother's name was Patsy, Patsy Dornick. The Dornicks were a family of Irish Catholics, originally from the west side of Cleveland. They moved to Tuttwyler during World War II, when Tuttwyler Mills was having trouble finding men with baking experience. Patsy's father had plenty of baking experience and having just lost his only son in North Africa, and his only wife in a streetcar accident, he was eager to escape the ghosts of his west side house. He bought the two-story frame on South Mill and went to work baking snack cakes.

Patsy was the oldest of four daughters, already a sophomore in high school when they moved to Tuttwyler. She had a tiny but well-proportioned frame.

She had her mother's perfect face. She did not miss her mother, since she was always with her, in every mirror she passed, and always in the sadness on her father's face. But she did miss her brother.

Howie Dornick's father was the war hero Artie Brown. The Browns were farmers, able to trace their ancestry to one of Connecticut's earliest families. They were a happy family, hard-working and patriotic, almost all of them living disease-free well into their eighties. The Browns considered their good health and longevity the result of good breeding rather than some sort of divine reward. Only the Brown women, recruited from other well-bred families, showed any interest in religion. The Brown men never set foot in a church unless it was a Saturday night and fried chicken was being served.

Artie Brown enlisted the same day he graduated from high school. Patsy Dornick had not yet arrived from the west side of Cleveland and his heart and his future belonged to Melody Ring. In the summer of 1942, Artie found himself in the U.S. Army's 164th Regiment, on the South Pacific island of Guadalcanal. On the day he was to become a hero he was sitting behind a Browning .30-caliber machine gun, on the banks of the Matanikau River, guarding a battalion of Seabees who had just finished building a swing bride and were now taking a much-needed bath in the moonlight.

Smoking a Camel and sipping a tin cup of cold bitter joe, Artie Brown watched the naked Seabees in the river below him, scrubbing the sweat from their pimply backs and the bugs from their itchy groins.

Suddenly Japanese soldiers exploded through the jungle along the opposite bank. Grenades and bullets ripped chunks of flesh from the naked and soapy Seabees. Artie Brown and his Browning came to their defense, ripping chunks of flesh from both palm trees and Japanese. The Seabees splashed ashore. The Japanese kept coming. Many of both were killed.

The Seabees reached the bank and kept going, naked and wet into the jungle without stopping to gather up their clothes or their weapons. Artie Brown kept firing. Japanese kept coming. Japanese kept dying.

It was now that Howie Dornick's future father became a hero. To his left he saw Japanese filing onto the bridge. It would have been like shooting starlings off a barbwire fence for him, had not one of the Seabees parked a bulldozer in the line of fire. Without thinking Artie Brown abandoned his Browning, and bent like a barn door hinge, ran to the bulldozer. As he ran, shrapnel from a Japanese grenade sliced his foot off at the ankle.

Artie Brown hadn't driven a bulldozer before, but he'd been driving farm tractors since he was five and by the time he was in the bulldozer's ass-shaped metal seat, he had the levers figured out. His bleeding ankle stump working the clutch, he drove the bulldozer straight onto the bridge. The bridge and the bulldozer and Artie Brown and a lot of Japanese collapsed into the river.

Artie rose from the river bottom like a coconut. He would have been spotted and shot for certain had he not come up under a face-down Seabee oozing blood. Sticking his nose out of the water between the dead Seabee's open legs, Artie Brown floated safely down the Matanikau. After a bend or two, he pushed the Seabee away and swam to shore. He hobbled for six miles until be reached the forward line of the 7th Marine Regiment. By noon of the following day, the Japanese advance was stopped and the surviving Seabees, wearing nothing but dried soap, were rescued from the jungle.

Artie found himself a hero. The morning he was to be evacuated back to Australia, Major General Alexander M. Patch found him among the other wounded and stooped over his stretcher. "You lost a foot, soldier," Major General Patch was reported to have said, "but you saved a whole gaggle of Seabees. I'm recommending you for a Congressional Medal of Honor Medal."

"Well, ain't that something," Artie was reported to have said.

And so one-footed Artie Brown came home to Tuttwyler. There was a parade and a special church service and an article in the local paper, and Melody Ring, so proud and so relieved, let him for the first time unhook her bra. Not too many days after that one-time event, Patsy Dornick began letting him unbuckle the belt on her dungarees, as many times as his heroism required.

Patsy Dornick went off to live with an aunt in Cleveland for a while. By the time she returned with young Howard Allen—last name still blank—Artie Brown, fitted with the best prosthetic foot the people of Tuttwyler could chip in for, was back on the farm plowing and milking and wondering why in the hell he'd married Melody Ring.

And so Howard Allen was christened a Dornick, though everybody in Tuttwyler, including the former Melody Ring, knew he was a Brown.

Howie Dornick washes down his bologna and Swiss cheese sandwiches with the last of the instant coffee in his Thermos. After *Jerry Springer* he watches the local news, and then the national news, and then *Wheel of Fortune* and *Jeopardy*. Then he brings in an armful of logs and builds a fire. The box elder wood is dead but wet, and no matter how far he opens the damper, smoke fills the living room.

Still, he stays by the fire until the logs are reduced to ash and then he goes to bed.

He hides his head between his two flat pillows. It has been one of those days when the plusses and minuses balance out, leaving you uneasy and ambivalent and awake for a long time. Despite the work and risk involved, being forced to cut that dead limb out of the box elder had been a plus. It had pleased the mayor. Pleased Delores Poltruski and the Knights of Columbus. Pleased God knows how many others.

But it wasn't the *pleasing* that made cutting that limb a plus. He doesn't care about pleasing people. What he cares about is *pressure*. He is under a lot of pressure. Terrible pressure. Pressure others in Tuttwyler can't begin to imagine. For most people the worst pressure of their lives is over the moment they pop free of their mother's vaginas. But he is still dangling from his mother's vagina, unable to be fully born, the only imperfection of a perfect father.

Being the war hero he was, Artie Brown was never required to take responsibility for the imperfection Patsy Dornick had named Howard Allen, neither legally nor financially. Not even morally. Boys will be boys. War heroes will be war heroes.

But Tuttwyler was required to take responsibility.

It was easy for the village to be responsible for Artie Brown's imperfection while the snack cake line was still operating. There was a job for anyone you needed one. An unmarried mother could have a job there. An illegitimate son could have a job there. They could slide into the production line unnoticed, hidden by the jangle of conveyor belts, the whoosh of wrapping machines and the growl of tow motors; hidden by the wonderful aroma of cakes baking and sweet icings squirting. But when the snack cake plant moved to Tennessee there were not so many jobs for women who seduced war heroes or for the illegitimate sons dangling from their vaginas. So Patsy Dornick and her son Howard Allen became wards of the village. She was given a job at G.A. Elementary School as cafeteria *manager*. He was hired as the village's maintenance *engineer*. Grand-sounding jobs no one in their right mind would want to do. Jobs that paid next to nothing. Jobs that would make Patsy and Howie Dornick forever beholden to the village's brutal benevolence.

Howie Dornick slaps some air into his flat pillows. If cutting the box elder limb was a plus, Mayor Woodrow Wilson Sadlebyrne's suggestion that he paint his house was an unsettling minus. Those raw, gray clapboards are all he has. They are his dignity. His legitimacy. No way in hell is he going to smother them with paint.

But there is the pressure of it. The teasing. The cajoling. The begging. The threats. So much pressure. As he folds one of his flat pillows and pounds some softness into it, Howie Dornick listens to his thumping heart commiserate with Woodrow Wilson Sadlebyrne. The mayor has pressures, too. He is a young Democrat trying to fill the shoes of an old Republican. He has D. William Aitchbone gnawing at his ass. So he will do what he can to help the new mayor. He'll take down Christmas decorations and cut dead limbs, do whatever is reasonably asked of him. But reasonably does not include painting his house.

Finally Howie Dornick falls asleep, comforted by his flat pillows and his Civil Service protection.

5

D. William Aitchbone carries his cappuccino to a table by the window. There is no wind tonight, not like the other night. The flakes, small and icy, are in freefall, bouncing off the roofs of cars and people's heads. On the speakers, a Pan flute plays ghostly Irish songs. Behind the counter the girl with blackcherry lips is counting the change in the tip jar.

D. William Aitchbone settles in for another important strategy session with himself. He knows that back at his impressive Queen Anne on South Mill, his wife and kids are just beginning to tease and complain and threaten their way through another blissful supper.

When his strategy session is finished, Aitchbone crosses the village square, noticing that the Christmas decorations are gone from the gazebo and the dead limb is gone from the box elder. "Sneaky bastard," he whispers to himself, meaning not Howie Dornick, but Mayor Woodrow Wilson Sadlebyrne. He crosses the street and shuffles down the slippery walk to the village hall. He makes sure he slides into his chair just as the meeting is scheduled to begin.

Everyone is there. Woody Sadlebyrne is there. Councilman Phil Tripp is there. Councilman Len Wilkinson is there. Councilman Tom Van Syckle is there. Councilwoman Victoria Bonobo is there. Everyone that D. William Aitchbone wants in the audience is there, too: Sam Guss from the *Wyssock County Gazette*; Katherine Hardihood.

Aitchbone bangs his council president's gavel and gets right to business. "The village budget is about go through the roof," he says.

While Sam Guss scribbles the great quote in his reporter's notebook, Victoria Bonobo loudly challenges D. William Aitchbone's dire prediction. "Through the roof, Mr. President? We're projected to have a six-thousand-dollar surplus this year. And with all the new commercial growth on West Wooseman—well!"

47

Victoria Bonobo has challenged D. William Aitchbone's dire prediction because D. William Aitchbone has asked her to. She owes him so much. He handled her divorce. He handled all the paperwork on her new business venture, the Tiny Toes Day Care Center. He handled the fund-raising for her election to the village council. Yes, she owes him a lot. And this morning he called her at Tiny Toes, before the mothers began showing up with their kids, to not only discuss his secret plan for the village budget, but also to ask her to meet him tomorrow for a secret lunch, at the Wagon Wheel Restaurant, way over in Wooster.

Now, as they discussed, Aitchbone responds to her challenge, his larynx vibrating with masculine confidence. "Six thousand bucks is not a surplus, madam councilwoman. Six thousand bucks is a train wreck waiting to happen. I've tracked this thing into the out years. The tax revenues from the new businesses won't begin to cover our additional outlays for police and fire, road and sidewalk repairs, and the like." Just in case Sam Guss of the *Gazette* missed it the first time, he repeats, "It's a train wreck waiting to happen."

D. William Aitchbone now passes out copies of a frightening flow chart he's drawn which shows the budget literally breaking through the village hall's historically accurate slate roof.

"What's the answer?" asks Councilman Phil Tripp, genuinely concerned, not part of the conspiracy.

"Privatization," D. William Aitchbone answers.

Sam Guss writes down the big impressive word and underlines it twice.

"Privatization, Mr. President?" Victoria Bonobo asks, another pre-arranged response.

D. William Aitchbone lifts his firm chin and runs all ten of his fingers through the head of thick hair Victoria Bonobo's husband hadn't been blessed with. "That's correct, madam councilwoman. Bid out some of the village's services to private vendors."

"You mean things like police and fire?" Tom Van Syckle wonders, all on his own.

D. William Aitchbone's smile is reassuring. "Well not right away, Tom. We could start with some of the costly little stuff, like cleaning storm sewers, grave digging, repairing sidewalks and trimming limbs, simple maintenance stuff. Then after we've seen if the savings are real, we can look at things like garbage and snow removal. Police and fire would be way down the road. Way way down the road." He passes out identical gray folders containing not only the details of his proposal, but Xerox copies of newspaper articles from other Ohio communities where privatization has been a big success. "Maybe this is the way we ought to go, and maybe it isn't," he humbly tells his fellow council members. "But I think it's something we ought to consider. Again, I'm suggesting we start small."

Mayor Woodrow Wilson Sadlebyrne sits back and folds his arms, both amused and terrified by Aitchbone's performance; knowing that while the village budget will indeed scrape against the ceiling tiles in two or three years, there is not a chance in hell it will ever break through the slate shingles; knowing that D. William Aitchbone's proposal to privatize is nothing more than his private war against Howie Dornick's unpainted house.

Katherine Hardihood leaves the council meeting bewildered. She, too, understands the wickedness of Aitchbone's privatization plan. Worse still—what is making her wrists and ankles quiver—is her realization that D. William Aitchbone knows she understands it, and that he's counting on her to explain his threat to Howie Dornick.

Walking down the dark sidewalks of Tuttwyler, icy snow bouncing off her noisy polyester coat, house key ready to pluck a rapist's eye, she more than once whispers, "That Machiavellian fart."

She reaches her house. Delores Poltruski's car is not in Dick Mueller's driveway. Rhubarb has not pissed the curio cabinet. She loves him up anyway. She puts on her nightgown and two pairs of socks and gets in bed. On the news, the Cleveland Indians' equipment truck is arriving at Winter Haven, Florida. The driver, still wearing his Chief Wahoo cap and jacket, waves at the camera. As he does every year, Ernest Not Irish has followed the truck south, and is now standing outside the Indian's spring camp, in summer shorts and a Hawaiian shirt, shaking a big homemade sign that shows Chief Wahoo holding not a baseball bat, but a plate of pancakes. AUNT JEMIMA IN REDFACE the sign reads.

In the morning Hardihood walks to the library. She turns on the lights and turns up the heat. Weekday mornings are not very busy. A few retired people. A few young moms with their preschoolers. A few people who work odd shifts. At eleven she takes ten minutes to eat her lunch, and then, invigorated by the small bites of egg salad and Wonder Bread floating in her stomach, in a subterranean lake of grape juice, she returns to her desk for the lunch-hour rush. By 1 p.m. she has checked out eleven movie videos, five computer games, four CDs of children's music, and three books, one of them a novel.

The library is dead until three. Then school is out. Dozens of kids tumble in. There is the din of magazine pages turning, the din of homework going undone, the din of computer keys as seventh-grade boys tap onto the Internet to research their favorite rock stars and—if the Reverend Raymond R. Biscobee is to be believed—to download dirty pictures and chat with European pedophiles. By five the library is empty again.

Katherine Hardihood has succeeded in keeping the Machiavellian Fart out of her mind all day. Then at five-ten, just as she is about to walk home for supper, leaving Megan Burroughs in charge for an hour or so, the wife of the Machiavellian Fart appears at the desk, her daughter Amy and son Cannon in tow. She is there to pick up her reserved copy of *Lake Toads and Land Frogs*, R.C. Corwin's young adult fantasy about mutlicultural tolerance.

"Aren't you so proud of Bill?" Karen Aitchbone says to Katherine Hardihood.

"Hmmm?"

Karen Aitchbone blushes loving-wife pink. "Stepping into Don Grinspoon's shoes, I mean. This is going to be the best Squaw Days yet, isn't it? Not that Donald didn't always do a great job. But he's had so much on his mind the past few years. I don't know how some people cope, do you?"

"No, I don't," Katherine Hardihood says. She hands *Lake Toads and Land Frogs* to Amy. "Be sure to return it by the 28th. There are lots of other children waiting."

"I will," says Amy Aitchbone.

Now the Machiavellian Fart that is the husband and father of these perfectly harmless people is stinking up the inside Katherine Hardihood's head. She worries and fumes all the way home. She worries and fumes all the time she is wiping down the curio cabinet with Pine Sol and all the time she is simmering a can of Campbell's Manhattan Style Clam Chowder and spreading margarine on eight saltine crackers. She worries and fumes while she is eating that soup and those eight crackers and sipping a half-glass of skimmed milk, scratching Rhubarb's ears while he sleeps next to the plastic roses on the table.

Knowing as many facts as she does, Katherine Hardihood can commiserate with any number of historic figures who faced similar damned-if-you-do, damned-if-you-don't predicaments. But with the demon responsible for her predicament being D. William Aitchbone, her heart instantly reaches out to the biggest schnook in all Christendom, Judas Iscariot. How Judas must have felt that night, she thinks as she plays with Rhubarb's head: If he betrays Jesus, as Jesus almost certainly wants, he'll be the most reviled man in all Judea, Jesus being the messiah and all; yet if he refuses to betray his lord, he might be mucking up God's grand plan for human salvation. Damned if you do. Damned if you don't.

She walks back to the library and checks out videos and computer games and CDs and even a few books. At eight-thirty she turns off the lights and locks the door. She goes home and takes a zip-lock bag of rhubarb stalks from the freezer and puts it in the sink to thaw, just in case she proves as weak-willed as Judas Iscariot.

The next morning she bakes a rhubarb pie.

Victoria Bonobo waits for D. William Aitchbone in the parking lot of the Wagon Wheel. At exactly noon he pulls in. Inside, they take the booth nobody wants by the restrooms. One restroom door says BUCKAROOS. The other says SCHOOL MARMS. Victoria Bonobo orders a light meal for her nervous stomach, tossed salad and hot tea. D. William Aitchbone orders a mushroom burger, fries and coffee.

"Thanks for last night," Aitchbone says when the waitress heads to the kitchen with their orders.

Victoria can feel her red blood cells spinning. "I think privatization is the way to go, too. It will take some doing to convince the others, but—"

The coffee and hot tea come. He waits for the waitress to pour and leave. "We'll get it done, I think." Then he smiles. "But that's not what I wanted to see you about."

Her red blood cells are somersaulting now. "Oh?"

D. William Aitchbone leans over his coffee steam. "When you were going through your divorce, I remember you telling me . . ."

Victoria leans into her tea steam.

". . . that your brother roomed with the Vice President when they were at Ohio State. And that they still keep in touch."

Victoria feels her red blood cells sink to the bottom of her veins like flakes of rust. "Oh."

While Katherine Hardihood worries and fumes at the library, the rhubarb pie cools on top of her stove, protected from her tomcat by the heavy lid of a turkey roaster. She does not go back to work after supper. For the first time since becoming branch librarian, she'll let Megan Burroughs lock up. She changes into a comfortable pair of slacks and puts on a huge, poppy-red turtleneck that hides her unappetizing trunk under thick folds and blazing color. She applies a thin coat of gloss to her lips then, thinking better, wipes it off, leaving her librarian's lips a bit pinker nonetheless. She brushes her teeth with baking soda, puts the rhubarb pie in a Rubbermaid pie carrier, and walks through the snowless night to the unpainted two-story frame on South Mill.

Howie Dornick, breath smelling of peanut butter, cracker crumbs on his flannel shirt, opens the front door without turning on the porch light. "Katherine?"

Katherine Hardihood stiffly offers him the rhubarb pie, the way Indians in old movies offer peace pipes. "I remembered how much you liked it," she says. "I found some this morning in the freezer—not pie but rhubarb—and said 'Jiminy Cricket, what the heck, I'll bake Howard Dornick a pie.'"

He takes the Rubbermaid container. "Isn't that thoughtful."

The heat escaping from the open door mixes with the outside cold, forming a noticeable vortex of spinning air that, if this uncomfortable moment lasts any longer, Katherine Hardihood fears, might erupt into a full-blown tornado, ripping the porch right off its foundation stones. "We need to talk, Howard."

He backs inside. She follows and closes the door. "Why don't you cut us some pie," she says, peeling off her noisy coat and white knit hat. The power of her poppy-red sweater sends him fleeing to the kitchen. "I've still got a little coffee in my Thermos, if you want some."

"Why not," she says.

And so they sit on the sofa eating rhubarb pie, drinking stale instant coffee. "I thought you might be at the Eagles club tonight," she says.

"Not on Fridays. Too many people go there on Fridays."

"Howard, did you read today's *Gazette*?"

"I don't subscribe."

"Did you hear about last night's council meeting then?"

"Nope."

"Howard, have you ever heard of privatization?"

"Nope."

She explains: "It's when the government turns public jobs like yours over to private businesses."

"Oh, I guess I've heard about that."

"Bill Aitchbone wants to privatize your job, Howard."

"Why would he want to do that?"

"He says to save the village money."

"Would it?"

"Howard, you'd be out of work."

"I've been out of work before. After the snack cake line was closed, remember?"

"And do you remember how long it was before the village finally hired you? You were on your final week of unemployment."

"I think I still had two weeks to go."

"Bill Aitchbone doesn't really want to privatize your job, Howard. His privatization plan is just a ploy to force you to paint your house."

"Why is everybody so concerned about my house?"

"Because it's an eyesore, Howard."

"Well, I ain't gonna paint it."

"Then Bill Aitchbone will push his privatization plan through the council. He owns them."

"He don't own the mayor. Mayor's got a veto, right?"

"He owns us all."

"He don't own me."

"The Bill Aitchbone's of the world own anybody they want to own."

"Well, he don't own me. You want more pie?"

"It's good, isn't it? Even with last summer's rhubarb."

Howie Dornick takes their empty plates to the kitchen, returning with fresh slices. "The coffee's all gone. I could make some more."

"None for me."

"So, if I paint my house, I keep my job with the village?"

"Yes."

"They can stick their job where the sun don't shine, for all I care."

"I'm not telling you what to do. I came as a friend. To tell you what's cooking, that's all. Bill Aitchbone's chairman of the Squaw Days Committee now, and—"

"I thought Donald Grinspoon was chairman."

"Not any more."

"You sure?"

"I'm on the committee, Howard. Bill Aitchbone is the chairman. And he wants to put his stamp on it. God only knows what else he's got planned, but he's got a real bug up his behind about your house."

"Well, I ain't gonna paint it."

"I'm not telling you what to do."

"I ain't."

"Then you'll lose your job."

"I'm Civil Service."

"Civil Service only protects people in jobs that exist."

"I ain't gonna paint it."

"I don't blame you for being stubborn, Howard. Not the way this town has treated you."

"I got this house free and clear when my mother died. Mortgage paid in full."

"You're lucky. I've still got nine years on mine."

"I ain't gonna paint it."

"I'm not telling you what to do."

"Not for Bill Aitchbone. Not for anybody."

"What about for yourself, Howard?"

"So, you think I should paint it?"

"It needs painting, yes. You know it does. But whether you do or not—"

"Well, I ain't."

"I'm all for being a thorn in Bill Aitchbone's side, Howard, but—"

"If you were me, you'd paint it?"

"I just wanted you to know what was going on."

"You use brown sugar in your pies? Mother always did."

6

There is a saying about the month of March in the Midwest: March comes in like a lion and goes out like a lamb.

But in fact, March in the Midwest has no discernible coming in or going out. March in the Midwest is wretched from start to finish. March in the Midwest is deep wet snow one day, razor-blade rain the next; crocuses and daffodils pushing through the thawing ground only to be withered by night frost; frogs burrowing from pond bottoms only to knock themselves unconscious on the ice; March in the Midwest is taking sweaters off and putting sweaters on; men itching to mate with any woman and to mow anybody's grass; women itching to rearrange anybody's kitchen cupboards; March in the Midwest is cloudy; 39 degrees; 31 long days.

No, there are no lions or lambs in a Midwestern March. Only dead skunks on the road.

On the first Tuesday of this March, Katherine Hardihood backs her boxy Plymouth Shadow from the garage and navigates over and around flattened skunks to New Waterbury for the county library meeting.

During her twenty-seven years with the library no one ever attended these meetings other than librarians and library board members. But since January these meetings are suddenly very popular. That's when the Reverend Raymond R. Biscobee first showed up to demand that the new computers be taken out. "The filthy books you folks put on the shelves for our children to read are bad enough," he told the board in January, "but now that you've hooked up to this Internet thing, our children can call up filthy pictures and chitchat with pedophiles from every country in Europe." The board promised to look into his concerns and went on to discuss the need for a new roof at the Pennville branch. "The Pennville branch hasn't had a new roof since 1971," board member Margaret Bale said.

In February, the Reverend Raymond R. Biscobee was back with a contingent of "good Christian mothers and fathers," as he loudly declared them, who had met at Darren Frost's house and formed a group of concerned parents called EDIT, Erase Destructive Internet Trash. Extra folding chairs were brought over from Barrow Brothers Funeral Home. The board promised to look into their concerns and went on to discuss the sewage problem at the Hillsboro branch. "You've got a sewage problem at all the branches," someone in the audience called out.

Now it is March and EDIT has grown from a contingent into a juggernaut, with a slate of officers and an agenda that includes not only the filth available on the new computers, but also the filth to be found in the library's magazines and videos and albums and books. Given this wider purview, EDIT now stands for Eliminate Destructive Influences Today. Katherine Hardihood has trouble finding a seat even though extra chairs have been brought over from not only Barrow Brothers Funeral Home, but the Moose Club as well. Sam Guss of the *Gazette* finds himself sitting between big city reporters from the *Cleveland Plain Dealer*, the *Akron Beacon Journal*, and the *Wooster Daily Record.*

The library board sits like a row of empty glass bottles on a fence as members of EDIT rise one by one to shatter their humanity.

One EDIT member, Eileen Shagreen, who lives three houses down from Katherine Hardihood on Oak Street, and has three children at G.A. Hemphill Elementary School, and a fenced-in backyard with two free-running rottweilers, tells the board she is particularly upset that the Tuttwyler branch put up a huge Halloween display with children's books about witches and goblins—the servants of Satan— while the Christmas display had only one little book about baby Jesus hidden among the Santa Claus and snowmen books. Eileen Shagreen sits down to a Gatling gun of applause, *clap-a-clap-clap.*

"I'm sure we try to treat all holidays equally," board member Paul Withrow answers.

"That's exactly the problem," someone in the crowd calls out. *Clap-a-clap-clap.*

The Reverend Biscobee rises and demands that *Lake Toads and Land Frogs* be taken off the shelves. *Clap-a-clap-clap.*

"I can't for the life of me see what's wrong with a book that teaches children to respect people different from themselves," board member Charles English says. "We live in a very diverse country."

"Thanks to New Worlders like you," someone in the audience calls out. *Clap-a-clap-clap.*

Carl Clegg, a hog farmer from Bartholomew Township, complains that his wife once saw a "boy no older than thirteen checking out a how-to book on homosexualism."

"We don't have how-to books on homosexuality," board member Margaret Bale answers.

"Queer," someone shouts. *Clap-a-clap-clap.*

Darren Frost, in whose house EDIT was born, rises with a stack of pornographic pictures he's downloaded from the library's computers. "Men having sex with men," he says, passing the pictures out. "Women having sex with women. People having sex with animals. Naked little girls and boys not even developed yet having sex. Too bad you don't have color printers in the libraries, then you could really see how disgusting they are." *Clap-a-clap-clap.*

After all the members of EDIT who want to speak, speak, and Darren Frost's pictures are gathered up and slapped down like God's gavel on the table, the president of the library board, smiling comfortably, introduces the library director, Dr. Venus Willendorf.

Dr. Willendorf unfolds her arms and stands up. As is always the case when she publicly presents herself like this, every woman in the room immediately feels as barren as Abraham's Sarah while every man immediately feels the need to father a thousand children. This is because Dr. Venus Willendorf's breasts have the dimension of ostrich eggs, and her narrow waist attaches these magnificent orbs to a high and wide set of hips that frame a lush and protruding lap. So men and women alike start to breath uneasily as she rises, knowing that her mind is just as fertile as her breasts and hips; that when her lake-blue eyes are finished washing over them, she will slowly part her heavily lipsticked lips, and drown them with her estrogen-enriched confidence.

And so Dr. Venus Willendorf begins: "What children read or look at—whether in a book or on a computer screen, whether at home or at the library—is ultimately the responsibility of their parents."

EDIT boos en masse.

"Librarians are neither censors, baby-sitters, nor surrogate parents."

EDIT boos en masse.

"Despite its obvious potential for abuse and misuse by some, the Internet is an important new learning tool. As President Franklin Delano Roosevelt once said, 'The only thing we have to fear, is fear itself.'"

EDIT boos en masse.

"Not counting the three successive nights your Mr. Frost spent surfing for his pictures, there have only been five reported incidents of anyone, adults or children, using the library's computers to view pornography. We need to keep our cool and not throw the baby out with the bath water."

EDIT boos en masse.

"Finally . . ."

EDIT applauds en masse.

" . . . while the Wyssock County Public Library District cannot in good conscience stop offering materials that some might from time to time find objectionable, we have heard your concerns, loud and clear, and we will study ways to discourage children from viewing adult-oriented material, without infringing on parental rights or responsibilities." Dr. Willendorf sits down and folds her arms over those breasts.

EDIT boos en masse. Hisses en masse, too.

"Please!" begs the president of the library board, holding up his hands in a half surrender, comfortable smile still spread across his face. "I hope you weren't expecting us to march over to the computer terminals with baseball bats right this minute!"

The president's attempt at humor falls flat and, en masse, EDIT demands that the library board do exactly that. "I'll supply the bats," Darren Frost, president of the Little League, offers. The meeting ends.

As EDIT retreats down the rows of folding chairs borrowed from Barrow Brothers and the Moose Club, the library board president goes straight for Katherine Hardihood. The library board president is D. William Aitchbone. "It's going to be hard to get the toothpaste back in the tube on this one, isn't it?" he says.

"I just hope the board doesn't fold," she answers.

Aitchbone chuckles, knowing exactly what she means. "Now Katherine, I may wear a politician's hat on the village council, but I wear a librarian's hat here."

Katherine Hardihood twists the white knit cap in her hands, wanting to pull it straight down over Bill Aitchbone's head, until only his Adam's apple is showing. "I hope so."

He changes the subject — to the subject he cares about most. "So, what do you think about my privatization plan, Katherine? I saw you at the council meeting."

"Of course you saw me. Other than Sam Guss, who else goes to those boring meetings?"

"It would be good if Howie Dornick went once and a while."

Katherine Hardihood pulls the knit cap over her own head. "I'm sure he hears what goes on."

"Let's hope he does more than hear," D. William Aitchbone says. "Let's hope he listens."

"Whether he listens or not is up to him."

"He needs a good friend right now, Katherine. Someone to help him do the right thing."

Katherine Hardihood puts on her mittens, wishing they were brass knuckles. She turns to leave. D. William Aitchbone puts his hand on her shoulder and swivels her about, just the way he had swiveled Woodrow Wilson Sadlebyrne that night by the gazebo when the February snow was blowing horizontally. "I'm ready to stand up to these EDIT people, whatever it costs politically. Between you and me, they're a bunch of nutballs. But they do have a right to have some input."

"Input, Bill?"

"Maybe put one of them on the board. There'll be an empty seat in the fall. Reverend Biscobee's a good man. Be good to have someone from the clergy on the board. What do you think, Katherine?"

What Katherine Hardihood thinks—what Katherine Hardihood knows—is that D. William Aitchbone is threatening her with her job, just as he is threatening Howie Dornick with his, just to get a coat of paint on that little two-story frame house on South Mill, just down the street from his impressive Queen Anne. "I'm just a branch librarian, Bill. Who sits on the board is up to somebody's else."

"But you know I count on you. You're one smart lady."

When Katherine gets home from the library board meeting she takes another package of rhubarb from the freezer.

Howie Dornick goes to the door. "Katherine? Not another rhubarb pie?"

"You enjoyed the last one so much, I figured, 'Jiminy Cricket, what the heck!'"

He leads her into the kitchen, feeling like a turd because he threw half of the last rhubarb pie away. "I've still got coffee in my Thermos, if you'd like some?"

"Coffee'd be nice."

He pours two cups. She finds the silverware drawer on the second try and slices the pie. He takes two of his mother's best plates from the cupboard. Each taking their own plate and cup, they shuffle to the living room. They eat as many forkfuls of pie as they can without talking. The silence gets to Howie Dornick first. "I suppose you want to talk about me painting my house again?"

"He's really turning the screws, Howard."

"Well, I ain't gonna paint it."

"He's holding me personally responsible," she says. She tells him of D. William Aitchbone's threat to put the Reverend Raymond R. Biscobee on the library board.

Howie Dornick feels a double turd now. "I didn't even know Bill Aitchbone was president of the library board."

"He's president of everything."

"Including my ass."

"He's president of everybody's ass."

Both having used the word *ass,* they go back to eating pie until their embarrassment passes.

"He's intent on being the next mayor," Katherine says when she has no more pie to eat. "That means Squaw Days has to be perfect."

"You wouldn't quit your job just because Ray Biscobee got on the board, would you?"

"Jiminy Cricket! No! And Bill Aitchbone knows I wouldn't. He knows I'd stay at the library even if Ray Biscobee got every book taken off the shelves but the Bible. Just like he knows I'll stay on the Squaw Days Committee no matter how much of a mockery they make of it."

"I've always thought Squaw Days was kind of fun," Howie Dornick admits. "I know what you mean, though. Celebrating an Indian woman and her papoose getting clubbed to death by two white men is kind of weird. And there is lots of clean-up afterwards."

Neither have anymore pie to eat. But they do have stale instant coffee to sip. And so they sip. As unappetizing as they are too each other, they are nevertheless a lonely man and a lonely woman, of approximately the same age, sitting alone together, in March, the month when more than the ground thaws. "I didn't come here to make you feel guilty,

Howard. I just want you to understand how adamant Bill Aitchbone is about this. That's all."

Howie Dornick, of course, is feeling guilty, though not about Katherine Hardihood's predicament. He is feeling guilty about his half birth and about his attachment to his mother after all these years. He rubs his eyes until a universe of miniature stars explode on his eyelids. "I can't afford to buy any paint. Not on what the village pays me. It's all I can do to eat and pay my utilities."

Katherine has spent her life learning facts and gathering them into truths. So she knows that Howie Dornick's refusal to paint his house has nothing to do with how little money the village pays him, just as she knows that D. William Aitchbone's obsession with Howie's unpainted house has nothing to do with Squaw Days being perfect, or even with his need to be mayor. This is all about Artie Brown's wayward sperm. Just as Howie Dornick is the illegitimate son of Artie Brown and Patsy Dornick, D. William Aitchbone's wife, Karen, is the legitimate daughter of Artie Brown and Melody Ring. Even though his wife's birth has been sanctified by both God and the Wyssock County Recorder's Office, the existence of Howie Dornick taints her. Taints their marriage. Taints him. The raw gray clapboards on this little two-story frame are not Howie Dornick's shame. They are D. William Aitchbone's shame and D. William Aitchbone's illegitimacy. "If it's just the money—"

Howie begins waving his arms, as if a swarm of wasps just flew out of the cracks in the ceiling plaster. "I'm not taking any of your money, Katherine. You don't make much more than I do."

Actually, Katherine Hardihood knows for a fact that she makes quite a bit more than he does. "I hate Bill Aitchbone as much as you, Howard. And I'd say stand up to him regardless of how much funny business he pulls, except—" She searches the bottom of her cup for a time-delaying swallow. There is only a single thick drop. She lifts the cup to her lips and waits for the drop to trickle onto her tongue.

"—except that your house is an eyesore, Howard, and everyone in Tuttwyler, including me, wishes for godsakes you'd paint it."

Howie Dornick's arms are now wrapped tightly around his waist, as if those invisible wasps have found their way down his throat and are now building a hive inside his belly. "I ain't gonna paint it."

Katherine Hardihood finds herself on his side of the sofa, her arms around his shoulders, her pencil-point librarian's chin dug into his maintenance engineer's clavicle. "Oh, Howie. Let's have some more pie."

7

Red.

Yellow.

Green.

The cars on Tocqueville stop. The cars on South Mill go.

D. William Aitchbone drives through the intersection. He's spent the day expediting divorces in New Waterbury again. March is getting on. Days are stretching out. Temperatures are rising. It hasn't snowed in three days. That morning he saw the heads of his wife's daffodils poking through the mulch. That morning he received the news from the Sparrow Hill Nursing Home that his uncle Andy has suffered another stroke. It was his third in two years and likely to be his last.

Andy was the last Aitchbone to make a living farming. Because he never married—strange since he was as manly as any Aitchbone male—his four-hundred acre farm on Three Fish Creek will go entirely to his nephew, one D. William Aitchbone, who is now driving past his wife and children and his impressive soapy white, green-shuttered Queen Anne, for a strategy session with himself at the Daydream Beanery. Then he will go to the March meeting of the Squaw Days Committee.

D. William Aitchbone hands his Coffee Club card to the counter girl with the blackcherry lips. All of the little boxes are punched. She makes him the free cappuccino he has coming. He pays for a raisin scone. "They say it's going to hit fifty tomorrow," the counter girl says.

Despite the dulcimer music and the anticipation of his uncle Andy's death, Aitchbone's strategy session goes well. At 7:25 he heads for the library, his Burberry open and flapping.

Everyone is there, even Kevin Hassock, who has just been served with divorce papers.

Aitchbone acknowledges him with a commiserating, "Kevin."

Kevin Hassock, eyes fixed on his shoes, nods back. "Bill."

"Oh, Bill," Delores Poltruski says, "thank you so much for getting that box elder limb cut down. The Knights of Columbus are simply walking on water."

"The real thanks goes to Mayor Sadlebyrne," D. William Aitchbone says, making sure there is a smidgen of humility in his voice. "I'm not sure how you did it, Woody, but thanks for getting Howie Dornick off his duff."

After the mayor nods, D. William Aitchbone initiates a round of applause. Only Katherine Hardihood doesn't join in.

"Now if we can just get Howie to paint his house," Delores Poltruski says.

"Amen," Dick Mueller says.

"If I were a betting man, I'd bet this will be the year Howie paints it," D. William Aitchbone says. His court-room smile flies around the table and lands on Katherine Hardihood's sour face like a bat on a barn beam. And so the meeting begins:

Dick Mueller reports that the Chirping Chipmunks unicycle troupe from Akron will indeed participate in the parade. "They'll be happy to come back as long as we don't put them behind the mounted color guard from the sheriff's department again."

Dick Mueller's discussion of the parade is a terrible temptation for D. William Aitchbone. Sweet Jesus, how he wants to tell them about his coup. But even though Victoria Bonobo has talked to her brother, and her brother has talked directly to the Vice President, and even though the VP says he'll be happy to ride in the Squaw Days parade if he can squeeze it in his schedule, he knows it would be imprudent to spill the beans just yet. "Sounds like the parade is shaping up, Dick. My only recommendation is that you stay fluid. You never know who might come in at the last minute, or who might have to cancel."

"No problem," Dick Mueller says, knowing only too well that the chairman is right. Two years earlier the parade order had to be changed at the last minute when two members of the Tuttwyler Senior Squares square-dancing troupe were sidelined, Calvin Dubin with a bad case of the shingles and Margaret Snyder with pinkeye.

Delores Poltruski reports that there will be at least three more crafts exhibitors than last year, proof, she says, that Squaw Days is growing by leaps and bounds.

If only she knew how big those leaps and bounds were, Aitchbone thinks, picturing himself seated next to the VP in one of Bud Love's classic Chevrolet convertibles, waving and waving and waving.

Paula Varney reports that financial contributions from the merchants are coming in slow but sure, and that the sidewalk sale will be bigger than ever. "Wal-mart is not only going to put out their leftover summer things, but some of their back-to-school clothes," she says. "I bet before it's all over, Kmart does the same."

"I bet they do, too," Delores Poltruski says.

Donald Grinspoon reports that the tobacco-spitting competition will be moved from Sunday to Saturday, even though the pie-eating contest also is held that day. "Reverend Biscobee has some real concerns about the use of tobacco being glorified on the Sabbath," he says. "I figured, why ruffle anybody's feathers?"

"I think you're right on target," D. William Aitchbone says, wondering if the VP could be talked into judging one, or both, of those events. Footage like that would surely give Squaw Days some national coverage.

"The fireworks will still be on Friday night, won't they?" Dick Mueller asks the former mayor.

"Oh, sure," Donald Grinspoon assures him. "Fireworks and Friday night go together like Limburger cheese and onions."

When Woodrow Wilson Sadlebyrne reports he'll be sending village employees a memo by the end of April regarding their assignments for the festival, the former mayor can't hold his tongue. "I'd get it out by the middle of April, if I were you. People plan their vacations early. I remember one year half the fire department was off walleye fishing during Squaw Days. If there'd been a fire, God only knows what would've happened."

The new mayor's Democratic pride gets the better of his manners. "I think the end of April is soon enough."

"I don't know," the old Republican answers. "You're cutting it close."

Aitchbone enjoys their joust. It is, after all, so meaningless. When the VP's visit is confirmed—probably in another month or two—there'll be Secret Service, White House advisers, and field people from the Republican National Committee running over Tuttwyler like ants at a picnic. He offers a compromise: "Maybe you could send out a memo in the middle of April telling everyone not to make any vacation plans until they get your end-of-April memo." The resulting laugh breaches the partisan divide. D. William Aitchbone now turns to Kevin Hassock. "How are the rides shaping up?"

Kevin Hassock tries, but is unable to make eye contact with the man overseeing the destruction of his eleven-year marriage. "Everything's hunky-dory."

Now it is Katherine Hardihood's turn to report. "The gazebo band started rehearsals last Tuesday and the Re-Enactment people start rehearsing Monday," she says. "Al Warner found six new arrowheads in his soybean field for the historic display. So everything's hunky-dory with me, too."

D. William Aitchbone crawls into bed and kisses his wife's ear. Spring is coming. Her ear isn't as cold as usual. "That woman has more brass than a marching band," he whispers between his kiss and a yawn.

"The nursing home called about an hour ago," Karen Aitchbone says. "Your Uncle Andy's died while they were spoon-feeding him rice pudding."

Aitchbone goes to sleep wondering how much developers will offer him for the farm. It will be a bundle. But how big a bundle? And how soon can he get his arms around that bundle?

Just as Katherine Hardihood reaches the parking lot of the In & Out, the muddy clouds that have been hanging low over Tuttwyler all day erupt. Key in hand, she runs up Oak Street, raindrops as fat and repulsive as the tobacco spit at Squaw Days soaking her white sweater. Jiminy Cricket, how she hates D. William Aitchbone!

Katherine was already a freshman in high school working weekend afternoons at the library when eight-year-old D. William Aitchbone—then called Dusty by his family and friends, his first name being Dustin—first came to the library by himself. "Hi, Dusty," she said. "Come all alone today?"

"Certainly," he answered, the word shooting out of his little-boy lips both brisk and brusque, as if spoken by a forty-five-year-old lawyer.

Even then, Katherine Hardihood was not surprised by D. William Aitchbone's intimidating maturity. He had been born a forty-five-year-old lawyer. In elementary school, when other boys were watching *Davy Crockett* and *Captain Kangaroo,* on their families' new black & whites, he was watching *Meet the Press* and *Lawrence Welk.* In junior high, when boys were buying Beach Boy records, and combing their bangs straight down like the Beatles, he was buying Sinatra, and wearing his hair like Sinatra. In high-school, when other boys were slopping around in bell-bottom pants, their hair down to there, he was seriously comfortable in cuffed stovepipe slacks and Hush Puppies, getting straight A's in civics and geometry, writing fan letters to Ohio's Republican Governor, the no-nonsense James A. Rhodes.

Even when D. William Aitchbone moved up to Cleveland to attend John Carroll University and then the

Cleveland Marshall College of Law, Katherine Hardihood saw him almost every weekend in the Tuttwyler library, determined eyebrows pointed into a textbook, determined right thumb clicking the button on his ballpoint. He was Dusty no longer. He was Bill. Forty-five-year-old Bill—even though the Selective Service mistakenly took him for nineteen-year-old draft bait.

But Vietnam never got D. William Aitchbone. Nosireebob. His 2-S deferment kept him out of the war's four worst years, and then, just when he figured his goose was *gooked*, as draft-aged Tuttwyler boys used to say back then, Richard M. Nixon, another no-nonsense Republican, decided that a lottery was the best way to determine who'd stay and who'd go. Katherine Hardihood remembers him coming into the library one Saturday as happy as a 4-F clam. "So, Katherine," he said. "guess what my lottery number is."

"High, I gather."

"Three-sixty-four," he said.

A week later D. William Aitchbone was even happier. "So Katherine, guess what my LSAT score was."

"High, I gather."

"One-fifty-eight," he said.

Spared from the war, spared from a life as an insurance agent or high school principal, D. William Aitchbone went off to law school. Four years later he came out, the same age as when he went in. Forty-five.

And now all these years later, when he really is forty-five, he still acts forty-five, and Katherine Hardihood, soaked to the bone with tobacco-juice rain, knows that no matter how old D. William Aitchbone gets to be—eighty-five or ninety-five or two-hundred and five—he'll still be forty-five. He'll spend his eternity in hell forty-five, too. Not that Katherine believes in a literal hell—eccept, that is, for her far-too-frequent encounters with D. William Aitchbone at this meeting or that meeting.

Donald Grinspoon had taken Bill Aitchbone under his political wing when he was still in high school. "That boy is just dripping with potency," Katherine overheard then-mayor Grinspoon tell then-sheriff Norman F. Cole as they sat reading hunting magazines in the periodical section. "And Tuttwyler needs some potency." That was, of course, long before the I-491 leg was built, when the village was just a hollow circle on the state map, a hollow circle with an empty snack cake factory.

And so when Donald Grinspoon got the brainstorm for a festival, he made sure the potent and perpetually forty-five-year-old D. William Aitchbone was on the committee. He'd made sure that Katherine Hardihood, with her love of facts, was on it, too.

Once Grinspoon decided that Tuttwyler's contribution to Ohio's summer festival season would be a festival commemorating the clubbing death of an Indian woman and her baby, the real work of his hand-picked committee began:

It became immediately clear that a catchy name for the festival had to be chosen; already committee members were clumsily referring to it was "our little festival" and "our festival thing" and even "our Indian-woman-getting-clubbed event."

The committee sat in the mayors office one December evening, squinting and digging their foreheads and playing with their chins, looking for the world, Katherine Hardihood thought, like sixth graders trying to convince the teacher that they were actually thinking. "How about Tuttwyler Days?" Phyllis Bastinado suggested, wedging her arms into the glacial grove that separated her basketball breasts from her sprawling belly.

"Pioneer Days," Dick Mueller suggested.

"Settlers Days," Sheriff Norman F. Cole suggested.

"History Days," Delores Poltruski suggested.

"Those names don't tell you anything," Donald Grinspoon said, "except that it's going to last more than one day. We need something specific. Something that tells you right off the bat what we're celebrating. Look at Hinckley, up in Medina County, they've got their Buzzard Day. Tells you right off the bat it's about buzzards. Or the Circleville Pumpkin Festival. Tells you right off the bat it's about pumpkins."

"How about Brothers Days, then?" Sheriff Norman F. Cole offered, drawing quizzical stares. "You know, after John and Amos Tuttwyler, the brothers who clubbed the Indian woman to death."

"Oh," said Donald Grinspoon on behalf of the others.

Katherine Hardihood, already regretting she ever went to Helen Smith's house in Berea and found Henry Howe's old history book, could not resist saying, "How about Brotherly Love Days?"

Everyone giggled nervously. Everyone but D. William Aitchbone, who was too focused on the problem at hand to appreciate her sarcasm. "Still doesn't tell us what the festival's about."

Again Katherine couldn't resist. "How about Dead Indian Days?"

No nervous giggle this time. Just the silence of guilt.

"Now, now Katherine," Donald Grinspoon said after pumping air back into his lungs. "But you're right. The focus needs to be on the Indian woman and her baby, not on the white men who killed them."

"Squaw Days," Delores Poltruski said.

Donald Grinspoon clapped his hands just once, making the same sharp crack a well-swung club might make coming down on a skull. "There you go! Squaw Days!"

With the name out of the way, the real planning could begin. First, when to hold Squaw Days? There was nothing in Henry Howe's book about when the Indian woman and her baby were clubbed by the Tuttwyler brothers, or when her ghost appeared to the stump burners. But the second weekend of August seemed perfect, falling, as it did, two weeks after the Wyssock County Fair and two weeks before the start of school. Next, how many days should the festival last? Certainly one day wasn't long enough. Nor was two. A week was certainly too long. So was four days. Was three days too long? No, three days was just right. Next, how those threes days should be filled, what kind of events and attractions? "There's clearly got to be some serious historical stuff," Donald Grinspoon said. "After all, a woman and baby getting clubbed requires a bit of sensitivity."

Everyone agreed with that. And since sensitivity was, as the mayor put it, "the bailiwick of women," Phyllis Bastinado, Katherine Hardihood and Delores Poltruski were appointed to a subcommittee to, as he put it, "sort out the handkerchief stuff."

That left Dick Mueller, Sheriff Norman F. Cole, D. William Aitchbone, and Mayor Donald Grinspoon to sort out the nuts and bolts of running the festival, nuts and bolts being the "bailiwick of men."

Everyone left that December meeting feeling their Wheaties, dreaming of the grand festival certain to put Tuttwyler back on the map, just nine months hence. But by the January meeting, with everyone fat and tired from Christmas, and northern Ohio looking and feeling much-too-much like the inside of an un-defrosted refrigerator, it was unanimously decided that eight months simply wasn't enough time to, as the mayor put it, "birth this baby."

Everyone was relieved. Waiting until the next year would give them time to plan, as the mayor put it, "a real humdinger."

At the February meeting, the all-male nuts-and-bolts subcommittee announced they were going to spend the summer visiting various festivals around the state to, as the mayor put it, "learn from their mistakes so we don't make too many of our own." The handkerchief subcommittee protested, especially Delores Poltruski. "So, you boys get to gallivant around the state while we've got our noses stuck in the history books? No way, José."

So, beginning that March with a trip to Hinckley's Buzzard Day—which celebrated the annual return of the township's famous flock of turkey vultures with a pancake and sausage breakfast and crafts fair—the Tuttwylerites spent their weekends criss-crossing Ohio, learning from others' mistakes and adding inches to their waistlines.

They went to the Festival of Flight in Wapakoneta, which annually honored hometown hero Neil Armstrong, first man on the moon; the 56-foot white dove in front of the Neil Armstrong Air and Space Museum gave Delores Poltruski goosebumps.

They went to the Pro Football Hall of Fame Festival in Canton; the museum had a 52-foot dome in the shape of a football and Sheriff Norman F. Cole wondered if the seven-foot bronze statue of Jim Thorpe was full-size.

They went to the Great Mohican Indian Pow Wow and Rendezvous in Loudonville and got the business card of a Navajo chief who could supply his troupe of authentically dressed Native American dancers anywhere, anytime, fee negotiable.

They went to the Melon Festival in Milan, where they not only ate their fill of melons, but visited Thomas Edison's birthplace. "Maybe we could make a museum out of Artie Brown's birthplace," Dick Mueller suggested through a mouthful of cantaloupe.

They went to the Ohio Swiss Festival in Sugar Creek, filling their bowels with too much cheese, and their bladders with too much apple cider.

They went to the Covered Bridge Festival in Jefferson and watched the plowing contest and ate Covered Bridge Pizza at a restaurant housed in a converted covered bridge.

They went to the Twins Day Festival in Twinsburg and ate vinegar-soaked French fries while watching hundreds and hundreds of identical twins march in the "Double-Take Parade."

They went to the Great Outdoor Underwear Festival in Piqua, a grand get-together celebrating the town's proud past as a major manufacturer of undergarments.

They went to Coshocton for the Canal Festival, which commemorated the first canal boat visit in 1830.

They went to the All-American Soap Box Derby races

in Akron and they went to Riverfest in Cincinnati for the Rubber Duck Regatta; a plate of Cincinnati-style chili gave Dick Mueller the squirts.

They went to the Valley City Frog Jumping contest.

They went to Rio Grand, to the farm of famous sausage-maker Bob Evans, for the Chicken Flying Meet, witnessing the longest flight by a chicken ever, 302 feet, six inches.

They went to the Woolly Bear Festival in Vermilion and ate elephant ears and taffy while people dressed as fuzzy brown and orange caterpillars paraded by.

They went to the Ohio Sauerkraut Festival in Waynesville. Sheriff Norman F. Cole bought a bag of sauerkraut fudge and ate it all the way home, a three-hour drive, getting such horrible indigestion that despite the emergency medical training he required of all his deputies, he didn't recognize the heart attack he was having the next morning while showering for work.

The Squaw Days Committee skipped the weekend after the sheriff's funeral, but the next Saturday resumed their research, driving down to Circleville for the Pumpkin Festival; Donald Grinspoon, signaling the end of their official mourning period, ate a piece of pumpkin fudge. Phyllis Bastinado and Delores Poltruski split a pumpkin burger.

They went and went and went that spring, summer and fall.

At their November meeting—held one year to the day of that first meeting in Donald Grinspoons office—they sat down to, as the mayor put it, "glean what we've learned."

Dick Mueller gleaned this: "You've got to have a parade. People love parades. And carnival rides. People love carnival rides."

Delores Poltruski gleaned this: "You've got to have plenty of food. Food you can't normally get."

"As long as it isn't sauerkraut fudge," Katherine Hardihood could not resist saying.

Phyllis Bastinado gleaned this: "You've got to have a busy schedule of events. One thing after the other. Something for everyone. Young, old and in-between."

D. William Aitchbone gleaned this: "A spoonful of sugar makes the medicine go down."

"Jiminy Cricket, Bill. What's that supposed to mean?" Katherine Hardihood asked on behalf of the other equally puzzled committee members.

"It means you can only push the history stuff so far. People come to festivals to have fun. To throw caution to the wind and let it all hang out. Fun, fun, fun 'til daddy takes the T-bird away, you know?" Realizing he was sounding much too young, D. William Aitchbone let the forty-five-year-old in him take control. "I guess what I'm saying is *balance*. We've got to find a way to let people enjoy themselves while they're remembering what a terrible thing happened to that Indian woman and her papoose. Balance. Balance. Balance."

Katherine Hardihood gleaned this: She wanted nothing to do with Squaw Days. "So, what did you glean, mayor?"

"That we've got our work cut out for us," Donald Grinspoon said. "And that we're going to have one helluva festival."

While Katherine Hardihood wanted nothing more to do with Squaw Days, she also knew she could not walk away. She was the one who found that Indian woman hiding in Henry Howe's old history book. She was responsible for her now. She'd have to stick it out, salvaging as much dignity as she could, not only for that poor Indian woman, but for poor Tuttwyler.

She knew it wouldn't be easy. And it wasn't.

"You know, Katherine," said Donald Grinspoon at the next month's meeting. "We've got to have a name for our squaw. A catchy name. A name folks can relate to. Pocahontas, Sacajawea, Little White Dove."

"Henry Howe doesn't say what her name was," Katherine Hardihood said.

"Donald's right," D. William Aitchbone said. "She's gotta have a name."

"We can't just make one up," Katherine Hardihood said. "We've got to be historically accurate."

"Accurate, schmaccurate," D. William Aitchbone said.

"How about Laughing Feather?" Dick Mueller offered.

"Jiminy Cricket, Dick."

"Katherine's right," Donald Grinspoon said. "It's got to be a real Indian name. Something she might actually have been called. Something people can relate to."

"Relate to a lie?" Katherine Hardihood asked.

"Not a lie, Katherine," Donald Grinspoon said. "We're just filling in the blanks."

"Donald's right," D. William Aitchbone said. "Just filling in the blanks. So, what's a good-sounding Indian name?"

"None of us speak Indian," Phyllis Bastinado pointed out. "We'll have to find a book on Indian languages. Find out what tribes were living around here in those years."

"Eries and Wyandots and Senecas and maybe Shawnees," Katherine Hardihood said. "Although by the time Wyssock County was settled by whites, most of the Indians had been pushed farther west already."

"That's all interesting, Katherine," Donald Grinspoon said, "but we don't have time for a big investigation into Indian languages here. I'm going public at the next council meeting with our Squaw Days plans. I've got to have a name. It's the first damn thing Sam Guss at the *Gazette* will want to know. Can't exactly tell him we're still making one up, can I?"

"No you can't," D. William Aitchbone said.

"I don't see what's so bad about Laughing Feather," Dick Mueller said.

Delores Poltruski could see that Katherine Hardihood was about to yell Jiminy Cricket or worse. "I've got a *great* name for the squaw—Pogawedka!"

"I like it!" Donald Grinspoon said immediately. He imitated a B-movie Indian chief. "Pog-uh-wed-kuh! Pog-uh-wed-kuh!"

Everyone but Katherine Hardihood started imitating B-movie Indians: "Pog-uh-wed-kuh! Pog-uh-wed-kuh! Pog-uh-wed-kuh!"

"Princess Pogawedka," Donald Grinspoon shouted.

"Prin-cess Pog-uh-wed-kuh! Prin-cess Pog-uh-wed-kuh!"

"What about her baby's name?" Phyllis Bastinado then wondered.

"I guess Little Laughing Feather is out of the question," Dick Mueller said.

"Was Princess Pogawedka's papoose a boy or a girl?" Donald Grinspoon asked.

"A boy," D. William Aitchbone decided.

"Then how about Kapusta?" Delores Poltruski offered.

"Kuh-poosh-tuh! Kuh-poosh-tuh!"

When Katherine Hardihood arrived at the library the next morning, she went straight for the language books and pulled down a Polish to English dictionary: Pogawedka meant nonsense. Kapusta meant cabbage. "Jiminy Cricket," she said. "Princess Nonsense and her Little Cabbage!"

Katherine Hardihood would wonder for the next thirteen years whether she had a playful ally on the committee. Or whether Delores Poltruski was just another fool.

8

April is a cold, muddy mess. May is not much better. Robins, forced to build nests and mate under these miserable conditions, are edgy and aggressive, ganging up on the sparrows and mourning doves. Goldfinches are refusing to turn gold, preferring to wear their melancholy winter brown. Squirrels are groggy from too much sleep. Canada geese are suffering from diarrhea. Tulips are dwarfed, their petals lackluster. People aren't washing their cars, or picking up the pop cans and cigarette wrappers littering their lawns, or cleaning the muck out of their gutters. The owners of garden centers, their greenhouses stuffed with unsold petunias and marigolds and impatiens, are pulling out their hair. Kmart and Wal-mart have more bags of topsoil and peat moss and cedar wood chips than they know what to do with. Denny's hasn't sold a single glass of iced tea. Frank and Carla Cooke, owners of the Dairy Doodle, are up to their elbows in frozen custard. Farmers can't plow. Men sit in their garages on their idle riding mowers watching the wet grass get higher and higher, while their wives rearrange cupboard after cupboard. The girl's softball team at West Wyssock High hasn't played half its games because of the rain, and in a one case, because of the snow.

Some blame the terrible spring on global warming. Some blame it on the coming of a new Ice Age. The Reverend Raymond R. Biscobee on Sunday, rain stomping up and down on the roof of his half-empty church, blames it on the filth available at the library. "God is warning us," he says.

Still, the people of Tuttwyler, Ohio, have to get on with their lives, Howie Dornick among them.

One Friday evening he takes a long shower with a new bar of Ivory Soap. He puts on his suit pants and a light blue shirt, and then, after watching the clock tick away to 8:30, gathers up the bag of fancy muffins he bought that afternoon at the Daydream Beanery and walks up South Mill, across the square, then down East Wooseman to North Grant. After stopping at the In & Out for a box of Tic-tacs, he forces his legs up Oak Street to Katherine Hardihood's two-bedroom ranch. He stands on the front step for a long minute and watches Delores Poltruski pull into Dick Mueller's driveway. Finally he rings the bell. And he knocks, just in case the bell isn't working.

Katherine Hardihood isn't at all surprised by his appearance at her door. She's invited him to stop by. The dress pants and blue shirt and bag of muffins do surprise her, though. Pleasantly surprise her. Also makes her more nervous than she wants to be.

"Smells like Pine Sol," Howie Dornick says, sniffing the living room air.

"My cat has a hard time controlling himself."

"Pisses things, does he?"

Katherine Hardihood takes the muffins to the kitchen and puts them on a pink depression glass platter. She pours two cups of freshly dripped coffee—freshly ground from the hazelnut-flavored beans she bought that morning from the Daydream Beanery—and putting everything on a reproduction tin Coca-Cola tray, returns to the living room.

Howie has positioned himself on the end of her sofa. "It's going to be just like last year, isn't it?" he says, putting down the *Newsweek* he wasn't reading. "It's going straight from winter to summer. No spring at all."

"Looks that way, doesn't it?"

Howie Dornick and Katherine Hardihood have been seeing each other quite a bit lately. D. William Aitchbone has seen to that.

"These muffins are wonderful," Katherine says, peeling back the sticky paper cup and taking a guppy bite out of her muffin's crunchy golden skin.

They talk about the Daydream Beanery for a while, he shaking his head at what a prissy place it is, she telling him that it's where she bought the coffee they're drinking, which, he agrees is pretty tasty. They talk about the trouble EDIT is causing for the library, including D. William

Aitchbone's ongoing threat to nominate Ray Biscobee for the board. They talk about his ongoing proposal to privatize village services—it looks like he has the votes to push it through at the June meeting—and they talk about the cause of all this trouble in their lives, Howie's unpainted clapboards.

"Do you really think I should paint?" he asks.

"It's up to you," she answers.

"I don't know," he says.

They finish all the muffins and half the coffee, and then, as if D. William Aitchbone secretly has implanted computer chips in their buttocks and brains, these two unappetizing people copulate right there on the couch, with the light on, and the drapes wide open, with Rhubarb watching from the top of the sofa, the scent of Pine Sol, Ivory Soap, and hazelnut wafting.

Howie Dornick walks home at one in the morning, wishing his mind was full of fresh memories of wonderful sex. But it hadn't been wonderful sex. It had been horrible sex. It was obvious from Katherine Hardihood's shaking knees that she had never had sex before. And his excessive sweating and inopportune passing of hazelnut-scented gas hadn't helped matters. Nor had his penis. It hadn't been in contact with a vagina since his year in Japan in the early sixties, and just like Japan, it had remained rubbery and ambivalent throughout.

Still, the kissing beforehand had gone fine, as had the hugging afterwards. After they each spent some time in the bathroom cleaning up, they had another cup of coffee, and shared a bowl of Cheez-its, letting Rhubarb lick their orange fingertips while they watched public television's umpteenth re-broadcast of Yobisch Podka's 1991 performance with the Santa Fe Symphony.

When he reaches the porch of his unpainted two-story frame on South Mill, Howie Dornick presses his face against the raw gray clapboards and cries. In the morning he drives all the way to Wooster. Passing the Wagon Wheel Restaurant, he spots a car in the parking lot that looks just like the American-made Japanese luxury job D. William Aitchbone drives—same pewter paintjob and everything. He drives on to Bittinger's Hardware and walks straight for the young man standing behind the cash register, who has shorn bootcamp hair, an earring, and a tee-shirt that reads BONE HEAD.

"How can I help you?" the young man asks in the friendly, efficient voice the hardware-selling Bittingers have been using for ninety years.

Howie frowns at the tee-shirt. "I need some house paint."

"You've come to the right place."

"I'm painting my house. On the cheap."

"Gotcha."

The Bittinger boy leads Howie Dornick down the wallpaper aisle to a pyramid of paint cans by the nail-nut-bolt-and-screw display. "Not our best, but the best for the price," he says, using a line he's heard his father and grandfather use a thousand times. He taps on the can lids as if they're a stack of bongo drums.

Howie stares at the pyramid of cans, in his head trying to multiply the sale price by the number of gallons he figures he needs. He doesn't like the total he comes up with. "Anything cheaper?" he asks.

"Nothing I'd feel right selling you," the Bittinger boy says, another well-practiced family line jumping off his tongue.

"I've got to do this on the cheap," Howie Dornick says.

The Bittinger boy knows the Bittinger credo: *Sell up if you can, sell at sale price if you must, but sell something if you call yourself a Bittinger*. And he wants to stay a Bittinger, at least until he graduates from Ohio University. He studies not only his customer's shabby clothes, but also the poverty in his eyes. "If this is too steep, we've got some stuff in the back I could give you at a real good price."

"I'm interested in a real good price."

The boy gives his customer the *follow-me* Bittinger wave and starts down the wallpaper aisle. "Once in a while somebody orders a custom color, then doesn't pick it up, for whatever reason." He turns down the garden tool aisle and gives the seed rack a spin just in case his customer might want to plant something. "Where you from?"

"Tuttwyler."

"I went to Squaw Days once. Almost entered the tobacco-spitting contest."

The small talk tempts Howie Dornick to ask the Bittinger boy about the message on his tee-shirt. "What makes you a bonehead?"

"My girlfriend had it made for me. I'm majoring in forensic anthropology, with a minor in archeology. I study bones and stuff."

"No kidding."

The Bittinger boy drums on the chest like a National Geographic gorilla. "Eventually I'd love to work with somebody like Donald Johanson. You know, from the Institute of Human Origins? The guy who discovered Lucy? *Australopithecus afarensis*? In Ethiopia? The little three-million-year-old hominid babe? Did you know Johanson used to work at the Natural History Museum in Cleveland? Working with a heavy hitter like Johanson is a long shot. Believe me, a reeeeaaaal long shot. I'll probably end up in a crime lab solving murders. But that's OK. More fun than selling hardware."

Bonehead, all right, Howie Dornick thinks.

The garden tool aisle empties into the heating and plumbing supply department. Between the air conditioners and the sump pumps stands the door to the back room. The Bittinger boy leads his customer through it. He knees in front of a stack of paint cans and twists them so he can read the labels. "I've got to warn you, some of these colors are reeeeaaaally something."

Howie Dornick squats next to him. "Let's see what you've got."

"Well, I've got four gallons of this yellow. The guy who took over the Klean Kar car wash on Route 3 wanted something that would really catch people's eye. Two days after he took it over, somebody shot him while he was emptying the quarter boxes. So we got stuck with this really bright yellow."

"How bright is it?"

"I can give you a real good price. I can give you a real good price on all this stuff."

And so Howie Dornick leaves Bittinger's Hardware with not only the four cans of car-wash yellow, but also with three cans of video-store blue (the electrician hired to rewire the old empty store burned it to the ground, the Bittinger boy told him), two cans of beauty-shop blue (the three women partners had a falling-out over what their shop should be called, Hairway to Heaven, Shear Magic, or Cheap Cuts), one can of gold (The Bittinger boy had mixed that one for a Wooster College fraternity house, but the brothers spent the entire fix-it budget on a propane grill, leaving repainting of the big peeling Greek letters above the front porch for another year), and one can of darkroom black (ordered by a freelance photographer who fell off a barn roof trying to take a panoramic shot of Holsteins coming in for milking, for the July cover of *Ohio Cow* magazine). Despite the misfortunes of these various Woosterites, Howie Dornick leaves Wooster a happy man. He's gotten all these cans for the price of one can of sale-price white.

As soon as his customer drives away, the Bittinger boy calls home. "Dad," he says, "you'll never guess what some guy from Tuttwyler just bought. All that paint in the back."

"Hope you gave him a good deal. You don't make your money on what people buy from you today, but on what they buy from you tomorrow."

"Gave him a real good deal."

"Good. You're not wearing that goddamn tee-shirt, are you?"

Bittingers never lie, not to each other, not to anybody. Still, they are skilled in the art of evasion. "Tee-shirt?"

"A hardware man can't be thought of as a bonehead," his father says. "People have to believe hardware men know everything. You sell him any brushes?"

"One of the cheap ones with the plastic bristles."

"Didn't you explain that a good brush is more important than the paint?"

"Twice. He said the cheap one was good enough."

"He'll be sorry."

"That's what I told him."

"And he still bought the cheap one?"

"We've got to keep our DC trip a secret," D. William Aitchbone says, after the waitress at the Wagon Wheel brings his scrambled eggs and wheat toast. "I don't want anyone to know until the VP's visit is chiseled in granite."

Victoria seals her lips with an invisible key. Reaching over the table, the yoke collar of her spring dress exposes her cleavage to the fake candlelight cascading from the wagon-wheel chandelier above their table. She drops the key into D. William Aitchbone's shirt pocket, the nail on her pinkie finger sliding over his nipple. "I haven't been to Washington for years. And never to the White House."

"Karen and I took a tour with the kids when we were there last summer," Aitchbone says, the touch of Victoria Bonobo's finger sending a watt or two of electricity up his spine. "We didn't get to see any of the offices or anything. Just the ceremonial rooms."

"The VP is just a regular guy," Victoria says. She presses her palm against her mouth to keep from giggling. "I can't believe I'm telling you this, but he tried to feel me up at my brother's wedding."

Aitchbone's estimation of the VP takes a nosedive. "You're kidding?"

Victoria takes her fingers away from her mouth and touches the back of Bill Aitchbone's hand before taking a packet of grape jelly from the bowl by the napkin holder. "Well, it wasn't really that bad. I was old enough to be felt up. And he wasn't married yet. Or in politics. And I didn't let him get that far!" She scrapes the grape jelly onto her toast. "I can't wait to go, can you?"

Katherine Hardihood stays in bed half the morning. She can still feel Howie Dornick's hairy belly on her ribs. She can still feel his hip bones on her hip bones. She can still feel the part of him that parted her. She can still smell the sticky stuff that went everywhere, the Ivory Soap and the hazelnut, the Cheez-its dust under her fingernails. Despite Howie Dornick's unappetizing appearance, he'd been tender and thoughtful and apparently quite an expert. She cannot wait to invite him over again.

The weather is suddenly better. Farmers can plow. Men can mow. Women stop cleaning their cupboards and start cleaning out their flower beds. Tuttwyler's collective edginess fades. A collective serenity sets in. Katherine Hardihood invites Howie Dornick over for pizza.

It is supermarket pizza, made on an assembly line in a faraway state, with a minimal amount of mozzarella and sausage, plastered to a cardboard disk and wrapped in plastic. Not much of a meal to offer your lover. So Katherine Hardihood doctors it with fresh mushrooms and fresh green pepper. Howie Dornick thoughtfully brings another bag of fancy muffins.

Between the pizza and the muffins they copulate for the second time in five days.

"You'll never guess what I did Saturday," he says, pants off, shirt on, crumbs of muffin sticking to his naked knees.

She looks up from the television listings. "What did you do?"

"I bought paint. In Wooster."

"You went all the way to Wooster to buy paint?"

"I didn't want anyone to know."

"You didn't want Bill Aitchbone to know."

"I'm not sure if I'm going to paint or not. He's put me in a real pickle."

She kisses him on the cheek. "Bill Aitchbone lives to put people in pickles. You heard his uncle died?"

"Think he'll sell the farm?"

"Jiminy Cricket, Howard, he's sure not going to farm it."

Howie brushes the crumbs off his knees. Rhubarb comes to lick them out of the carpet fibers. "I don't think I bought enough paint, anyway," he says.

9

Even though Katherine Hardihood invites him over for supper twice more before the end of May—they are getting nearly as regular as Dick Mueller and Delores Poltruski, they joke—Howie Dornick is no more confident with his sexual performance than the first time. Nor is he any closer to deciding what to do with his clapboards. Then walking home from work on the first Monday in June, stopping to scrape a pancake of chewing gum from the heel of his work-boots, he overhears Paula Varney, standing in the open doorway of Just Giraffes, telling someone on her cellular phone that Bill Aitchbone and Victoria Bonobo have gone somewhere together. "Really," she is insisting, "Vicki Bonobo and Bill Aitchbone! Suitcases and everything!"

At dawn the next morning Howie Dornick calls Mayor Woodrow Wilson Sadlebyrne at home. "Woody, I won't be at work today. I'm sicker than a dog with something."

"No problem," the mayor tells him.

With that out of the way, Howie Dornick puts on the worst clothes he has— he has plenty to choose from— and after a quick cup of instant coffee goes to his garage. He rolls out an empty fifty-five gallon drum. He sweeps out the dead flies with a broom. Then he carries out the paint he bought at Bittinger's in Wooster, and can by can pours it into the barrel: the car-wash yellow and the video-store blue and the beauty-shop blue and the fraternity-house gold and the darkroom black. He stirs the paint with the broom handle until his growing worry stops his arms. But it isn't the color that's worrying him. It's the amount of paint. It isn't going to be enough.

And so he goes to his basement and finds a can of satin finish peach his mother once bought with the intention of painting the kitchen. He also finds the two-quart can of shellac she bought with the intention of refinishing the upstairs baseboards and door casings. While he's at it, he gathers up the bleach jug by the washing machine.

From under the kitchen sink he gathers up bottles of floor wax and furniture polish. From the bathroom he takes bottles of rubbing alcohol and Listerine and hydrogen peroxide. He empties it all in the barrel and stirs with the broom handle. It thins the paint but doesn't add much volume.

And so he goes into the garage and collects six cans of 10W-30 motor oil, an almost full jug of windshield wiper fluid, a quart of Kingsford charcoal lighter, and three, two-gallon containers of something everyone in Ohio has plenty of, antifreeze. Into the barrel it all goes. He stirs with the broom handle until the mixture is mixed. He goes inside and pours himself a cup of coffee. He sits at the table sipping, still unsure whether he is actually going to paint. When his cup is empty, he pulls down a bag from the top of the refrigerator and takes out the cheap brush with the plastic bristles that the Bone Head warned him not to buy. He rams it in his back pocket, walks timidly to the garage and pulls his ladder from the rafters. He leans it against the back of his two-story frame.

Only now does Howie decide to paint. He dips one of the empty paint cans into the barrel, and with the cheap brush in his back pocket, climbs, all the way to the top of the gable. His first brushful of paint sinks into the raw gray clapboards like oleo margarine into a slice of hot wheat toast.

When Howie Dornick paints things for the village—the dark green park benches on the square, the egg-yolk yellow crossing lines in front of G.A. Hemphill Elementary School, the smoke-gray walls of the mayor's office—he paints carefully, and slowly, hardly ever dribbling or splattering or smearing, his left hand guiding the brush in smooth even strokes from right to left, his puckered lips blowing away spiders and ants and ladybugs, the nail of his little finger flicking away scabs of bird shit. And he always prepares the surface first, carefully sanding or scraping, puttying or caulking. Now he paints like van Gogh at his maddest.

By nine the back is finished. By two the west side is finished. By seven-thirty the east side is finished. At ten he is finishing the front, standing on the porch roof, flashlight sticking out of his mouth like a thick silver cigar. When the last little corner is covered, he throws what is left of the cheap plastic-bristled brush into his untrimmed shrubs. He carries the ladder back into the garage and slides it up into the rafters. He walks the 55-gallon drum back into the garage, too. It is as empty as when he started, every drop of the brew now slathered on the clapboards of his two-story frame. He washes his face and hands in gasoline and dries off with a greasy rag.

He crawls into his bed feeling proud, feeling potent, feeling fully free of his mother, wishing Katherine Hardihood was under him right now, wishing that D. William Aitchbone's severed head and limbs and trunk were stuffed in that 55-gallon drum. But once his sheet is tucked around his neck, once the cool has faded from his pillow, these fresh and wonderful feelings are gone and his brain is crawling with the same old maggots of doubt: Why in *thee hell* did he paint his house that god-awful color? What in *thee hell* is wrong with him? Why in *thee hell* didn't he paint it white? He could have bought that white paint on sale at Bittinger's. He could have bought the most expensive paint they had. He has $18,500 in the bank—not in a CD he can't touch without paying a penalty—but in a regular old fashioned savings account he can tap any time he wants. He could buy vinyl siding for godsakes. No doubt about it, Bill Aitchbone will have a fit when he comes back from wherever he is with Victoria Bonobo, and sees that god-awful color. What in *thee hell* is wrong with him? Why in *thee hell* did he do it? To please Katherine Hardihood? To show her what a man he was? So she'll continue copulating with him? One thing for sure, there'll be no more copulating with Katherine once she sees that god-awful color! What in *thee hell* was he thinking? Bill Aitchbone will privatize his job and Katherine will put his private parts back in cold storage. What in *thee hell* was he thinking?

Howie Dornick turns his pillow over, to bury his head in the side still cool. He laughs into the dark. What would Artie Brown say about all this? Would he appreciate his son's courage, for standing up to Bill Aitchbone the way he stood up to those Japs on Guadalcanal? Who knows what Artie Brown would say? Probably nothing. Artie Brown never said a word about his son—or to his son—from the day Patsy Dornick returned from Cleveland with her newborn baby until the day he died of a heart attack hobbling across a cornfield with a five-gallon can of gas for his tractor. Artie Brown was a hero in war. But not in life. If his last will and testament was a true measure of his desires, he would rather have spent his life copulating with Patsy Dornick, not Melody Ring. The will was nicely typed by a lawyer's secretary, but at the bottom of the last page in Artie's faltering hand were the most embarrassing words ever put to paper by a Tuttwylerite, and therefore known to just about everyone: *To Patsy Dornick I leave my crank, who loved it so much more than Melody Ring ever did. But before anybody goes running to my casket with a butcher's knife let me state clearly that I leave the above mentioned appendage to Patsy Dornick only symbolically. I have already lost one appendage and neither dead nor alive do I wish to be separated from another.*

Again Howie Dornick laughs into the dark. What anger Artie Brown must have carried around inside him to scribble those words so late in his life, words that spread through Tuttwyler like a wildfire and prevented Melody Brown from ever going to church again. He wonders if it was anything like his own anger. Good God! What in *thee hell* was he thinking, painting his clapboards that god-awful color?

10

D. William Aitchbone watches the suitcases chug along the carousel. He spots the two-suit leather-trimmed Hartmann he bought for his very important trip at the new mall at the I-491 interchange. "There's my Hartmann," he loudly announces.

Victoria Bonobo spots her Samsonite. "There's mine," she says.

They ride the people-mover to the parking garage. It takes seven or eight long minutes. They stand apart from each other. Neither says a word. Neither knows what to say. They get in his luxury sedan and fasten their seat belts. They leave Cleveland Hopkins Airport and take the southbound ramp to I-71.

They pass the Strongsville exit.

They pass the Brunswick exit.

They pass the Medina and Lodi exits.

They pass the New Waterbury exit.

They swing onto I-491 and drive to the Tuttwyler exit.

It's been a long and silent drive. But now they are sitting in Victoria Bonobo's driveway, in Woodchuck Ridge, and D. William Aitchbone has already popped the trunk and somebody has to say something.

"Well, we did it, Bill," Victoria Bonobo says.

"The Democrats are going to shit a brick when they find out the VP is coming to Squaw Days. Sweet Jesus, I wish we could announce it right way."

Victoria opens her door but does not get out. "You know I'm sorry about the other thing."

"It's OK, Vicki. I'm just as attracted to you as you are to me."

"But walking out of the bathroom naked—what was I thinking?"

"Don't beat up on yourself. We'd just come from the White House. Had a great dinner and too much merlot."

"Not that much merlot. I guess when you've had a bad marriage, you think everybody has a bad marriage."

"Sometimes I wish I had a bad marriage."

"No you don't. Karen is terrific." She reaches over and squeezes his knee. "And so are you. You want to come in for coffee or something?"

"I do need to use your bathroom. I can never pee on airplanes."

"Me neither."

So D. William Aitchbone follows Victoria Bonobo inside and uses the bathroom and comes out fully clothed. When they stand at the front door and discuss the village council's upcoming privatization vote, he wants to latch onto her shoulders and never let go, just as he wanted to latch onto them at the Washington Hyatt. They are wonderful shoulders, sloping wonderfully from her wonderful neck, just fleshy enough, just bony enough, just round enough and just square enough, and just strong enough to support a pair of breasts far larger than his wife's. As soon as there is nothing more to say about the upcoming privatization vote he retreats to his car.

Driving toward Tuttwyler he calls home on his cell-phone. "I just dropped Vicki off," he tells his wife. "I thought I'd stop at the farm for a while."

"Don't be too long," Karen Aitchbone says. "I want us to have a nice lunch with the kids. Tacos, OK?"

"Better than OK. All I had for breakfast was airplane peanuts and a Sprite."

Then Karen Aitchbone remembers. "You haven't heard, have you? Howie Dornick painted his house yesterday."

D. William Aitchbone says "Love you, babe" and clicks off. What a couple of days! He's finagled the VP for Squaw Days! He's resisted Victoria Bonobo's wonderful shoulders! He's forced Howie Dornick to paint his house! "Am I on a roll or what?" he says to himself. As much as he wants to drive straight into town and see for himself that white paint on Howie Dornick's clapboards, he knows he needs to stop by the farm. Uncle Andy's will is moving quickly through probate. The court-appointed appraiser is coming to look it over on Friday. A developer is coming to look it over on Saturday. Other developers will be coming after that. So everything out there's got to be ship-shape. He turns onto Three Fish Creek Road.

Three Fish Road is about sixty percent developed now: three-acre estates crowed with big new houses; pole barns for pet ponies and cute little pigmy goats; front yard ponds as round as pancakes; newly planted trees that won't provide a lick of shade for another thirty years. The forty percent that isn't developed lays fallow: cowless cow pastures; pigless pig yards; fields that once grew corn and soybeans now thick with wild carrot and thistle. Some of the old farm houses are still standing, some still lived in. Some of the old barns are still standing, too, though there is no hay or straw in their mows; no fodder in their silos; no corn in their cribs; no tractors with attached plows, waiting greased and gassed for the rain to stop; no cows to be milked; no pigs to be slopped, no eggs to gather, no sheep to shear; just mice and bats and mold and rot.

D. William Aitchbone turns into his Uncle Andy's driveway. In a few months it will be his driveway. It will be his house. It will be his barn. It will be his four hundred acres. But not for long. Nosireebob. With a little luck his name will be on the deed for only a few days, maybe only for a few hours. As soon as humanly possible this driveway, this house, this barn, these four hundred acres, will belong to a developer. He has been in contact with several already. By Thanksgiving the old Aitchbone homestead will be cash in the bank. Even after the state and the federal governments take their unfair shares, he still will be a millionaire, two maybe three times over.

D. William Aitchbone trots to the house. He checks the doors to make sure they're locked. He checks the windows to make sure none are broken. He does not go inside. The last time he was inside is the day he took Uncle Andy to the Sparrow Hill Nursing Home.

The house, built in the 1830s, is one of the older houses in Wyssock County. It was built by the original Aitchbone from Connecticut, Jobiah Aitchbone, but not before the barn was built or the fields and pastures cleared. For nearly twenty years those original Aitchbones—six sons, three daughters and wife Almira—lived in a log house, which, according to the family's oral history, had been located somewhere along the creek; not far, D. William Aitchbone surmises, from where the Tuttwyler brothers clubbed to death Princess Pogawedka and her poor little Kapusta.

Although the old house always smelled like someone hadn't flushed the toilet, it was a grand place for a boy to visit. So many little rooms, with their lopsided walls and slanting ceilings and creaking floors; so many old drawers to snoop in; attics full of old trunks and boxes; attics and drawers and cupboards filled with antiques that he sold to one of the state's top dealers the same week he moved Andy to Sparrow Hill. He made enough money from those antiques to cover six months of Andy's care. The only thing he kept was the little dresser that had first belonged to Andy's grandmother. It had glass handles and a cracked oval mirror. It would have brought three hundred bucks but Karen wanted it for Amy's bedroom.

So, D. William Aitchbone does not go inside. He walks to the barn. The padlock is still on the big sliding doors. The side door that Andy's cows once used is padlocked, too. No need to go into the barn, either. Unfortunately, the door on the granary has been jimmied open. He goes inside. He finds a few pages ripped out of a *Hustler,* and an empty beer can. He looks at the dirty pictures and goes back outside.

He walks to the fence behind the barn and slides between the loose strands of barbed wire. He heads across the pasture. Andy sold off the last of his herd three years ago, so the pasture is waist-high with weeds and the cowflops are as gray and hard as granite. He walks to the end of the pasture and again slides through the barbed wire, this time snagging the knee of his Dockers. He is not particularly concerned. Dockers are always on sale at the new mall at the I-491 interchange. He walks across the rolling fields where Andy—and God knows how many Aitchbones before him—once grew corn. He keeps is eyes peeled for arrowheads, even though most of the ground is covered with weeds and rotting stalks. After he moved Andy to Sparrow Hill, he sold a whole shoe box full of Indian artifacts to that same top dealer. He was amazed at how much those worthless things went for.

He walks all the way to Three Fish Creek. Most of the creek here is on Aitchbone land, though some of it wiggles onto the old Tuttwyler homestead. He stands on the shale bank and looks into the shallow water, hoping to spot a crayfish or a school of minnows. All he sees is a crushed Dr Pepper can. On the ridge above him are the backyards of new houses. A year from now the spot where he is standing will be in someone's backyard, too. He heads upstream through the burdock, well aware that he is the luckiest sonofabitch alive.

He is a lucky sonofabitch because he was born with good Connecticut Yankee genes. He is a lucky sonofabitch because his parents made sure he got the best education the Wyssock County public schools could offer, so he was ready for the best education a private college could offer. Never once at John Carroll or at the Cleveland Marshall College of Law did he get drunk on beer or high on marijuana. He kept his hair short, his mind sharp, his nose in his books, and his name on the dean's list.

He is a lucky sonofabitch because he married a good, level-headed woman. A woman who, despite the weakness of her father, the war-hero Artie Brown, had the good sense to keep her knees together until she had an engagement ring on her finger. A good, level-headed woman who gave him two good level-headed children, cute-as-a-button Amy, handsome-as-his-dad Cannon.

He is a lucky sonofabitch because he turned down those offers from those big Cleveland law firms and returned to practice in Tuttwyler. He is lucky because while other students followed George McGovern over a cliff, he stayed connected with the local Republican Party. That got him Donald Grinspoon as a client. And having Donald Grinspoon as a client got him all the clients he'd ever need.

He built his political career slowly, patiently carrying Donald Grinspoon's waterbucket. That patience paid off in spades. Today he is president of the village council, vice-chairman of the Wyssock County Republican Party, president of the county library board, and— *Yeeeessss!*—chairman of the Squaw Days Committee, just back from the White House where he charmed the Vice President of the United States into attending that summer's festival. The luckiest sonofabitch alive, that's what he is. Sure, he isn't mayor yet. But that's Donald Grinspoon's fault, for not knowing when to hang it up, for falling off the stage during the Meet the Candidates Night at G.A. Hemphill Elementary School. But there is always another election. And when that next election is over, Woodrow Wilson Sadlebyrne will be back connecting TV cable. And a patient and disciplined lucky sonofabitch named D. William Aitchbone will be running the village. He'll be the best mayor Tuttwyler, Ohio ever had. Better than Donald Grinspoon ever was. He'll be a mayor who personally knows the VP. The same VP who in just three short years will be elected President of the United States of America, having carried Ohio's fast-growing 26th congressional district in a landslide, a landslide orchestrated by a lucky sonofabitch who by then will be a congressman-elect. And thanks to Andy Aitchbone's decision never to marry, he'll be a millionaire two or three times over. The luckiest sonofabitch alive, that's what he is.

He wades out of the tall grass and burdock and climbs the highest hill on the farm. There is a fantastic elm up there. Next spring some two-income couple will eagerly pay a premium to have that fantastic elm in their front yard. Come Saturday, he will have to point out this hill and that elm to the developer.

As he reaches the top of the hill, and the shade of that fantastic elm falls over him, he lifts his clenched jaws and with angry disappointment growls "Shit!" Just beyond the elm is something he'd forgotten all about: the old Aitchbone family cemetery.

Breathing hard with worry, he trots toward the cemetery. The gravestones and the wrought-iron fence surrounding them are barely visible above the weeds. He orbits the fence until be finds the gate. Weed-bound, it won't swing open. So he hops it, snagging the ass of his Dockers on one of the iron points. He kneels by the nearest gravestone. It is the grave of Henry Aitchbone, one of Jobiah's six sons. Born July 1802. Died February 1878. His wife, Blanche, August 1805 to March 1881, is buried next to him. He kneels by other gravestones. Some are broken, some flat on their backs, some leaning, some as straight as the day they were planted. There are maybe fifteen gravestones in all. He looks until he finds the stone where the original Ohio Aitchbones are buried. Isn't that something, Jobiah and Almira were both been born in May 1782; both died in May 1861.

D. William Aitchbone cannot help but think about Jobiah and Almira walking their brood all the way from Connecticut, through forests and across rivers, worried about wolves and bears and how much flour was left in the wagon; maybe even worrying about Indians, though if Katherine Hardihood is right, the Indians were long gone from the Ohio frontier by the time Wyssock County was settled. Indians or no Indians, the genetically blessed Aitchbones made it. They chose this land above all the rest, paying $1.50 an acre. They felled trees and burned stumps and maybe it was right around here somewhere, where that Indian squaw appeared in the smoke, forgiving the Tuttwyler brothers for clubbing her and her baby to death, wishing the white settlers nothing but the best—not that such a silly thing really happened, of course.

Surrounded by the graves of his ancestors, how can D. William Aitchbone not think about these things? How can he not think about them plowing their fields with teams of oxen? Or shooting squirrels and raccoons to save their precious corn crops? Or crowding into their first little long house? Or building with their bare hands that big house and big barn down there? How can he not think about them sitting around the table eating pork roasts and potatoes? Pies stuffed with the apples they grew themselves? Washing it down with the milk they squeezed from their own cows? How can he not think about them chopping wood and spinning flax and dipping candles and having no such thing as toilet paper when they headed for the outhouse? How can he not think about those nine Aitchbone children growing into adults and marrying somebody from an adjoining farm and copulating and copulating and copulating, creating new generations of Aitchbones and Browns and Warners and Grinspoons and Randalls and Goodes and Sprungs, spreading across Wyssock County like windblown milkweed seeds? How can he not think of them dying of the ailments people now take over-the-counter pills for, of them being buried on this hill on terrible February mornings, horizontal snow pelting their disciplined Connecticut Yankee faces?

And how can he—being who and what he is—not think about the problem this collection of ancestral bones is going to create for him? Will developers want a farm with a cemetery on it? Will it affect the price? Will voters vote for someone who sells his ancestors' remains? What will it cost to dig these bones up, and bury them somewhere else? How much will fifteen cemetery plots cost? Will he have to buy fifteen new caskets? What would that cost? And what kind of a stink will Katherine Hardihood raise about all this? "That woman has more brass than a marching band," he tells his long-dead relatives buried there, afraid that maybe he isn't the luckiest sonofabitch alive after all.

This new predicament requires an immediate strategy session. Those tacos with the kids will have to wait. He walks straight and fast for his car, as straight and fast as those early Aitchbone men walked when an Aitchbone woman rang that dinner bell he sold for one hundred bucks to that top antique dealer.

D. William Aitchbone drives into Tuttwyler. He waits impatiently for the light at Tocqueville and South Mill.

Red.

Yellow.

Green.

As he drives up South Mill the impressive Victorians and Greek revivals click by like perfect teeth. Then he pounds the brakes. The car squeals and twists, narrowly missing the fender of a Jeep Cherokee. "That crazy bastard," he screams, the bastard being, of course, Howie Dornick, owner of the freshly painted clapboards in front of him.

And so D. William Aitchbone finds himself out of his car, screaming "Crazy bastard!" over and over, charging the freshly painted two-story frame, invading its rotting porch, banging on its door with two fists, grabbing the man who opens it by the sleeves of his undershirt, shaking and jerking him about, screaming "Crazy bastard!" square into the man's stunned, crazy-bastard face. Then he finds himself retreating back across the grass. He finds himself swiveling and pointing a single sharp finger at the man, the way the Japanese on Guadalcanal pointed their bayonets at the man's war hero father. "That isn't white, Howie! That is a far cry from white!"

PART II

"By convention colors exists, by convention bitter, by convention sweet, but in reality atoms and void."

Democritus

11

Hugh Harbinger closes the front door and jiggles the knob to make sure it's locked. He drags himself down the sidewalk and folds himself into the back seat of an 1984 cinnamon-gold Ford Crown Victoria station wagon. Back in the house his Jack Russell terrier, Matisse, is running back and forth across the sofa, growling, yipping, abandoned.

"Did you take your pill?" Eleanor Hbracek whispers to him over her headrest.

Hugh Harbinger, thirty-seven since the fifth of June, squirms like a boy of twelve. "I took my pill."

Now Bob Hbracek growls over his headrest. "Buckle up."

"You don't have to buckle in the back seat," Hugh Harbinger protests.

Bob Hbracek ignites. "You do in my car."

With the help of Eleanor Hbracek's persuasive eyes, Hugh Harbinger surrenders. "I'm buckled."

Having successfully laid down the law, Bob Hbracek backs his Crown Vic down the driveway and heads up Delano Drive to Pearl Road.

Bob and Eleanor Hbracek are Hugh Harbinger's parents. Hugh's last name used to be Hbracek, too. For reasons Bob and Eleanor still can't understand, he changed it to Harbinger about ten years ago.

They turn left on Pearl. It's August. It hasn't rained for fifteen days. Thanks to the city water ban, every lawn in Parma, Ohio is as cinnamon-gold as Bob Hbracek's Crown Vic. Parma is a Cleveland suburb, populated primarily by Eastern Europeans who, enriched from their union jobs at the steel mills and auto plants, bought up street after street of bungalows in the fifties and sixties. Poles. Slovaks. Ukrainians. Slovenians. Germans. Lithuanians. Hungarians. Their taxes built good schools and good parks and paid for top-notch police and fire protection. Their spending power attracted one of the first covered malls in Northern Ohio.

Parmatown it's called. Retired from Ford two years ago this September, Bob Hbracek now spends a lot of time at the Parmatown mall, sitting in the food court with his UAW buddies drinking coffee and shaking their heads at all the strange people moving in. The Hindus. The Chinese. The Koreans. The Vietnamese. The Arabs. And the blacks. Yes, even the blacks are moving in.

Pearl takes them south through a corridor of fast-food restaurants, auto dealerships and discount stores. The Saturday morning traffic is horrendous. It's 10:30 before they reach the Interstate 71 interchange. Eleanor Hbracek has already sucked her way through half a roll of pineapple Lifesavers. "We're going to be on time for the parade, aren't we?"

"With plenty of time to spare," her husband answers, merging onto the highway, free at last to let the eight cylinders under the big hood of his Crown Vic do their stuff.

"Wait until you see Princess Pogawedka," Eleanor Hbracek says to her son. "She'll give you goosebumps."

In just thirty-eight minutes they are whooshing across Wyssock County, new housing developments as far as the eye can see. "If I was a younger man I'd move out here," Bob Hbracek says. "This is like Parma used to be."

Hugh Harbinger can't resist. "White?"

Eleanor Hbracek quickly offers both her husband and her son a Lifesaver. "You father just means there's more elbow room out here."

Hugh Harbinger waves off the peace offering. "White elbow room."

"Let's not argue about the Negroes again," Eleanor Hbracek pleads. But Bob and Hugh do argue about the Negroes. They cover every Negro topic Bob is proficient in: real estate values, affirmative action, welfare reform, drugs, babies having babies, foodstamps and professional basketball. When Bob runs out of Negro topics, they argue about immigration, Ronald Reagan, Richard Nixon, gun control, homosexuality, and seat belts. They argue all the way to Tuttwyler. It takes Bob Hbracek ten angry minutes to find a place to park. Finally out of the Crown Vic, they follow the crowd toward the village square.

Hugh Harbinger can't believe he's come to Squaw Days. Then again, these days there are so many things he can't believe he's doing. He can't believe he's back in Parma living with his parents and that he doesn't have a fucking penny to his name after so many six-figure years. He can't believe he's eating red meat and drinking Pepsi again. He can't believe he's reading the *Parma Post* instead of the *Village Voice* and is no longer walking Matisse down to Washington Square for a nightly romp in the dog run, or sipping expresso with Jean Jacques Bistrot at the Peacock, meeting Buzzy at Zulu Lulu for hummus and pita. He can't believe he's no longer copulating with Zee Levant, popping 100 milligrams of Solhzac every morning, antidote for the clinical depression that crippled him at the height of his genius. More than anything, he can't believe he's no longer the design world's most coveted color consultant, no longer deciding what color clothes people will be wearing, what color cars they'll be driving, what color sheets they'll be sleeping on, what color they'll be painting their walls and their fingernails, what color food dehydrators and bread-makers they'll be wasting their money on.

Hugh Harbinger has never been to Tuttwyler before. At first the old brick buildings surrounding the square reminds of him of Greenwich Village. But the display of giraffes in Paula Varney's shop remind him this isn't The Village. The wooden Indian in front of the Pizza Teepee, holding that big wooden pizza with the intricately carved pepperoni slices reminds him this isn't The Village. The hundreds of straight, white, overweight Ohioans milling about remind him this isn't The Village. He spots the Daydream Beanery. That does remind him of The Village. "I'm going in for an espresso."

"You just stay put," his mother says. "The parade's going to start."

Hugh Harbinger twists his face like a disappointed twelve-year-old.

"You can have your espresso when we get home," his mother says.

Hugh Harbinger surrenders and accompanies Bob and Eleanor Hbracek to the curb. The Squaw Days Parade begins.

The first parade unit is a black sheriff's car. Its rack of blue lights is blinking. Its siren is blaring. The crowd applauds. The deputy driving the car waves as if he's the Queen of England.

The next parade unit is the VFW color guard. Two of the veterans carry a long canvas sign between them. ARTIE BROWN POST, the sign reads. The crowd applauds. When Eleanor Hbracek asks who Artie Brown is, Bob Hbracek answers, "How in the hell should I know?"

The next parade unit is a brand new school bus fitted with a hydraulic lift for handicapped students. A long sign on the side reads: SCHOOL STARTS IN 16 DAYS. The adults in the crowd cheer. The kids in the crowd jeer. Then everyone laughs as if they're in an old movie directed by Frank Capra. "So far," Hugh Harbinger whispers to his mother, "I think the school bus wins the governor's trophy."

The next parade unit is a troupe of young unicyclists. For some reason they're dressed like chipmunks. The crowd applauds them.

The next parade unit is a clump of cub scouts. They're followed by a clump of brownies. They're followed by a clump of 4-H kids, some of them pulling goats, some carrying chickens and rabbits, some just waving like the Queen of England. The crowd applauds them all.

Next comes a candyapple-red Ford mustang. There's a boom box sitting on the roof, blaring "Mustang Sally." The crowd sings along. Some in the crowd dance. Bob Hbracek tells his son, "It's a '66." A sign on the door of the Mustang reads: BILL BLAZEK FORD. Even parades have commercials these days.

Next comes someone in a cupcake costume. There is a large plywood butcher's knife sticking from its back. Fake whipped cream is dripping from the wound. The crowd applauds defiantly. "I don't get it," says Hugh Harbinger.

Bob Hbracek, the union man, does get it. "They used to make snack cakes here until the workers organized with the AFL-CIO. The bastard owners moved the whole kit and caboodle to Tennessee."

"So the cupcake's a protest," Hugh Harbinger says.

"Yeah," Bob Hbracek says. "A protest."

"I like it," Hugh Harbinger says. "Very Salvador Dali."

This Bob Hbracek doesn't get. "Huh?"

Hugh Harbinger now hears the *clicky-clacky-click* of drumsticks on metal. The crowd claps and cheers. Suddenly there's a whistle. *Threet-threet-threet-threet.* Then there's an off-key blast of trombones and clarinets, sousaphones and flutes. He recognizes the tune. It's "Louie-Louie." *Bomp-bomp-bomp. Bomp-bomp. Bomp-bomp. Bomp-bomp. Bomp-bomp-bomp.* The sign carried by two meaty majorettes—who, in their shimmering red and gold bathing suits look for all the world like a pair of ornamental carp— tells the crowd that this is the MARCHING WILDCAT BAND OF WEST WYSSOCK HIGH. The band director, dressed like Davy Crockett, urges the crowd to sing along: *"Lou-eeeea, Loooo-i, ohhhh no! I godda go. Yah yah yah-yah."*

The next parade unit is an American-made Japanese luxury sedan. Hugh Harbinger recognizes the paint job.

"That's one of my colors," he tells his parents.

"It is?" Eleanor Hbracek says proudly, as if her son had just brought home a drawing of a seven-legged cat from kindergarten.

Bob Hbracek is not proud. "It's gray. Gray has been around forever."

"Actually, it's pewter," Hugh Harbinger says.

"Pewter's been around forever," Bob Hbracek says.

"Not that shade of pewter," Hugh Harbinger says.

The pewter-colored car reaches them. Everyone but Hugh Harbinger starts to clap. The sign on the car's door tells everyone that the man in the back seat waving like the Queen of England is none other than Danley McCutcheon, Secretary of the U.S. Department of the Interior.

Everyone in Tuttwyler is thrilled that Interior Secretary Danley McCutcheon has come to Squaw Days. Everyone except for the driver of the pewter-colored luxury sedan. While he is smiling for all he's worth, he's feeling like the unluckiest sonofabitch in the world. He knows something the crowd doesn't. He knows that the waving man in the back seat should have been the Vice President of the United States, not the secretary of the measly goddamn Interior.

Many more parade units pass by. Scouts. Clowns. Little League baseball teams dangling their legs over flatbed trucks. Mayor Woodrow Wilson Sadlebyrne waving like the Queen of England from a fire truck. Former Mayor Donald Grinspoon, wearing a scarf and goggles, bouncing by on an oil-farting old Harley. Sheriff's deputies on prancing appaloosas. The Senior Squares square-dancing club do-si-doing through the horse biscuits.

Hugh Harbinger now hears the *DOOM-doom-doom-doom* of Indian drums. The crowd, merely enthusiastic up to now, grows ecstatic. Hundreds of necks stretch in unison. A cheer rattles up the street. Then there she is, Princess Pogawedka, standing high on the back of a farm trailer, pulled along by a huge blue tractor. The princess is wearing a white buckskin dress, long fringe cascading from her sleeves and hem. A single feather rises straight up from her beaded headband. Princess Pogawedka—the woman portraying her, that is—has stained her skin the color of butterscotch pudding. She wears a black wig with waist-length pigtails. A baby is strapped on her back. As far away as he is, Hugh Harbinger can make out the baby's Cabbage Patch face. Princess Pogawedka is not alone on the trailer. All around her sit people dressed as Indians and pioneers. There also are a pair of ceramic lawn deer on the float. And a full-size teepee. And a few evergreen shrubs still in their black plastic garden-center tubs.

The happy cheers suddenly give way to a heavy *Booooooo!* Walking behind Princess Pogawedka's trailer are a pair of men. They are weaving back and forth across the street like drunken Neanderthals. Their faces are painted white. They are wearing fake frizzy beards. They are wearing felt Lil'Abner hats and baggy bib overalls. They are carrying enormous papier-mâché clubs. They are throwing candy into the crowd.

"Who are those two clowns?" asks Hugh Harbinger.

"They're not clowns," Bob Hbracek says. "That's the Tuttwyler brothers."

"John and Amos," Eleanor Hbracek says.

"The ones who clubbed the squaw and her papoose to death," Bob Hbracek says.

"Why are they throwing candy?" Hugh Harbinger asks, swatting away a miniature Tootsie Roll.

"It's just a little treat for the kids," Eleanor Hbracek says.

Even in the East Village Hugh Harbinger never saw anything this perverted. Not even in Soho. Not even on Gay Pride Day. Not even on St. Patrick's Day. "Why would parents let their kids take candy from a couple of guys who clubbed a woman and her baby to death?"

"For christsake, Hugh, they're not the real Tuttwyler brothers," Bob Hbracek says.

The next parade unit is the West Wyssock Junior High School Band. They are wearing Indian headdresses made out of colored construction paper. They squeak and honk their way through "America the Beautiful."

The parade ends. The crowd follows the junior high school band out South Mill. Bob and Eleanor Hbracek join the juggernaut. "Where we going now?" Hugh Harbinger wonders.

"To the cemetery for the memorial service," Eleanor Hbracek says.

"Memorial services for who?" Hugh Harbinger asks.

"For everyone who's died since 1803," she says. "It'll give you goosebumps."

Hugh Harbinger is impressed by the big houses on South Mill. Impressed with the Victorians. Impressed with the Greek Revivals. Impressed with the Tudors and the colonials and the arts-and-craft bungalows. "You know," he says, "these houses shouldn't be painted white."

"They're pretty painted white," Eleanor Hbracek says. "They make you feel like you're living in the past."

"In the *past,*" Hugh Harbinger informs her, "these houses would have been painted every color imaginable. Especially the Victorians. When those babies were built, they were painted up like cheap whores."

Eleanor Hbracek hopes no one in the crowd has heard her son's language. "What a thing to say."

"It's true," her son says. "You know what they used to call Victorians? Painted Ladies."

"Which ones are the Victorians?" Bob Hbracek asks.

"Even the Greek Revivals were painted in bright colors," his son says. "Yellow ochre. Pumpkin orange. Indigo blue."

"Which ones are the Greek Revivals?" Bob Hbracek asks.

Eleanor Hbracek defends the homeowners. "I think they look nice all white."

The word *nice* eats through Hugh Harbinger's Solhzac-numbed nerve endings like sharks through a school of San Francisco Bay grunion. He has hated that word since high school Latin, when Brother Peter Paul Tummler, explaining how old words often take on new meanings, said that *nice*, now meaning pleasing or good, is from the Latin word *nescius*, meaning ignorant. Everything else Brother Tummler taught that semester farted right out Hugh's ears. But the fact that *nice* really meant *ignorant* could not escape his ears. It soaked into his brain, prickling his already tender synapses, transfixing him, supporting his earliest suspicions about life's terminal absurdity, justifying his adolescent withdrawal and rebellion. From that right-after-lunch Latin class on, Hugh would reject anything deemed nice by others: Nice clothes, nice music, nice girls, nice times, nice thoughts, nice art, nice words. No longer could he conform or be average. Conformity and averageness were nice things, ignorant things. How, he wondered, could anyone intentionally accept ignorance? And so he went go off to the Cleveland Institute of Art where his aversion for all things nice was immediately recognized as genius. And where does a brilliant American art school graduate go but into advertising? Where to but New York City? Where to but the anything-but-nice, anything-but-ignorant streets of the East Village? To friendships with people like Jean Jacques Bistrot and Buzzy. To rampant, unemotional copulation with the very rich Zee Levant.

But now Hugh Harbinger is no longer among his fellow un-nice in New York City. He is in Tuttwyler, Ohio, following a junior high school band and a whipped cream-bleeding cupcake, and his parents, to the cemetery, to memorialize everyone who's died since 1803.

The slate sidewalk takes Hugh Harbinger and the Hbraceks up a slight knoll. At the top of the knoll Hugh lets out a bedazzled "Oh Momma!"

Ernest Not Irish dos not follow the parade to the cemetery for the memorial services. He stays on the square, walking slowly along the row of food tents. He buys a Coke and a big cookie from the Knights of Columbus. "Enjoy," the woman working the counter says to him. She is wearing a gold badge with red ribbons. DELORES POLTRUSKI SQUAW DAYS COMMITTEE, it reads. She also is wearing a construction paper headband and feather, just like the kids in the junior high band.

Ernest Not Irish, with his Coke in one hand and his I'M A REAL INDIAN placard in the other, has to let Delores Poltruski stick the big cookie between his teeth. "Are you really a real Indian?" she asks.

He nods that he is.

"Well, thank you so much for coming," she says.

Earnest Not Irish walks to the gazebo and sits on the steps. The Coke is good and cold. The cookie tasty. He takes a letter from the back pocket of his Levis and reads it for the umpteenth time:

> Dear Mr. Not Irish,
> If you think Chief Wahoo is a disgrace to your people, you should come to Squaw Days.

The letter is not signed. But there is a PS:

> Be sure to stick around for the Re-Enactment!

Ernest Not Irish finishes his cookie and walks back to the Knights of Columbus tent. "What time is this Re-Enactment?" he asks the woman named Delores Poltruski.

"Nine sharp at G.A. Hemphill Elementary School," she tells him.

"What exactly do they re-enact? Not the clubbing I hope?"

"Goodness no," Doris Poltruski laughs. "Princess Pogawedka's rising out of the smoke. You'll love it."

Ernest Not Irish buys another big cookie.

The same bedazzling sight that forces an "Oh Momma!" from Hugh Harbinger's lips also stops his feet. He notices that it has not only stopped his feet, but also his parents feet, and, momentarily at least, the feet of almost everyone else flooding towards the cemetery. "Tell me, mother," he says. "Do you think that house looks nice?"

"Nice?" she says. "It's the ugliest house I've ever seen." She and Bob hurry down the sidewalk.

Hugh Harbinger does not hurry on. He wobbles off the sidewalk. He sits on the unmowed grass. His eyes fix on the great shimmering truth before him. Inside him the sharks are still feasting on the grunion. "Now that is *green*," he says.

He has never seen such a green. It is not, thank God, hunter green, the green that for a decade now has permeated every product line from polo shirts to potato peeler handles; permeated every economic class, so that even the poorest of the poor are these days wearing hunter green jogging shorts and drinking coffee brewed in hunter green coffeemakers. Yes, thank God, it is not hunter green. Nor is it the festive green of cups and saucers made during the fifties. Nor the green of sixties' miniskirts or seventies' polyester leisure suits. Nor is it the green of eighties' punk-rock hair. Nor the green of all those shutters on the impressive houses up and down this street, the green of grass dripping spring dew, the green of grass coated with autumn frost.

It also is not the green of April leaves or May leaves or June leaves or July leaves or August leaves or September leaves, not the green of pine needles or fern fonds or cactus or palm, nor the green of plastic Easter eggs. It is not the green of the pants middle-aged men wear to play golf, not the green Girl Scouts wear, not the fertile green the Irish love so much. It is not the rainforest green Amazonian Indians hunt monkey in, nor the green of tundra moss Eskimos track caribou across, or the green of deep water. It is not the sugary green of Kool-Aid, the anemic green of hospital walls, the green of iceberg lettuce, the green of canned peas. It is not the green of guacamole, of cabbage rolls, of olives. Or the green of traffic lights, ambulances, or Army tanks. It not the green of Eleanor Hbracek's puffy Christmas slippers, the green of the clip-on necktie Bob Hbracek wears to Christmas mass, or the green of the highway signs that point you east toward New York. It is not any of the greens you'd find in even the biggest box of Crayolas, any of the greens you'd find on an artists' pallet. It is not the green of American money.

It is a green such as Hugh Harbinger, renowned genius of color, has never seen before. To the trained technician in him, it is a mysterious green that refuses to stay at a fixed position on the color spectrum—from 490 to 570 nanometers its fickle wavelengths are flying, at once yellowy and blue, at once warm and cool, at once transparent and opaque, at once glossy and flat. To the artist in him, it is a green at once soothing and irritating, at once feminine and masculine, yin and yang, kind and cruel, obstinate and submissive, envious and generous, at once filled with and devoid of hope, of love and hatred, love and loneliness, love and the absence of love. It is a green not only racing back and forth along the color spectrum, but also a green balanced precariously on the spectrum of precious *Time*, between the verdancy of life and the fly-infested rot of death. It is the green of God's fluttering cape and Satan's stomping boots. It is the green of Hugh Harbinger's depression and the green of his resurrection. It is a green he understands better than anyone alive, save maybe the owner of this little two-story frame house.

It is a green that keeps Hugh Harbinger seated on this unmowed lawn while Bob and Eleanor Hbracek drift with the crowd toward the cemetery for the Squaw Days memorial service, where all those buried beneath the green grass will be remembered.

12

The Ferris wheel is still turning, but the midway is all but empty. The food tents on the square are still open, but the sloppy joes and French fries go unsold. Talented village women still man their craft booths, but their quilts and Christmas decorations go unmolested. It is 8:45, the sun is falling, and the crowd is gathering at G.A. Hemphill Elementary School for the Re-Enactment.

It is an old brick school, built in the thirties when, despite the raging depression, schools were still considered monuments to the future; and therefore its temple-like entrance and the sandstone reliefs cornicing the entire three-story building like a halo were not seen, as they would be seen today, as a waste of taxpayers money, but as the very best possible use of it.

Erected right in front of the school's temple-like entrance is a stage. There is a backdrop of painted trees and hills and log cabins with chimneys trickling frozen smoke. In the center of the stage is a pile of real tree stumps. On the corners of the stage sit magnificent stacks of speakers, borrowed from The Gizzard Girls—a local rock band comprised of four despondent high school boys from the expensive new developments. To the left of the stage sits the high school band, the legs of their folding chairs slowing sinking into the ground. To the right of the stage sits the Singing Doves, an ad hoc chorus comprised of the choirs from every church in Tuttwyler, save the Reverend Raymond R. Biscobee's non-affiliated Assemblage of the Lord, which believes Christian voices never should be lifted for secular purposes—not even for a worthy event like Squaw Days.

It is three minutes after nine now and the Davy Crockett band director raps on his music stand. The band erupts into the very recognizable *Star Wars* theme: *Bum-BUMMM, bum-bum-bum-bum BUMMM-bum.*

This first piece is just to get the crowd's attention. And it does. And now as the sun is all but spent, and blue flood-lights turn the stage ghostly, the band takes the crowd back to the early nineteenth century with a dirge-like rendition of the Beatles' "Yesterday." The boy playing the bass drum, who after school is the drummer for the Gizzard Girls, is thumping out an Indian pow-wow beat: *DOOM-doom-doom-doom, DOOM-doom-doom-doom.*

The Singing Doves beings to howl eerily. Canisters of dry ice are opened, drowning the stage in unruly smoke. People dressed as pioneers drift into the smoke, completing the tableau. Most of the pioneer men have axes over their shoulders. Most of the pioneer women are carrying baskets. "Yesterday" drags to an end. One of the ax-carrying men walks to the microphone. "Well," he almost shouts, "we've worked all day a-cuttin' these trees and a-pullin' out these stumps with our horses and oxen, the same beasts of burden that brought us west from our homes in Connecticut. Now let's set these stumps a-blazin', so all the world knows where Tuttwyler is, and will always be!"

A basket-carrying woman joins him at the microphone. She holds up a plaster of Paris roasted chicken. "And let us feast," she almost shouts, "as our forefathers and fore-mothers feasted at the first Thanksgiving in faraway Plymouth, Massachusetts, thankful for this bountiful land, which God hath bequeathed."

Now an old man steps to the microphone. He is wearing a tattered Revolutionary War uniform. Many in the crowd applaud. They know who this old man really is. He is Donald Grinspoon, the former mayor, former owner of Grinspoon's Department Store, until this year, chairman of the Squaw Days Committee. He waits for the applause to die, then almost shouts: "And let us not forget the men who gave their lives so that this nation could be born. Nor should we forget the men who will die in wars to come—the War of 1812, the Mexican War, the Civil War, the Spanish-American War, World War One and World War Two, the Korean Police Action and the Vietnam War, and Desert Storm and all the little wars in between."

Two children step to the microphone. They carry old-fashioned school slates and they are dressed like Tom Sawyer and Becky Thatcher. Donald Grinspoon adjusts the microphone stand for them, sending a screech of feedback across the crowd. The boy almost shouts first: "What about the Indians? We must never forget that this was their land first."

"That is right," almost-shouts the girl. "Nor should we forget Princess Pogawedka or tiny Kapusta."

Another pioneer man, ax over his shoulder, strides to the microphone. "Princess Pogawedka and tiny Kapusta?" he actually shouts. "I am new to this land. Who were they?"

Now another pioneer woman steps to the microphone. She is not carrying a basket, but a huge book. Many in the crowd applaud. They know who this woman really is. She is Katherine Hardihood, head librarian at the Tuttwyler branch, and founding member of the Squaw Days Committee. For ten minutes she reads aloud about the Western Reserve and the coming of the first white settlers. She reads about how John and Amos Tuttwyler who, while hunting for a spot on Three Fish Creek to build their grist mill, happened across the Indian squaw Pogawedka, and perhaps thinking they were in danger of being attacked by other noble savages hiding in the great trees, clubbed her and her baby to death, only to have great remorse afterwards, and to suffer for their mistake the rest of their lives, though they did help build a prosperous village, a village that prospers still, and remembers still poor Princess Pogawedka and tiny Kapusta. As the crowd applauds, many of them snorting away tears, Katherine Hardihood retreats into the billowing dry ice, visibly relieved her part in the Re-Enactment is finished.

The Marching Wildcat Band begins to play a peppy martial version of Pachebel's "Canon in D major." From the back of the crowd comes a pioneer man with a real torch. He is preceded by a sheriff's deputy who parts the crowd so no one accidentally gets burned. Once on the stage, the man holds the torch high, first to his left, then to his right, then full center, and then, as if this were the opening ceremonies of the Summer Olympics, lowers the torch into the stumps. There is the sudden buzz of electric fans as strips of shimmering yellow, red and gold plastic are blown skyward.

The band switches suddenly to "Turkey in the Straw" and the Senior Squares trot onto the stage and begin to dance. Now the Singing Doves offer a medley of "My Country 'Tis of Thee," "She'll Be Coming Around the Mountain," the famous Shaker hymn "Tis A Gift to Be Simple," and finally a rousing rendition of the Woodstock generation anthem, Canned Heat's "Going Up the Country."

Suddenly there is an explosion of smoke, as if the Wicked Witch of the West is about to appear on that rooftop and send a ball of fire into the Scarecrow's straw-stuffed chest. Instead Princess Pogawedka rises above the stumps in her white buckskin dress, tiny Cabbage Patch Kapusta strapped to her back. The pioneers on the stage cower dramatically. The crowd applauds and cheers.

Princess Pogawedka does not need to come to the microphone this year. This year she is wearing a wireless mike, courtesy of The Gizzard Girls. In a voice that blends the chopped cadence of Tonto with the regal tones of a fairytale queen, the princess speaks: "Do not be afraid. Come near! Come near!"

The pioneers crawl reverently through the dry ice to the stumps.

"I am Pogawedka, mother of Kapusta, daughter of the trees and rivers, sister to the soaring hawks and sprinting dear. Long ago, when the sun and moon and stars were young, when the first wood duck quacked, when the first turtle thrust his curious neck, when the first black bear growled himself awake, the Great Spirit, the one you call God, gave this land to my people. And we cared for it as if we had created it. Now the Great Spirit in his wisdom has given this land to you. Pioneers! I beseech you! Care for this land as if you created it! Mold it into the vision that the Great Spirit has given you! Love it and cherish it and prosper upon it! And be happy, pioneers. As once we were happy!"

The pioneers sing out: "We will! We will!"

Tom Sawyer and Becky Thatcher now bravely rise. "But how can we be happy," almost-shouts the boy, "when our hearts are filled with so much guilt?"

Princess Pogawedka turns to Tom and Becky and lovingly opens her arms as the Virgin Mary might. "Guilt? What guilt have you, little ones?"

"For the way we treated you and your child," the girl almost-shouts.

Princess Pogawedka presses her hands over her heart. She smiles as wide as she can, so even those at the back can see her forgiving white teeth. "Do not feel guilt, little ones. And do not feel sorrow, for tiny Kapusta and I are in a better place. You also must not feel hatred for those who did this deed. Forgive them as I have forgiven them, and as the Great Spirit has forgiven them. For they knew not what they did."

"Thank you, Princess Pogawedka," Tom and Becky almost-shout in unison.

Princess Pogawedka raises her arms as Moses surely did when he parted the Red Sea. In the tongue of her people she says: "Teh-nay-goo Winne-bago, Cuy-a-hoga-Chau-tau-qua, Mosh-kosh-kee-pop." Then for those in the crowd speaking only English, she translates: "May the Great Spirit be with you! Live long and prosper!"

There is another explosion of smoke and when it clears Princess Pogawedka and Kapusta are gone. The Marching Wildcat Band launches into Deep Purple's '70s heavy metal classic "Smoke on the Water." *Doot doot DOOT Doot-doot DOOT-DOOT.*

The crowd cheers and applauds and starts to disperse. One of the pioneer men steps to the microphone and reminds them that the midway, as well as the food tents and craft booths, will be open until eleven.

One of those dispersing is Hugh Harbinger. As Salvador Dali as the Re-Enactment was, he paid very little attention to it. The whole time his head and heart were filled with the green paint on that two-story frame on South Mill. They are filled with it still as he trails behind the Hbraceks. Bob is anxious to get on the road before the traffic backs up.

Another of those dispersing is D. William Aitchbone. He, too, paid very little attention to the Re-Enactment. His head and heart were filled with anger that the Vice President of the United States reneged on his promise to attend; anger that Victoria Bonobo didn't vote for his privatization plan; anger that CNN featured Mayor Woodrow Wilson Sadlebyrne in their report on small town strategies for economic survival; that Cabrini Brothers Development Corp. was making him bear the cost of moving the bones of his ancestors; that Kevin Hassock let the Happy Landing Ride Company bring their small Ferris wheel, and not the big one they always brought when Donald Grinspoon was Squaw Days chairman; and that Howie Dornick's two-story frame was still that God-awful green. Yes, D. William Aitchbone is still filled with all these angers as he heads for the Daydream Beanery.

Another of those dispersing is Darren Frost, still wearing his cupcake costume. His head and heart were too full of his angry love for God to pay much attention to the Re-Enactment. His head and heart are still filled with this love as he trots to his car and his appointment with the Reverend Raymond R. Biscobee. Tomorrow EDIT will interrupt the tobacco spitting contest with a protest against the library's Satanic policies, and there are still many plac-ards to make.

Also dispersing is Katherine Hardihood. She has already stuffed her pioneer bonnet into her pioneer apron. Her head and heart are filled with shame for participating once again in this miscarriage of history. She heads straight for Howie Dornick's green house where, Howie willing, she will copulate her shame away.

Howie Dornick also is among those dispersing. He paid great attention to the Re-Enactment, especially Katherine Hardihood's reading. Head filled with lust, heart filled with love, he is rushing home to copulate away his dear Katherine's shame.

Dispersing, too, is Ernest Not Irish. The hatred in his head and heart did not keep him from devouring every horrible second of the Re-Enactment. He flees to his car knowing that Chief Wahoo is small potatoes now. He knows that next year the whites responsible for Squaw Days will pay for Wounded Knee, the Trail of Tears, and a million other indignities to indigenous peoples.

"Smoke on the Water" finished, the Marching Wildcat Band reprises "Louie, Louie." The Singing Doves clap in time and sing the only words anybody knows: *"Lou-eeeea, Loooo-i, ohhhh no! I godda go."*

13

Howie Dornick is curled up in his bed listening to Katherine Hardihood's whispery librarian's snore when the *pling-plingy-plong* of the door bell echoes up through the heating ducts. He looks first at Katherine's face—her lips pushed out like the petals of a wilting tulip—and then at the clock radio he won at the Eagles Club raffle. It's only 8:37. *Pling-plingy-plong.*

He puts on his pants and goes down to the door. On the porch he finds a man with a brown and white dog under his arm. The man is tall and vegetarian thin. His hair is concentration camp short. He is maybe thirty-five. The dog is maybe the size of a Hungarian rye. "My name is Hugh Harbinger," this man says. "I'd like to talk to you about your house."

Suddenly Howie Dornick can feel last night's coffee in his liver and in his Sunday morning delirium he supposes that this man has been sent by D. William Aitchbone. "I ain't gonna repaint it."

"Good God, I hope not," says Hugh Harbinger. "I think it's fabulous."

Howie Dornick studies him more closely now. This man has beseeching eyes. This man has a hopeful smile. While he is a nervous man, there is also a listlessness about him. If D. William Aitchbone has sent this man to harass him, then clearly he has not chosen wisely. This man is no more threatening than the little rye-bread dog under his arm.

Within three minutes Howie Dornick is in the kitchen grinding expensive African coffee beans in the expensive German-made grinder Katherine Hardihood gave him for his birthday. Katherine and this man named Hugh Harbinger are sitting at the table. The rye-bread dog is running free in the living room, barking at the prosthetic foot on the mantle. "Who wants peanut butter toast?" Howie asks.

And so they eat peanut butter toast and drink freshly ground African coffee and talk first about the little dog named Matisse, then about Squaw Days, and finally the color of the house they're sitting in.

"You see," Hugh Harbinger explains, "I design colors."

"I thought that was God's job," Katherine Hardihood cannot resist saying.

Hugh grins. He explains that he consults with companies about what colors they should make their products. Color can make or break a product, he tells them.

"And you really like the color I painted my house?" Howie Dornick asks.

"I think it's fabulous."

People in Tuttwyler do not say *fabulous* very often, not the way this Hugh Harbinger is saying it. "Where you from?" Howie asks.

The simple question opens Hugh's soul like the key on a tin of Norwegian sardines. He confesses that he is from Parma. He confesses about his years in New York ping-ponging between advertising agencies and corporate marketing departments as a graphic artist. "I got this gig with this Mexican-owned bathroom fixture company, designing their brochures," he says, "and this guy in R&D liked my color sense and before I knew it I was the crown prince of toilets and bidets. My reputation snow-balled overnight—in New York reputations can do that—and before I knew it I was no longer Hugh Hbracek, lowly graphic artist, but Hugh Harbinger, coveted color designer. I've done just about everything. Cars. Clothes. Appliances. Furniture. Paper products. Everything. Most of it high end. I'm also one of those rare birds who's demographically versatile. Boomers. Gen-X. Ethnic. Gay. Hetero. East Coast, West Coast. Urban, Leafy. I've got good Euro instincts, too. I can out-Italian the Italians. The last few years before I had my breakdown—don't worry, I'm not going to freak on you—I got into cosmetics big time. I'm responsible for that whole black thing."

"The girl at the Daydream Beanery wears black lipstick," Howie Dornick observes.

"No doubt one of mine. I've done over three hundred shades of black. A lot of the epic shades. Bullet Hole. Virtual Death. Decompose. Black Maggot Woman. They're all mine." Suddenly Hugh Harbinger's mood goes black as well. He drinks half a cup of coffee before speaking again. "Then my life took the L train to Loserville. Clinical depression. Slam dunk, I'm in a funk. Now I'm just a thirty-something zeke living with his parents."

"And you really like the color I painted my house?" Howie Dornick asks.

"I think it's fabulous," Hugh Harbinger assures him. "Absolutely fabulous."

And so they finish their coffee and toast and go outside. The sun is over the treetops now and the house is shimmering. Already the traffic on South Mill is heavy. Locals are heading for church. Daytrippers are already filtering in for the third and final day of Squaw Days. "Where did you get this paint?" asks Hugh Harbinger. "I've never seen a green like this."

While Howie Dornick has understood very little of his guest's breathless confession, he feels the need to confess himself. He confesses how his house went unpainted for decades and how the president of the village council, the same evil man who's in charge of Squaw Days now, threatened to eliminate his job as maintenance engineer if he didn't paint it, how he drove all the way to Wooster and bought the cheapest paint he could from a kid wearing a BONE HEAD tee-shirt—the car wash-yellow and the video-store blue and the beauty shop-blue and the fraternity-house gold and the darkroom black—and mixed it together in a rusty old drum, with all kinds of other stuff—his mother's satin-finish peach kitchen paint, the two-quart can of shellac, the jug of bleach, the floor wax and furniture polish, the rubbing alcohol, the Listerine and hydrogen peroxide from the bathroom, the six cans of 10 W-30 motor oil, the jug of windshield wiper fluid, the charcoal lighter, and the three, two-gallon containers of antifreeze. He confesses that he didn't scrape or prime, that he painted over mold and moss, over bird shit and bugs.

"So this green color was just a serendipitous thing," Hugh Harbinger says.

Katherine Hardihood can see that her man doesn't know this word, serendipitous. "Out of the blue," she says in a sort of whisper.

Howie Dornick now understands. "That's right," he says. "Out of the blue. And the yellow and the gold and the black and all that other stuff I dumped in. Serendipitous for sure."

Hugh Harbinger thanks Howie Dornick for the coffee and peanut butter toast, helps Matisse wave good-bye to Katherine Hardihood, and drives off in Bob Hbracek's cinnamon-gold Crown Vic.

The traffic on I-71 is light. Hugh Harbinger speeds northward, in the left-hand lane, as restless as the green on Howie Dornick's clapboards, his mood dancing back and forth on the spectrum of possible human emotions. When he reaches the Hbracek's bungalow on Delano Drive, Eleanor is grating mozzarella for a Sunday lasagna. Bob is on the sofa, watching *This Old House* and eating a huge bowl of Neapolitan ice cream.

Hugh goes straight to the phone in his parent's bedroom. He starts to dial Buzzy in New York. His fingers get no farther than the area code. He flops back on the bed. He sits up and dials his psychiatrist, Dr. Pirooz Aram. He waits for the beep and leaves a message.

In the morning Dr. Pirooz Aram's secretary calls back and an emergency appointment is made. Late the next afternoon Hugh Harbinger slumps into a comfortable leather chair. He hears the faraway flush of a toilet and a half-minute later Dr. Aram enters the office, huge hands wrapped around a fragile demitasse. "How are you, Hugh Harbinger?" He has been in the United States half his life, some thirty years, yet his accent is as obstinate as the weave in the expensive Persian rug on the floor. "Can I get you an espresso?"

Hugh hears himself answer "no."

Dr. Aram finishes his espresso and deposits his tiny cup on the silver tray resting on the corner of his mammoth desk. He scratches his white beard and sits in his throne-like leather chair. "Caffeine is no good for a man with your problems, anyway," he says. "Tell me, Hugh Harbinger, what is so important that I must work until 5:30 on a Monday?"

Hugh tells him about going to Squaw Days with Bob and Eleanor Hbracek.

"You should avoid associating with those two," Dr. Pirooz Aram says. "They will love you straight into a mental ward."

Hugh tells him about the green house he has discovered. He tells him about the mercurial nature of its hue. He tells him how this green is tearing away at his soul.

"This must be some green," says Dr. Aram.

Hugh goes on and on about the green, and about the man, Howie Dornick, who so serendipitously concocted it.

Dr. Pirooz Aram smiles proudly. "Did you know that this wonderful word you use—this *serendipity*—is taken from an old Persian fairy tale? The Three Princes of Serendip, who made wonderful discoveries by accident?"

"I didn't know that."

Dr. Aram frowns. "Americans do not know anything important." Suddenly his frown somersaults into a grin. "Like all good fairy tales there are many versions of it, of course. But essentially it is about a wise king who sends his three sons into the world to perfect their educations. Even though they encounter many dangers—a three-headed snake, an evil hand as big as a mountain, a stubborn merchant who accuses them of stealing one of his camels— they always manage to stumble upon something wonderful, something serendipitous, Hugh Harbinger, that make their lives worth living—a beautiful princess, a grateful queen, a magic mirror, a bird with golden wings, a silver box that contains a poem for chasing dragons away."

Now the doctor rubs his chocolate eyes and laughs as only a wise Persian can. "So, my good prince of Serendip, you have stumbled upon this wonderful green house. And now you make me work until 5:30 on a Monday."

"Sorry."

Dr. Pirooz Aram continues to laugh. "Do not feel sorry. Just hurry up and tell me what you want me to tell you! My sweet Sitareh and I are going out for fish at six."

Hugh Harbinger feels suddenly small and numb. He wishes he had accepted that demitasse of espresso. "I'm not sure what I want you to tell me."

Dr. Aram jumps up. "Boool-shit! You know exactly what you want me to tell you. You have come to me for permission to end your exile and take this serendipity green of yours to the world."

Hugh no longer feels small and numb. He feels huge and his skin is prickling. "I could make the world go nuts for that color."

"If you were not already nuts yourself?"

"Bingo."

"Bingo, nothing. You are no longer nuts."

Hugh Harbinger scratches his nose and laughs sardonically. "This green has cured me, has it?"

"Ah! You are a student of Avicenna!"

"Who?"

Disappointment wrinkles Dr. Aram's face. "Let an old man from a very old country lecture you for a moment," he says. "You are a young man from a young country, and accordingly you have never heard of anybody who does not score lots of points in some pointless game, or who does not shout obscenities into a microphone while a guitar electrocutes his fingers. Avicenna was one of the greatest scientists of all time. And naturally he was a Persian."

"Naturally."

Dr. Aram is not deterred by his patient's sarcasm. "A thousand years ago this *Persian* wrote a book on medicine that is marveled at even today—even by American doctors who know everything and nothing. You think you are an expert on color, Mr. Hugh Harbinger? Avicenna was the expert of all experts! He not only used color to diagnose the afflictions of his patients, he used color to cure them. Potions made of red flowers cured the blood. Yellow flowers reduced pain and swelling. So when you joke that this green has cured you, you are not joking at all. Of course it has cured you! It has awakened you and transformed you, and just perhaps it will make your life worth living again."

Hugh can feel his heartbeat in his eyes and ears and even on the end of his tongue. "So you think I should take this serendipity green to the world, do you?"

Dr. Aram closes his briefcase and clicks off the lights. He hurries his patient to the door. "It is not my job to tell you what to do. It is my job to help you get back to a place where you can tell yourself what to do. As much as I enjoy taking your money, Hugh Harbinger, I'm afraid this green has interfered with the lengthy and expensive treatment I had planned for you. Admit it, you knew you were going to take this color to the world the second you saw it."

"I guess so."

Dr. Aram explodes with affection. "Do not guess! Know, dammit! Know!" He hurries Hugh to the parking lot. "Now that you are no longer my patient, would you like to join Sitareh and me for some fish?"

Hugh is too excited to eat fish and he drives off in the Crown Vic.

Dr. Pirooz Aram drives off in a sports car so red that even the mullahs now ruling his homeland would be forced to praise God for Western technology.

"Buzzy? It's Hugh."

"Hugh! How the hell—"

"Listen, Buzzy. I've got a fabulous new color."

"That's fabulous."

"You've got to do a show for me."

"Yum! How soon?"

"ASAP."

"Where's the bread coming from? You're not the only one who's a penniless wretch these days."

"Zee Levant, I suppose."

"Zee's still talking to you?"

"I don't know yet."

"You left us all high and dry, Hugh."

"Easy on the guilt. I'm clinically depressed, remember."

"All's forgiven if this color is as fabulous as you say."

"Oh, it is."

"Hugh Harbinger rides again!"

"I'll be in New York in three, maybe four days. Okay if I sleep on your couch?"

"No problemo."

"So, Buzzy, do you see Zee much?"

"Every once."

"She sleeping with anybody?"

"Not with anybody of your gender, I don't think."

"Good. Now you book some wacky spot for a show. And start lining up models. All boys, Buzzy. Masculine, Wall Street types."

"We're breaking this fabulous color of yours on boys in business suits? Boooor-*ringgggg!*"

"Boring, my ass. Start sketching some thirties and forties Cary Grant stuff. As conservative as your trashy little mind can manage. Cuffs. Hats. Vests. Industrial-strength lapels. And overcoats, Buzzy. Big-ass overcoats."

"Whatever you say. Youz da boss."

"Just keep telling yourself that and I'll be at your door with the most fabulous green you've ever seen."

"Green?"

"Green."

"But Hugh, green is so *ambiguous*."

"Bingo, Buzzy. Green is ambiguous. And my green is the most ambiguous green on God's green earth. And if there's one thing I'm sure about, it's that New York loves ambiguity. Green is refreshing. Green is quieting and peaceful. Optimistic. Green is life. But green is also the color of greed and envy and fear and death. Ambiguity out the wazoo, Buzzy. Every clothes horse in the city will go gaga for serendipity green. You can take that to the bank."

"Serendipity green?"

"Just start drawing, Buzzy."

Red.

Yellow.

D. William Aitchbone bullies through the intersection at South Mill and Tocqueville before the light turns green. His CD of Yobisch Podka's *Insipientia*, uplifting as it is, has not chiseled a single chip out of his foul granite mood. "That bastard," he curses over the electrified violins, meaning, of course, Howie Dornick. "That woman has more brass than a marching band," he curses over the electrified oboes and French horns, meaning, of course, Katherine Hardihood. He drives right past his impressive soapy white Queen Anne—Karen, Amy and Cannon Aitchbone patiently waiting inside for their supper—and pulls into the driveway of the impressive soapy white Gothic of former Tuttwyler mayor Donald Grinspoon.

"For a man who's just put one of the best Squaw Days ever to bed, you don't look very happy," Donald Grinspoon says to his protégé when they are seated across from each other at the dining room table, sipping warm 7UP.

"Who you kidding, Donald, the entire festival was a disaster," Aitchbone says to his mentor. "A goddamn disaster." He brings up the Ferris wheel first: "After all my preaching, that idiot Kevin Hassock let the Happy Landing Ride Company bring the small one. I hope his company downsizes his ass all the way back to North Carolina."

"I liked the small Ferris wheel," Donald says. "It goes a lot faster than the big one. I rode it four times."

D. William Aitchbone brings up the cupcake: "I told Dick Mueller not to let Darren Frost march in the parade as the cupcake again. We've got to get that snack cake shit behind us."

"Everybody loves the cupcake," Donald says.

D. William Aitchbone brings up Ernest Not Irish: "And

that asshole Indian with the I'M A REAL INDIAN sign. What was that all about, anyway?"

"It's a free country," Donald points out.

D. William Aitchbone brings up moving the tobacco-spitting contest to Saturday: "Big mistake, Donald. There were six fewer contestants. And the winning spit was the third shortest on record. "

"I know," Donald Grinspoon says sadly. "I was sure we'd set a new record this year. But, what the hell."

D. William Aitchbone brings up Interior Secretary Danley McCutcheon: "I never told you about this, Donald, but that was supposed to be the Vice President! Victoria Bonobo and I went all the way to Washington to see him."

Donald grins like someone passing gas on a crowded bus. "Everybody figured you two were off diddling."

Aitchbone puckers sourly. "The VP promised to come. We shook hands on it. He had his aide take notes on it. Then the day before I'm going to announce it, his aide calls and says the Interior Secretary is coming instead. I could have crawled under a rock."

"Well, it was nice that Secretary McCutcheon stayed long enough to judge the pie-eating contest," Donald Grinspoon says. "I doubt the Vice President would've done that."

Aitchbone stands up and puts his hands in his pockets, jingling the quarters he always carries for the meters outside the court house in New Waterbury. He strolls to the hutch and studies the rows of antique English plates. "And that goddamn green house! Did you see the crowd? They skirted that goddamn house like it was a huge block of radioactive limburger cheese. I'd like to shove that goddamn green house right up Howie Dornick's goddamn ass. Sweet Jesus, I would!"

Donald pours himself another glass of warm 7UP. He doesn't offer a refill to his protégé. "To be fair, Bill, you're the one who forced Howie to paint it."

D. William Aitchbone notices that his mentor hasn't offered him a refill. "He was suppose to paint it white."

"Was he now?"

"Every goddamn house in town is painted white."

"Every house but one."

"And why that color? Where do you even buy paint like that?"

"It's some god-awful color, all right."

Now the crises in D. William Aitchbone's life twist together like one of the stale pretzels the Tuttwyler Optimists' Club sold in their food tent: "I should've won that privatization vote. Damn that Bonobo!"

"It's hardly Vicki's fault that Woody vetoed your bill," Donald Grinspoon says.

"I'm not talking about the goddamn veto. I knew that pimply assed socialist would veto it. But the override vote, Donald, the goddamn override. She knew I needed her vote for that."

Donald Grinspoon starts working his protégé toward the front door. "You can't blame Vicki for getting the flu."

D. William Aitchbone's hands are out his pockets. He slaps at the air as if it's lousy with black flies. "In July? Nobody gets the flu in July! She intentionally skipped that council meeting. She wanted me to lose that override."

"And why would that be?" Donald asks, opening the door for his protégé.

"Because I wouldn't sleep with her," Aitchbone confesses. "Do you know, when we were in Washington, she came out of the bathroom naked? She's punishing me, Donald. Punishing me for being faithful to my goddamn wife." They're on the porch now. The late afternoon sun is shooting through the decorative spandrels that arch between the posts like fancy spider webs. "I'll never be able to prove it, but I think she called the VP off."

Donald herds him down the sidewalk. "Because you wouldn't sleep with her? Come on, Bill, Vicki Bonobo is too classy for that."

"Oh, really? Do you know that the VP once tried to feel her up?"

The revelation shocks Donald Grinspoon. He opens the car door for his protégé. "If she's as ruthless as you say, maybe you should diddle her."

"One thing I am not going to do is diddle Victoria Bonobo. Not literally, anyway."

"Sometimes literally is necessary, Bill. Remember that exclusive contract I had with Weideman Boots? I had to diddle Bud Weideman's wife six or seven times to land that baby. She looked more like a mule than a donkey does. But it got me that exclusive contract. Anybody in a fifteen-county radius who wanted a pair of Weideman boots had to drive to Grinspoon's. Best boots in the world back in the fifties and sixties when best counted for something. Those boots bought me that condo in Key Largo. Penny and I had lots of wonderful vacations there. Romantic vacations." He closes the car door as soon as his protégé's legs are out of harm's way. "There are bumps in every road, Bill. Squaw Days went just fine."

"Did you know that Katherine Hardihood and Howie Dornick are—"

"Everybody in Tuttwyler knows that. I can't imagine what ever brought those two got together. Can you?"

"That woman's got more brass than a marching band," D. William Aitchbone says to his mentor. "Howie never would have painted his house that goddamn color if she wasn't whispering in his goddamn ear."

Donald Grinspoon reaches into the car and pats his protégé on the shoulder. "You're worrying too much. Nobody's going to blame you for Howie house. In fact, you can blame it on Woody in the next election."

"Oh, you bet I will."

"Woody's a flash in the pan," Donald says. "You'll win the next election."

"Oh, I'll win it. Howie Dornick's days as maintenance engineer are numbered, Donald. Goddamn numbered."

"Howie's a decent guy."

Aitchbone wrings the blood out of his steering wheel. "He's a bastard. And Katherine Hardihood's a dried up old bastard bitch. And Victoria Bonobo's a bitch, too. Half the people in this town are bastards and bitches. I may not be the mayor yet, Donald, but I'm goddamn everything else in this goddamn town, and goddamn it, Donald, the whole lot of them are going to rue the day they ruined D. William Aitchbone's first Squaw Days!"

"Revenge is fine in politics," the mentor reminds his protégé, "as long as you show your enemies a little respect. And respect yourself a little, too."

Aitchbone puts his car in reverse. He smiles warmly. "How is Penny?"

Donald Grinspoon smiles back. "Her emphysema is about the same. But her mind, well, it's as brittle as her bones."

D. William Aitchbone eases up on the brake. The car rolls toward the street. "You'll give her my love?"

"I will. And you give Karen my love. Amy and Cannon, too."

After D. William Aitchbone leaves, Donald Grinspoon gets into his dusty rose Oldsmobile and drives forty miles north to the Sparrow Hill Nursing Home. He sits at his beloved Penelope's bedside and tries to kiss the ache out of her knuckles. "I'm starting to worry about Bill Aitchbone," he says. "Since taking over Squaw Days he's really gone over the edge. Very sad."

Penelope Grinspoon's Alzheimer's is settling in for the evening. "Who's Bill Aitchbone?"

"That's a good question," answers Donald Grinspoon.

After supper with Karen and the kids, D. William Aitchbone hurries to the Daydream Beanery for a strategy session with himself. It's a long session. He drinks two double cappuccinos and picks at a banana muffin. He watches the counter girl with the blackcherry lips. He's never noticed how wonderful her shoulders are. They're almost as wonderful as Victoria Bonobo's shoulders. He goes home and crawls into bed and kisses Karen Aitchbone's cold ear. "I'm getting worried about Donald," he says. "Since giving up the Squaw Days chairmanship he's really lost his edge. Very sad."

14

Early Tuesday morning Hugh Harbinger sneaks out of Bob and Eleanor's house. Under one arm he carries a shopping bag containing two empty cereal bowls and a one-liter bottle of mineral water. Under the other arm he carries Matisse. He drives the Crown Vic into Cleveland, to the funky Tremont neighborhood on Starkweather Avenue, where gays and Hispanics and artsy bohemians live happily among the poor Irish. He parks and hurries into Quintessential Art. He waves to the owner of the shop. "Casey! Yo!"

Casey Quinn "Yos!" back. They know each other from their days at the Cleveland Institute of Art.

Hurrying straight to the Winsor & Newton rack, Hugh Harbinger gathers up several dozen tubes of gouache, an opaque water-based paint that's just the ticket for the work ahead. He not only chooses various hues of green, blue and yellow, but many other colors, too. He grabs an inexpensive pallet for mixing. He grabs an expensive pad of thick paper. He selects three very expensive sable brushes. Matisse runs free, sniffing his way up and down the aisles.

"Back in Cleveland to stay, are you?" Casey Quinn asks, stuffing what Hugh has just paid $157 for into a bag made of recycled paper.

"I'm Amtrakking back tonight."

"You've at least got time for us to get drunk, don't you?"

"Love to, Casey, but I've got a lot of shit to do."

"Ah man, don't we all."

Hugh Harbinger now drives south on Interstate 71. He takes it all the way to Tuttwyler, to the two-story frame on South Mill. He knocks on the door for a long time, but Howie Dornick is not home. Permission or no permission, he nestles himself in the tall grass in the back yard, morning sun at his back, Matisse nestled between his legs like an enormously swollen prostrate. He fills the two cereal bowls with Evian. One bowl is for cleaning his brushes. The other is for Matisse. He loads his pallet with squirts of gouache. He opens his pad. He clenches one sable brush between his teeth. He clenches one in his left hand. He begins making green circles.

He knows replicating the green on Howie Dornick's house won't be easy. He knows this may take hours. He implores Matisse to be patient. And Matisse will be patient, because he knows from long experience that his master is as crazy as the squirrels in Washington Square.

Hugh knows this may take hours because he knows color. He knows that color isn't a real and tangible thing. He knows that color is more than paint on the side of a house or the paint on a thick piece of paper, that color is only light and that light is nothing but ghostly waves of ancient energy, radiating and reflecting and bouncing and bending and advancing and retreating, zigzagging and spinning, appearing and disappearing, no more easy for a mortal man to capture than a cat chasing a flashlight beam.

Hugh Harbinger also knows that this green is more than the serendipitous result of what Howie Dornick mixed in his 55-gallon drum, the car-wash yellow and the video-store blue and the beauty-shop blue and the fraternity-house gold and the darkroom black he bought at Bittinger's in Wooster. He knows it is more than the other stuff he mixed in, the kitchen peach, the shellac, the bleach, the floor wax and furniture polish, the rubbing alcohol, the Listerine and hydrogen peroxide, the 10 W-30 motor oil and the wind-shield wiper fluid, the charcoal lighter and all those gallons of antifreeze. He knows it is more than the rotting gray clap-boards Howie Dornick slathered his concoction over; more than the moss and the mold and the bugs and the splatters of bird shit, more than the sweat dripped from Howie Dornick's forehead, more than the rays of sun stabbing Tuttwyler that particular day. He knows it is more than the radiation riding the northwinds from the nuclear power plants along Lake Erie and more than the gritty steam oozing from Cleveland's steel mills, more than the exhaust of cars and trucks and buses whooshing bumper to bumper on I-491.

He knows better than anyone alive that this green comprises the collective hues of Howie Dornick's life. Yet Hugh Harbinger is confident he can capture this serendipity green. He is confident because he understands Howie Dornick's fears and frustrations, his feelings of worthlessness. He understands because he has a hunch that Howie's goblins are personal friends of his own.

As the sun changes its position, Hugh is forced to change his position, too. By noon there are several buttock-sized circles smashed into the unmowed grass, each a little farther west than the other. Matisse is restless now. And angry. He wants to run and sniff and salute some bush with his back leg.

His master also is growing restless. Also growing angry. Despite his mastery of color and his kinship with Howie Dornick's goblins, he is unable to replicate the green on Howie's house.

All afternoon Hugh Harbinger works. The westward sliding sun moves him from the back of the house to the side of the house and to the front of the house. He is running out of paint. Running out of paper. Running out of sun. Then at ten after five a narrow shadow falls over Hugh's pad of green circles. He lifts his chin until his upside down eyes see an unappetizing face. "Hey, Howie! Hope you don't mind I came by."

Howie Dornick does not appear the least bit upset. "You paint really good circles," he says.

Hugh explains that he's trying to capture the green, as perfectly as he can, so he can take it to New York and make it the biggest color in years. "With your permission, of course," he says. "I figured I'd give you half of everything I make. If that's OK."

Howie Dornick studies the pages of green circles. "Just what is it you're planning to make? Beach balls? Dinner plates?"

Hugh Harbinger laughs and explains what he intends to make is money. "We'll do it legal, of course. A contract spelling it all out."

"I guess that would be OK," Howie Dornick says.

So while Hugh Harbinger goes back to painting green circles—each a slightly different hue than the last, each a far cry from the serendipity green soaked into the clapboards of the two-story frame—Howie Dornick goes inside and empties two cans of Franco-American Spaghetti into a sauce pan. He'll also boil some wieners. "Can Matisse eat hotdogs?" he yells out the window.

Yes, Matisse is permitted to eat hotdogs, and the three of them eat their supper on the front lawn. The evening flies by. Hugh Harbinger's hope of capturing the color is flying by, too. He'll have to take tomorrow night's train to New York.

Howie Dornick is not an artist. He is a practical maintenance engineer. He walks to the side of his house and breaks one of the clapboards off the wall. He hands Hugh Harbinger four feet of serendipity green. Together they laugh like the worthless bastards they know they are.

"You wouldn't want to watch Matisse for a while, would you?" Hugh asks.

D. William Aitchbone and Victoria Bonobo slide into a booth at the Wagon Wheel. "This is a pleasant surprise," she says. "I figured after my stunt in Washington I'd be exiled to an iceberg."

"We've been through all that."

They order. She orders feminine, a garden salad—hold the onion—poppyseed dressing on the side. He can play the gender game, too. He orders a steakburger and steak fries. She orders a diet Coke. He orders a regular Coke.

"Squaw Days really kept me hopping," he says.

"You were magnificent."

He counters with a sexual innuendo of his own. "Even with the small Ferris wheel?"

She gets it and they both laugh. The Cokes come. They unsheathe their straws and sip.

D. William Aitchbone has rehearsed this rendezvous at two separate strategy sessions. "I've been meaning to tell you this all summer," he begins. "I really appreciate your looking out for me on that privatization thing."

Victoria Bonobo hasn't had time to rehearse—he invited her to Wooster for lunch just that morning—and he can see that she's flummoxed. "Well," she says. "Well."

"I must say I'm impressed with your political instincts."

"Well," she says. "Well."

"Pretending to have the flu. Very Nixonian, Vicki. Nixonian as hell."

"Well, thanks, but I really wasn't feeling good."

"Well, you sure were thinking good." He takes a long smooth suck on his straw, emptying half his glass. He hopes it has the sexual connotation he intends. "You knew putting Howie Dornick on the street without a job would be bad for me politically. Knew Woody and the Democrats would turn him into a cause célèbre. Sledgehammer me with it in the next election. 'There's Bill Aitchbone, the cold-hearted SOB who put Artie Brown's son on the street,' etcetera, etcetera. You knew I was just thinking about saving the village some money, overlooking the emotional side of it. That's my one political flaw, Vicki. I'm not emotional enough."

Victoria Bonobo protests. "You're a very sensitive man."

He knew she would say something like that. He puts a blush on his face. "Well, I just wanted to thank you."

"Well, you're welcome." Her hand comes down on his, like the heavy lid of a waffle iron. "You know how much I admire you."

He waffle-irons her hand right back. "And I admire you."

Their feminine and masculine lunches arrive.

"The upside, of course," says D. William Aitchbone, his molars grinding away at a huge bite of ground beef, "is that with Howie Dornick still on the village payroll, we can still exert some pressure on him. Help him reconsider that god-awful paintjob on his house."

Victoria Bonobo now does exactly what he knew she would: She accepts his version of reality. "I should have been more direct with you," she says, "instead of trying to protect you. I'm not your wife, after all."

D. William Aitchbone laughs, with her, and at her, and he springs for the kill like the shrewd meat-eater he is. "I wish my wife was more protective like that."

Victoria Bonobo is flummoxed anew. "Well," she says. "Well."

Three entire steakfries go into D. William Aitchbone's mouth before he speaks again. He does not know for sure whether the Vice President's sudden change of plans was Victoria Bonobo's doing or not—Vice Presidents do, after all, get occasionally busy—but he will raise the VP issue nonetheless. "Squaw Days went well enough, little Ferris wheel or no. I just wish the VP could have been there."

"Me, too," Victoria says. "I feel so responsible."

They make another hand waffle.

"Do you think we can get him to come to next year's festival? It would do everyone a lot of good. Help me win the mayor's race. Help him carry Ohio when he runs for the big enchilada. Help you win the council president's seat. You know I want you in that chair when I'm mayor."

"You do?"

"God yes, Vicki, I want you in that chair more than anything."

D. William Aitchbone cannot remember ever seeing a woman so flummoxed. He enjoys the rest of his steakburger and steakfries as he has never enjoyed a steakburger and steakfries before. Donald Grinspoon would be proud of him, he thinks. God knows he is proud of himself. Next Squaw Days the VP will be in his car, not the goddamn secretary of the Interior. Next Squaw Days Howie Dornick's house will be as soapy white as every other house in Tuttwyler. Next Squaw Days the Happy Landing Ride

Company will bring the big Ferris wheel. And the next election! Next election D. William Aitchbone will be goddamn mayor! And one thing Victoria Bonobo *won't be* is president of the goddamn village council. "You know, Vicki, maybe you and I could go down to Washington again, to twist the VP's arm a little harder."

"I'd love to."

"Still hungry? Want to split a piece of pie?"

"Love to."

And so D. William Aitchbone shares a piece of peach pie with Victoria Bonobo, knowing as he chews and swallows that her mind is filled with images of them in bed together, in a big Washington, DC hotel, the Washington Monument right out the window, copulating and copulating and copulating; knowing as he chews and swallows that a year from now he will be a very rich man, that the old Aitchbone family farm will have been annexed into the village, and that hundreds and hundreds of big two-income, marriage-wrecking, lawyer-needing houses will be springing up; knowing that the second Squaw Days under his leadership will be even better than the first. "I love peach pie," he says.

"Me, too," says Victoria.

"Karen hates it," says D. William Aitchbone.

"Tiny Toes!"

"Hello, Vicki? Donald Grinspoon."

"Well, what a nice surprise! How are you, Donald?"

"Oh I'm fine, Vicki. Just fine. How's everything at the day care center these days?"

"Just fine."

"That's good. Say, Vicki—"

"Yes, Donald."

"I'm calling about Bill Aitchbone."

"Oh?"

"I wouldn't want him to know I called."

"I understand."

"He's like a son to me, Vicki."

"He's very fond of you."

"Yes, and he's very fond of you, Vicki. I guess that's why I called. I'm afraid Bill may be a little too fond of you."

"What are you saying, Donald?"

"I'm not really sure. It's just that I'm an old man, been around for a long time. Too long maybe. And I sense things, Vicki. I sense that our Bill is attracted to you. Not just physically, either. He talks all the time about how simpatico your political instincts are with his."

"Donald, I'd never—"

"Oh, I know that, Vicki. I know that."

"I hope so."

"Believe me, I do. But this is a rough time for Bill. His law practice. Council. County Republicans. Squaw Days. All that library board crap with those EDIT people."

"Oh, Donald. Bill's a happily married man. He'd never—"

"Karen's one helluva woman, Vicki. Good mother. Good wife. But she knows less about politics than the Man in the Moon. And I know Bill's taken you under his wing the same I way I took him under mine. And you're one helluva good-looking woman and—"

"Well, Donald, thank you."

"You're also a smart woman. You know how easily men can confuse one thing with another. And with things between Bill and Karen not being what they should—"

"I didn't know that."

"Unfortunately."

"That's too bad."

"I guess what I'm saying is this, Vicki, that if Bill suddenly gets a little too friendly, makes a fool out of himself, well—"

"I understand."

"You're a smart woman, Vicki."

"Hello, Bill?"

"Donald."

"Just finished talking with Vicki."

"And?"

"Hook, line and sinker."

"Thanks, Donald."

15

Howie Dornick goes to work thirty minutes early, not because there is still much to clean up after Squaw Days, not because the privatization vote is keeping him on his toes, but because he has a Jack Russell terrier named Matisse to let out for a noontime piss, lest his two-story frame on South Mill takes on the same aroma as Katherine Hardihood's two-bedroom ranch on Oak Street.

He begins his day scrubbing the gazebo clean of spilled soda, splotches of ice cream, cigarette butts and gobs of foul ground meat that plopped from sloppy joes and chili dogs. He works slow, putting off as long as he can the ritual hosing of the village hall parking lot, site of both the pie-eating and tobacco-spitting contests. But the morning rolls by and the inevitable must be faced. He is unrolling a hundred feet of red hose when he spots D. William Aitchbone waving and walking in his direction.

"Howie!" D. William Aitchbone sings out. "Got a minute?"

In case the council president pulls a gun, Howie Dornick readies his hands on the nozzle. "Bill."

D. William Aitchbone surveys the gelatinous lumps of blueberry and tobacco and just has to shake his head. "They can really make a mess, can't they," he says, the they, of course, meaning the people of low self-esteem who swallowed the pies and spat the tobacco. Now he grabs the lapels of his suitcoat and wiggles his fingers. "If I wasn't dressed up I'd give you a hand."

Howie Dornick hears himself say "Thanks."

D. William Aitchbone puts a well-practiced smile on his face. "Look, Howie, I know I've really put you through the grinder the last few months. That privatization thing. Blowing my lid over the color you painted your house." His well-practiced smile slowly contorts into a well-practiced pout of contrition. "I owe you an 'I'm-sorry,' Howie. A big one."

"No need," Howie Dornick hears himself say.

"Don't get me wrong, the village may very well have to privatize some services a year or two down the line. God knows there's still a lot of support for it on council. Vicki Bonobo for one. She's gung ho about it. Thank God she came down with the flu just before the vote. God was looking out for both of us that day."

"Both of us?"

"Yessireebob. Both of us. You know me, Howie. Always looking at the bottom line. Frankly, when I put that privatization plan together, I wasn't thinking of the human equation. What a kick in the balls it would be to you personally. Middle-aged. No real skills. Not that well-liked. All that illegitimate son of Artie Brown stuff."

"I think I could find another job," Howie Dornick hears himself say.

"Oh, I'm not saying you couldn't. Sure you could, Howie boy."

Howie Dornick really wants to twist that nozzle now. He can pretend it was an accident, he thinks.

"So, I can't blame you for slapping that crappy green paint on your house." D. William Aitchbone says. "I had it coming. Touché!"

The hundred-foot red hose suddenly ejaculates on the front of D. William Aitchbone's well-creased pants. "Oops," says Howie, taking his time twisting the nozzle off. Unbeknownst to D. William Aitchbone, he has jumped back into a plop of blueberry pie, speckling the back of his well-creased pants. "Now someday soon I hope you'll put about six coats of white over that green. But no more pressure, Howie. You do what you think is best for you."

Howie Dornick is surprised when he hears himself answer, "Oh, I will." He can tell by the weak unpracticed smile on D. William Aitchbone's face that he, too is surprised.

"So, the bottom line is this, Howie: No privatization without advance warning. No pressure on repainting your house. Your looking at the new, more-humane Bill Aitchbone."

Howie Dornick wants to let the nozzle slip again, just to see how new the new Bill Aitchbone really is. But he doesn't. He knows exactly how new he is.

The subject of their conversation suddenly changes: "Say, Howie, did I tell you I sold my Uncle Andy's farm? Oh, I made some good money, I'll tell you." D. William Aitchbone now whips the air with his erect index finger, to signal that his ever-alert brain has just stumbled on a very good idea. "Here's something you might like. You know, there's a little family cemetery on the farm."

"I didn't know that."

"Oh yeah. Some of the graves go way back to the early eighteen hundreds. Anyway, under my deal with the developer, I've got to move those graves. To the village cemetery. Sweet Jesus, Howie, I don't know why they won't leave those poor souls rest in peace. But you know how developers are, they want a house on every square inch. Anyway, I was thinking, why don't I hire you to move the graves?"

"Uhhhhhh—"

"I can give you, what, fifty buck a grave? Hell, Howie, seventy-five. And these are old graves, Howie. No rotting flesh or anything. Just some dirty old bones."

Howie Dornick wonders if the hose in his hands could be tied into a noose—for himself. "Uhhhhhh—"

"Once the land gets annexed into the village, you'd have to do it anyway, for no extra money."

"I'd have to do that? Move graves from private property?"

"Well, you wouldn't have to. Except that if that privatization thing comes up again, say in the spring, and Vicki Bonobo and others on council start asking which village employees are team players and which aren't, well, council president or not, I'm just one vote. So, hell, Howie, you might as well let me pay you for it. I'm sure the village would even look the other way if you used the village backhoe. I know I would."

"Uhhhhhh—"

D. William Aitchbone offers a final "Think it over,

Howie" and retreats to the village hall, pantlegs soaked and splattered, but creases still as sharp as ever. Howie twists the nozzle and starts herding the blueberry and tobacco plops toward the storm sewer drain. He must finish by noon and then rush home to walk Matisse, whose master is on his way to New York City, with a piece of green clapboard.

"Hey, Bill!"

D. William Aitchbone, having just been told by village secretary Molly Kellogg that he's got blueberry pie filling stuck to his pants, continues on into the men's room.

Mayor Woodrow Wilson Sadlebyrne follows him in. "I think you should see this," he says, extending a folded letter.

D. William Aitchbone lets the letter hang in the Democratic mayor's hand while he wets a paper towel and goes to work on his pants. The damage is beyond the help of a paper towel. He'll have to stop at home and change his suit before driving into New Waterbury for his court appointments. He snowballs the paper towel into the waste can and takes the letter.

"It's from some Indian in Cleveland," Woodrow Wilson Sadlebyrne tells him.

And so D. William Aitchbone reads the letter:

> Dear Mayor Sadlebyrne,
>
> This Squaw Days thing of yours is an insult to all Indian peoples. No Indian woman clubbed to death by white men would ever appear above a pile of burning stumps to bless the whites for raping sacred Indian lands with their axes and plows and greed.
>
> You whites have humiliated our Indian women for the last time. We will not let you do to Pogawedka what you have done to Pocahontas and Sacajawea. Squaw Days must go!

Sincerely,

Ernest Not Irish
President, Cleveland's Real Indians.

D. William Aitchbone hands the letter back. "They're the bunch who don't like Chief Wahoo, right?"

"That's them. I think this Not Irish guy was at this year's festival. Delores Poltruski sold two big cookies and a Coke to some Indian-looking guy carrying and I'M A REAL INDIAN sign."

"Maybe if we invited them to dance next year—one of those rain-dance deals—they wouldn't cause any trouble for us."

Woodrow Wilson Sadlebyrne's eyes close. His head slowly swings back and forth. "Invite them to dance? You Republicans never cease to amaze me."

His political heritage insulted, D. William Aitchbone pushes past his foe and throws the men's room door wide. "Next election, Woody boy, you're going to be amazed right back into the cable TV business."

Sadlebyrne follows him out, yelling. "We're going to be attacked by Indians and all you're concerned about is the next election?"

"Sweet Jesus, Woody, Tuttwyler isn't Fort Apache. We're not going to be attacked by Indians."

"They'll picket."

"They? Five or six fools with pigtails shuffling around in a circle? Woody! Take a reality pill!"

When Dr. Pirooz Aram comes into his office, demitasse of espresso in his huge hands, he notices that his patient is sitting differently than during previous visits. She is no longer stiff-spined. No longer are her knees clenched like a bulldog's teeth. "Katherine Hardihood, how are you today?"

"I'm good."

"Just good? On such a perfect day?" Dr. Aram takes a final sip and puts the tiny cup on the silver tray on the corner of his desk. He slumps into his own chair. "The last time you were here you had just baked a rhubarb pie for some gentleman."

"Howie Dornick."

"Yes, Howie Dornick. Did this Howie Dornick like the pie?"

"We had sex."

"Ah! That is wonderful!"

"We have sex all the time."

Dr. Aram ponders this development, wondering what kind of man this Howie Dornick must be to copulate with such an unappetizing woman on a regular basis. "Are you able to enjoy it, Katherine?"

"You are asking whether my uncle is in bed with us?"

Dr. Pirooz Aram rubs his chocolate eyes and laughs as only a wise Persian can. "I ask a cloudy question and I get a clear question in return. How am I supposed to treat you, Katherine, if you are more honest than me?"

Katherine Hardihood laughs as only a librarian can. "Sometimes I think about my uncle before we do it, and sometimes after, but never during. I guess I get totally enmeshed in the moment."

"Enmeshed in the moment? Very nice. You are a poet. Now tell me, Katherine, do you love this Howie Dornick?"

"He's growing on me."

Dr. Aram now listens in amazement as she tells him about Howie's pitiful life: about his illegitimate birth; about his famous war-hero father; how Tuttwyler both shuns and protects him; about his unpainted two-story frame on South Mill; how a ruthless lawyer named D. William Aitchbone conspired to get that eyesore-of-a-house painted before Squaw Days; how this D. William Aitchbone had manipulated her, sending her to that unpainted house with a rhubarb pie; how Howie Dornick drove all the way to Wooster to buy paint, and for some mystifying reason came back with a car-load of ungodly colors and mixed them together into an ungodly concoction of ungodly green, and slathered his clapboards with it.

Dr. Pirooz Aram, of course, has heard about this house before, from Hugh Harbinger. But he is a proud and conscientious psychiatrist and cannot betray the confidence of another patient. "So, this Howie Dornick of yours is both brave and cowardly at the same time? He buckles but he doesn't buckle?"

"I guess that's right."

"And this is why he is growing on you, Katherine?"

"I suppose." She tells him now about the strange man from Parma who showed up for breakfast, a strange man with a small dog who thought the ungodly green paint on Howie Dornick's house was both fabulous and serendipitous.

Dr. Aram's lips freeze between a frown and a grin. "It sounds like this man from Parma should see a psychiatrist."

"We're all a little crazy, I suppose."

"Not a little crazy, Katherine," Dr. Pirooz Aram says, leap-frogging disciplines, psychiatry to philosophy. "A lot crazy. Our specie is genetically insane."

"That's a bit rough, isn't it?"

"Rough but true," he says "When trouble comes, mules kick and rabbits run. Turtles grow shells. And they think they are surviving! But our human ancestors with their big monkey brains could see from Day One that all the kicking and running and shell-growing in the world would not spare them from the predator called death, from rotting like a forgotten pistachio nut. Unlike the mule or the rabbit or the turtle, our ancestors knew they were doomed. Knew that like the pistachio they were prone to rotting. Knew they were mortal, Katherine, mortal! And knowing this terrible secret, they understandably went insane, en masse, and passed along their collective insanity from generation to generation, eventually inventing the rewards of heaven and the punishments of hell, inventing countries and nationalities and politics and professional sports franchises, filling silos full of corn and wheat and canning beans and peaches, inventing lifejackets and fire alarms and lucky rabbit's feet, as if somehow all these things are going to save us. Rotting pistachios, that's what we are." Dr. Aram has enjoyed listening to himself, but now that he has run out of breath, he is quite embarrassed. "Of course, I don't talk to my other patients like this. But you, Katherine, you are so perceptive, and such a poet. So I make a fool out of myself."

But apparently she does not think he has made a fool of himself. She picks up where he leaves off. "And so we demand that the illegitimate sons of war heroes keep their houses painted. For the sake of our own false immortality."

Dr. Pirooz Aram walks across the room on his knees, taking Katherine Hardihood's librarian's hands in his huge Persian hands, as if he were holding a pair of fragile espresso cups. "Whether you can admit it or not, you are in love with this Howie Dornick. He has awakened and transformed you. And you have awakened and transformed him. This serendipity green you tell me about is the color of your love for each other. It is a powerful color, Katherine, a powerful color."

Katherine feels the heat from his hands moving up her forearms like mercury up a thermometer. She withdraws her hands and pats his cool balding head. "Now who is the poet?"

Still on his knees, Dr. Pirooz Aram begins to dance. "Yes, I am a poet. In fact, sometimes I think I am the reincarnated soul of Jalaluddin Rumi, the great Persian poet. Do you know of him, Katherine?"

"His poems are very popular today."

"Very popular *today*? You are such an American! Yes, Rumi is very popular in America today. In the same way that Russian Matruska dolls are popular in America today. We Persians knew of Rumi's greatness when *America* was nothing but the name olive-picking Italians gave their third sons." As he continues to dance, he recalls one of the Rumi poems he read as a youth in Tehran: "I remember this one poem about a chickpea who tries and tries to leap over the rim of a boiling pot of water. 'Why are you doing this to me?' the chickpea asks the cook. And the cook just knocks the chickpea back with his ladle. 'Do not try to jump out,' says the cook. 'You think I'm torturing you. But I'm giving you a favor. So you can mix with spices and rice and be the loving vitality of a human being.'" Dr. Pirooz Aram pulls his patient from her chair and wraps his arms around her bony back. "Neither you nor Howie must be afraid of this serendipity green. It is giving you a favor. Allowing you to mix with spices and rice. Mix, Katherine! Mix and mix and mix!"

Katherine Hardihood is not taken aback by any of Dr. Pirooz Aram's peculiarities, not the dancing, not the poem about the leaping chickpea, not even his rant about rotting pistachios and the genetic insanity of monkey-brained humans. These peculiarities are exactly why she continues to visit him several times a year; these and the prescription for antidepressants, which, since Reagan's first term, have kept her from ripping the last chapters out of the library's mystery novels. Her session ends and on the way out she writes the secretary a check and makes a appointment for February. She drives home to Tuttwyler.

Howie arrives at her two-bedroom ranch at exactly 6:30. He is not alone. With him is Hugh Harbinger's Jack Russell. "He asked me to watch Matisse while he was in New York," Howie says.

As he preheats her oven to accommodate a supermarket pizza, Howie tells Katherine about finding Hugh Harbinger in his yard the previous afternoon, painting little circles of green in a tablet. He tells her how he ripped a piece of clapboard from his house and gave it to the strange man from Parma, so he could take it to New York and make it one of the hottest colors in years. "He's going to give me half of everything he makes."

Matisse likes Katherine Hardihood's little two-bedroom ranch. Likes it fine. Likes the broad-backed chairs. Likes the rubber cat toys lying about. Likes the catty smells. Likes the cat.

The cat, however, does not like the dog. The dog's sudden and unexpected appearance has thrown Rhubarb off balance, like a bad case of ear mites. After a long back-bending hiss, he has fled to a shoe box in his mistress' closet.

Howie and Katherine eat the pizza while they watch *Jeopardy*. As soon as a winner is declared they copulate on the sofa, as is their custom. Later, after watching a PBS show on Australian railroad journeys and eating a bag of Fritos, they retire to the bedroom, not to copulate, but to snuggle and listen to Cleveland's only big band radio station. And to talk.

"I shouldn't have ripped that clapboard off my house," Howie Dornick says, one hand scratching his woman's bare shoulder, the other scratching Matisse's belly. "I shouldn't have painted my house that color either."

"Sure you should have," she tells him. "Both things."

Now Howie, fed and bed and ready for confession, tells her about D. William Aitchbone's visit while he was hosing the tobacco spit and blueberry pie off the parking lot. He tells her about his fresh threats, how D. William Aitchbone is going to rub his illegitimate nose in the dirty bones of his ancestors. "Bill Aitchbone has not yet begun to fight," he says.

"And neither have we," Katherine hears herself saying.

Howie Dornick buries his illegitimate nose into the hollow space just above her collar bone. "No, Katherine, we have yet begun to lose."

Katherine Hardihood is not the least bothered by his fatalism. Dr. Pirooz Aram's words are still burning in her brain, as vigorously as the pepperoni burning in her throat. According to the wise old Persian, she has been awakened, transformed and is in love. And whether her man knows it, the two of them are as genetically insane as D. William Aitchbone, and therefore, if they put their minds to it, they can be just as ruthless. "Jiminy Cricket, Howie, where's your vinegar?"

Howie Dornick allows himself an evil chuckle. "Know what I did? Sprayed him with the hose. Made him jump back and get blueberry on his suit pants."

Katherine hugs him and fills her lungs with his Frito breath.

They fall asleep.

Matisse goes into the living room, where he finds Rhubarb licking Frito crumbs off the sofa cushions. There is the obligatory growling and hissing, and the mutual suspicious sniffing of both ends, but with so many crumbs to lick, the two kept-beasts quickly make peace and share the bounty.

16

The Lakeshore Limited leaves Cleveland's humble Amtrak station at 1:36 in the morning. North of the tracks Lake Erie's black waves are crashing. South of the tracks the city's skyscrapers are having their wastebaskets emptied. Hugh Harbinger has nothing with him but a chunk of green clapboard, a duffel bag stuffed with wrinkled clothes, and a half-bottle of butter-yellow Solhzac.

Erie 3:07. Buffalo 4:42. Rochester 6:00. Syracuse 7:25. Utica 8:12. Schenectady 9:30. Albany 10:05. Three-plus hours of not toppling into the pewter-blue Hudson River. Penn Station 1:24. Six minutes on a subway platform. Six minutes on a subway train. Buzzy's garden apartment 2:04. Buzzy's refrigerator 2:08. Buzzy's slippery leather couch 2:18. Hugh Harbinger is back in New York, back in The Village, sleeping like a New York baby.

Buzzy shows up at six with a portfolio full of sketches. Charcoals of manly men in Cary Grant suits. Manly men in Gary Cooper suits. Manly men in Ray Milland suits and Jimmy Stewart Suits. "Perfect," says Hugh Harbinger.

"Do you like the big-ass overcoats?" Buzzy asks. "You said you wanted big-ass overcoats."

"Fabulous," says Hugh.

"I am soooo relived," says Buzzy. "Now show me that Greeeen of yours."

Hugh Harbinger retrieves his precious chunk of clapboard from the closet.

Buzzy hooks his fingers over his teeth. Then he splays his bespittled fingers across his pounding heart. "Fabulous."

They rush out to meet Jean Jacques Bistrot at the Peacock. After a round of espressos as rich and thick as river silt, they maneuver the sidewalks to Zulu Lulu. Over baba ghanoush they plot the campaign which they're certain will, as Hugh Harbinger now says, falling into his color-talk as if he'd never spent those colorless months in exile with Bob and Eleanor Hbracek in Parma, Ohio, "Enrage and engage" marketing vice presidents worldwide.

Jean Jacques Bistrot, the gifted leftist who since fleeing the death squads in his native Haiti has become New York's most important fashion writer, promises in advance to go gaga over their line of serendipity green business wear. Hugh and Buzzy smile at each other without moving their lips. They knows this is quite a coup. They know Jean Jacques Bistrot sells his soul to very few devils.

Jean Jacques Bistrot confesses that he is "sick to death" of brown and black and gray. He tells them that he's "sick to death of having nothing new to say *fabulous* to." He tells them sight-unseen that he's certain serendipity green will be "*simply* fabulous."

By eleven Hugh Harbinger is copulating with Zee Levant. It has indeed been a fabulous day.

At nine the next morning, Hugh Harbinger is in the office of patent attorney Carl Jablonsky. He knows he can't protect Howie Dornick's concoction—you can no more claim ownership of a color than you can claim the oceans—but he can protect the name he gave it. And so serendipity green becomes Serendipity Green®. Carl Jablonsky also drafts a contract giving Howard Allen Dornick half of everything.

At 11:30 Hugh Harbinger takes his chunk of clapboard to his old friend Karl Bice at McDougall & Kline. They small talk until everyone else in the tech department goes to lunch, then run the clapboard through the scanner, letting the firm's Macintosh do what Hugh Harbinger could not do with his little circles of gouache: decipher Howie's serendipitous concoction. At 2:15 Hugh Harbinger is on the New Jersey side of the Hudson, at Zildenheim & Pavli, formula in hand, blank check from Zee Levant in his pocket, ordering the proper dye. It takes four days for Zildenheim & Pavli to mix and deliver the dye to Westerman & Klup in Chelsea, where bolts of wool and cotton and hemp are waiting.

Even as the Serendipity Green® dye is soaking into these natural fabrics, Jean Jacques Bistrot is heralding the Second Coming of Hugh Harbinger. His articles praise the new color. His articles praise the suits, the big-ass over-coats. and hats. He uses words like *bodacious* and *unrepentant, apoplectic* and *scandalous,whoomp* and *duggy, cool beans* and *jiggy,* and of course he uses *fabulous*. His articles not only promise a new fashion *paradigm*, but a new cultural *Zeitgeist* as well. His articles brazenly recount Hugh Harbinger's slow descent into clinical depression during the years he was designing his 300-plus shades of black; they recount his miserable, Solhzac-controlled exile at Bob and Eleanor Hbracek's house in Parma, Ohio; they recount his journey to Tuttwyler for Squaw Days; they recount his serendipitous discovery of the two-story frame on South Mill and his immediate epiphany; and with all the spiritual drama of the King of Kings riding his donkey into Jerusalem for his final showdown with the powers that be, he recounts Hugh Harbinger's all-night Amtrak ride to New York with his chunk of precious green clapboard.

One of Jean Jacques Bistrot's nuggets is even selected by *Newsweek* for its page of pithy and ironic quotations:

> "Hugh Harbinger's 300 shades of black gave individual expression to our generation's collective narcissism. Now Double H is back from the Ohio hinterlands with a dazzling and disturbing new hue that will force us to shed the snake skins of our angst and admit that we are about as goddamn happy as a person can be." *Fashion writer* **Jean Jacques Bistrot** *on colormeister Hugh Harbinger's latest creation, Serendipity Green®.*

By the time Buzzy's designs are cut and the invitations sent, Serendipity Green® has already piqued the interest of anybody who is anybody in the color world, not only in New York, but in Paris and London and Milan and LA. Even automotive executives in Detroit and Tokyo are intrigued.

September flies by. The trees in Washington Square start dropping their leaves on the chess players. October blows in from Pennsylvania. One month after Hugh

Harbinger's return, two hundred of the world's most influential marketing, manufacturing and media gurus are trekking into a sweaty old warehouse house in the trendy Meat Packing District. As they enter they are handed tiny flashlights. The warehouse is cold and damp and dark. With the help of their tiny beams, the privileged 200 find the rows of metal folding chairs. Somewhere in the blackness a klezmer band is playing Jewish funeral tunes. Slowly, as the clarinet wails, a wintergreen wind mixes with the faint stench of beef. Green laser beams begin to slice. Then a great square of flood lights, everyone of them green, explodes into the eyes of the privileged 200. The klezmer band, now joined by a shirtless steel drum band from Trinidad and Tobago, breaks into a throbbing rendition of Kermit the Frog's "It's Not Easy Being Green." Three men in black business suits appear on the catwalk. Three women in green spider suits—a green no one has ever seen—bungee jump from the high ceiling and squeeze the three men in black until the catwalk is dripping with what for all the world looks like green blood. The wintergreen wind reaches gale force. Fluorescent ceiling lights pop on. For the first time the privileged 200 realizes they are sitting on green chairs in a warehouse with a green floor and green walls and a green ceiling—the green a green none of them has ever imagined. Now three meat hooks descend from the ceiling and the spider women run them through the backs of the three bloodless men in black. As they are hauled into the rafters, a choir of green-robed Gregorian monks wind through the aisles, chanting "Serendipity Green®" over and over while the Klezmers and steel drummers maintain a blistering tempo. Suddenly, New York's currently most famous transvestite, Pippy Monroe, flutters down the catwalk in a shimmering Serendipity Green® gown scooping handfuls of green M&Ms into the crowd from a Serendipity Green® basket. "Yo-yo-yo, everybody," she sings out. "Y'all ready for Serendipity Green®? Serendipity Greeeen®? Serendipity Greeeeeeeen®? Ahhhh can't heeeeaaaar y'all!" The privileged 200—the most jaded gaggle of fashion and manufacturing elites ever assembled—screams "Yes!" Begs "Yes!" Demands "Yes!" And so in this painful cacophony of sound and light and heat and orgasmic anticipation, amidst the dueling scent of wintergreen and beef, the first Wall Street type marches manfully down the catwalk in a three-piece Cary Grant suit of Serendipity Green®.

There is a fabulous gasp.

Howie Dornick has been watching Matisse for two weeks when a contract arrives in the mail from Hugh Harbinger. There's no small print in this contact to worry about, or see a lawyer about. In the clearest English it simply guarantees one Howard Allen Dornick of 185 South Mill St., Tuttwyler, Ohio, fifty percent of all royalties derived from the licensing of the color therein known as Serendipity Green®. Embarrassed that he has consented to such a foolhardy agreement, he signs the contract as soon as he finds a ballpoint. He stuffs it into the self-addressed stamped envelope his new partner has provided him. With Matisse trotting alongside on his leash, he walks the envelope to the out-of-town drop-off box outside the Post Office.

The next morning he drives the village truck to the old Aitchbone family farm on Three Fish Creek Road, to fulfill an even more foolhardy agreement—to dig up and re-plant Bill Aitchbone's ancestors at seventy-five bucks a pop. "Why in *thee hell* am I doing this?" he yells at himself as he drives. "Why in *thee hell*?"

He reaches the Aitchbone farm much too soon. The house and barn have been flattened by bulldozers. A huge plywood sign has been planted: SETTLER'S KNOB. EXQUISITE EXECUTIVE HOMES. He drives past the earthmovers waiting to scrape the precious topsoil off the land, drives all the way to the hill overlooking the creek, where the village's faded yellow backhoe and a stack of inexpensive coffins are waiting. He crawls over the wrought

162

iron fence and climbs aboard the backhoe. The tractor, with its great digging claw poised like the tail of a giant scorpion, starts up on the first try. Diesel fumes spoil the crisp October air.

As skillfully as Artie Brown drove that Seabee bulldozer into the Japanese-infested Matanikau River, Howie Dornick sends the backhoe's claw into the six feet of good earth atop the bones of Henry and Blanche Aitchbone. Little by little he peels away the dirt until he finds traces of rotted wood. Now comes the hard part, the shovel work. It's noon before he has Henry and Blanche in their new caskets. With chains and skill he lifts them into the truck. Next he lifts their old weather-worn headstone into the truck. He drives to the Tuttwyler Village Cemetery where, with only a pair of squirrels as witnesses, he lowers Henry and Blanche into their new eternal resting place. When they are covered with dirt and their headstone resting firmly atop them, he goes back to the farm for another Aitchbone or two.

In three days Howie Dornick digs up seven of D. William Aitchbone's ancestors. He is accustomed to the sight of dirty old bones by now, accustomed to handling skulls with gold-plugged teeth. He is accustomed to his recurring dream of opening a rotting box and finding the decaying bodies of Artie Brown and Patsy Dornick copulating like there is no tomorrow.

On the fourth day the backhoe eats into the dirt over one Seth Aitchbone. Only four feet down the claw strikes bone. "Well, that's not right," Howie Dornick says. He jumps off the backhoe to remove the yellowy femur dangling from the claw. What he finds in the hole sends him driving like a madman into Tuttwyler, to the Tuttwyler Branch of the Wyssock County Library, to the desk of branch librarian Katherine Hardihood who is completing a report to the board on how many children were caught looking at pornography on the Internet the previous month. It will be a short report, there having been only one offender, Darren Frost Jr., son of Squaw Days cupcake and Christian crusader Darren Frost Sr.

Howie does not let his woman complete the report, short as it is. He drives her back to the Aitchbone farm and the bones only four feet down. Katherine Hardihood crawls into the hole and like an ambidextrous Hamlet lifts two dirt- and worm-filled skulls high into the bluer-than-blue October sky. "Jiminy Cricket," she says.

By Halloween Hugh Harbinger has signed two dozen licensing agreements. By Thanksgiving week investment bankers and stock brokers are showing up at work in Serendipity Green® suits, checking their Serendipity Green® hats and big-ass Serendipity Green® overcoats at the city's toniest restaurants. Posh Christmas parties on both coasts are wall-to-wall with men and women in Serendipity Green®. Hugh, wearing a Serendipity Green® Santa suit appears on the cover of *GQ*. That same week *Newsweek* puts him buck naked in a Serendipity Green® wheelbarrow full of fifty dollar bills. *Time* doesn't put him on the cover—that honor goes to Yobisch Podka who is about to perform his commissioned symphony at the ceremony celebrating the completed restoration of the Sistine Chapel's ceiling frescoes—but there is a three-page feature inside documenting the color world's jealousy over the Second Coming of Hugh Harbinger: FABULOUSLY GREEN WITH ENVY the headline reads. A photograph of a perplexed Howie Dornick shoveling snow outside his Serendipity Green® two-story frame accompanies the story. Just a week before Christmas, the nation's Gap stores are piled high with Serendipity Green® socks, Serendipity Green® jockey shorts, Serendipity Green® polo shirts, even stacks of Serendipity Green® chinos. On December 23, Hugh flies back to Cleveland to claim Matisse and hand Howie Dornick a prototype Serendipity Green® food blender stuffed with very real royalty checks. "This is just the beginning," he tells his partner as they sip a couple of brown beers.

And it is just the beginning. On New Year's Eve Dick Clark broadcasts from Times Square wearing a big-ass Serendipity Green® overcoat. A Serendipity Green® Goodyear blimp flies over Miami's Joe Robbie Stadium on Superbowl Sunday. On January 3, both Jay Leno and David Letterman tell their first Serendipity Green® jokes. On January 6, the President of the United States wears a Serendipity Green® necktie while welcoming the prime minister of Mozambique to the White House. On January 8, Prince Charles attends a Yobisch Podka concert at The Albert Hall wearing a Serendipity Green® tuxedo. On January 11, *The Today Show* unveils its new Serendipity Green® couch. On January 12, Oprah Winfrey wears a Serendipity Green® pantsuit for her interview with Hugh Harbinger. On January 17, PBS viewers watch the hosts of *This Old House* slather Serendipity Green® paint on a newly restored Queen Anne in Vicksburg, Mississippi. On January 23, Hugh sends Howie Dornick a Serendipity Green® bread maker stuffed with more royalty checks. On January 27, the first copycat color debuts, assuring Hugh Harbinger that his comeback is complete; Serenity Green the manufacturer of plastic raincoats calls it. On February 1, *Sixty Minutes* correspondent Carolyn Carlucci-Plank profiles a village maintenance engineer from Tuttwyler, Ohio, named Howie Dornick.

Carlucci-Plank: "You're father was a war hero."

Dornick: "He hobbled six miles."

Carlucci-Plank: "And saved a lot of Seabees. The Army awarded him a Congressional Medal of Honor."

Dornick: "That's his wooden foot on the mantle."

Carlucci-Plank: "And when he returned home a hero, he got your mother pregnant. She was still in high school. He never married her."

Dornick: "No. But he willed her his penis."

Carlucci-Plank: "And so you grew up—how can I put this, Mr. Dornick—as a local embarrassment. Like some crazy old aunt locked away in the attic."

Dornick: "They gave me a job with the village when the snack cake line moved to Tennessee."

Carlucci-Plank: "Shoveling snow and digging graves."

Dornick: Somebody's got to do it."

Carlucci-Plank: "I heard that as recent as last summer the village council tried to fire you."

Dornick: "Some thought it would be a good idea to privatize village services. To plug future shortfalls in the budget."

Carlucci-Plank: "Then you painted your house this—how else can I put it—this atrocious green. And this famous color designer from New York, Hugh Harbinger, who's being treated for clinical depression, happens by one day and . . ."

Dornick: "He came to Squaw Days with his parents."

Carlucci-Plank: ". . . and he falls in love with that atrocious color, what he now calls Serendipity Green®. He turns it into the color rage of the decade."

Dornick: "That's about it."

Carlucci-Plank: "In a few short months Serendipity Green® has made you a wealthy man."

Dornick: "I don't know about wealthy."

Carlucci-Plank: "And yet you keep your degrading job with the village. Shoveling snow. Digging graves."

Dornick: "So far. But there's still talk of privatization."

PART III

"So tractable, so peaceable are these people, that I swear to your majesties there is not in the world a better nation. They love their neighbors as themselves, and their discourse is ever sweet and gentle, and accompanied with a smile; and though it is true that they are naked, yet their manners are decorous and praiseworthy."

Christopher Columbus,
Letter to King Ferdinand and Queen Isabella

17

Green.
Yellow.
Red.
The cars on South Mill stop. The cars on Tocqueville go.

It is February and the snow is horizontal again. D. William Aitchbone is returning from New Waterbury, once more missing dinner with Karen and the kids, on his way to the year's first meeting of the Squaw Days Committee.

D. William Aitchbone desperately needs a strategy session with himself. Yet he won't be going to the Daydream Beanery. Nosireebob. Not since they started serving their coffees in Serendipity Green® mugs he won't. Not since the counter girl changed her lipstick from blackcherry to Serendipity Green®. So when the light goes from red to yellow to green, he does not drive straight through the intersection, nor drive past his impressive soapy white Queen Anne. He does not drive past Howie Dornick's repulsive green clapboards where, despite the purple-black February sky and the gooseshitting snow, tourists and television crews are most certainly causing traffic problems. Instead he turns left on Tocqueville and winds his way through Tuttwyler's side streets to the throbbing commercial strip on West Wooseman. At Burger King he sits in a cold booth next to the condiment counter. As high schoolers with larynxes surely transplanted from rutting moose fumble for ketchup packs and straws, he sits in his Burberry overcoat sipping a large black coffee, honing his plans for what will be the best Squaw Days ever. As he plans and shivers and sips, he notices that three of the four girls sitting under the twirling bacon-cheeseburger mobile are wearing Serendipity Green® socks.

At 7:20 he drives to the square and parks in front of Just Giraffes. In the window two dozen Serendipity Green® giraffes are circling a JUST ARRIVED! sign. He crosses

169

the square. The gazebo is still trimmed with Christmas garlands. "Conniving bastard," he growls through his thin blue lips, the conniving bastard being, of course, one Howie Dornick, scheduled to be featured that coming Sunday on *Sixty Minutes.*

At 7:30 he barges into the library community room. He sits at the head of the table, thinking he is seducing his flock with his perfected lawyer's smile. In reality he is scaring the bejesus out of them with the giddy grimace of a maniac. "Everybody here then?" he asks.

Everybody is.

Delores Poltruski is there. Dick Mueller is there. Mayor Woodrow Wilson Sadlebyrne is there. Donald Grinspoon, Katherine Hardihood, and Paula Varney are there. So is the Serendipity Green® giraffe Paula brought along to show the others. Kevin Hassock, the buffoon who let the Happy Landing Ride Company bring their small Ferris wheel is not there. Two weeks after his divorce was final, he accepted a transfer to Duluth, Minnesota. But his replacement, Paul Kreplach, is.

D. William Aitchbone simultaneously gives him a nod and a thumbs up. "We're delighted to have you on the committee, Paul. I'm sure you'll have lots of good ideas for us."

Paul Kreplach responds with a confident Popeye the Sailor Man wink. He has every right to feel as confident as Popeye. In just the past six months he's been named Midwestern sales manager for the nation's largest manufacturer of tamper-proof medicine bottles, gotten married for the second time—to a woman not only younger but infinitely better-looking than his first wife—and purchased a monstrous brick colonial in Woodchuck Ridge.

Delores Poltruski knows all about Paul Kreplach. She was, after all, the real estate agent who convinced him his salary could handle the 30-year adjustable mortgage. "Paul's new wife used to dance with the Youngstown Ballet," she informs the others. "She's thinking of opening a dance school."

"I hear Dottie Dunkle's bagel shop is going under," Dick Mueller says. "That'd make a great dance studio. High ceiling. Right on the square."

Delores Poltruski pats Dick Mueller's arm. "Oh, Dick! That's a great idea! Isn't it, Paul?"

"Yes, it is," Paul Kreplach says. Being new to Tuttwyler, Ohio, he does not know what others know. He does not know that Dick Mueller owns the soon-to-be-empty storefront in question. He does not know that Dick and Delores Poltruski have been copulating twice a week for years. Nor does he know that the maniacally grimacing chairman of the Squaw Days Committee plans to ignore and humiliate him for the next seven months, and probably, if all goes as plans, handle his young, good-looking, ballet-dancing second wife's divorce.

"I suppose the first thing we need to do," begins D. William Aitchbone, "is to make sure everybody is happy with their subcommittee assignments."

Everybody is extremely happy with their subcommittee assignments. Their February faces show it. One by one they make their presentations:

Dick Mueller dutifully reports that the parade units will line up on Mechanics Street, proceed up East Wooseman to the square, go once around, then proceed out South Mill to the cemetery for the memorial services. Both the high school and junior high bands will march again, he says, and the Chirping Chipmunk unicycle troupe from Akron has expressed interest in returning for a third year. Now he folds his hands on the table. His neck turns to steel. His eyes lock on the wall just above D. William Aitchbone's head. "I think we ought to put Howie Dornick in the parade," he says. "I can't tell you how many out-of-towners have come into the auto parts store for directions to his house."

Delores Poltruski immediately offers her support. "He's becoming a national celebrity. Did you know that *Sixty Minutes* is—"

"We know," says D. William Aitchbone. "But just because the liberal media is falling for—"

171

Before his protégé can ridicule Dick and Delores into submission, Donald Grinspoon offers his support for the idea. "Howie's going to end up more famous than his father."

Dick Mueller doesn't especially like that. "You can't compare a guy who loses his foot on Guadalcanal to a guy who paints his house."

"I'm not comparing their accomplishments," says Donald Grinspoon, "just their fame."

"I'm not sure putting Howie in the parade fits the Squaw Days theme," D. William Aitchbone says.

"Fits about as much as Darren Frost and his cupcake suit," Delores Poltruski points out.

D. William Aitchbone cannot believe Delores said that, and not Katherine Hardihood. Nevertheless he's happy to have an ally. "I agree. No Howie Dornick and no cupcake."

"Overruled," Mayor Woodrow Wilson Sadlebyrne says. "Both are a part of our history. As much as Princess Pogawedka."

"Absolutely," says Donald Grinspoon.

D. William Aitchbone cannot believe he's lost the debate. It's the first debate he's ever lost in his life. "OK folks, but don't come crying to me when Tuttwyler becomes the laughingstock of Ohio." He asks Delores Poltruski for her report on the food and craft booths.

"My people are bombarding me with oodles of good ideas, "she begins. "Just oodles and oodles!" She tells them how the G.A. Hemphill Elementary School PTA plans to sell Serendipity Green® snow cones. She tells them how the Knights of Columbus plans to sell Serendipity Green® macaroni salad. She tells them how Ethel Babcox is already making little Serendipity Green® houses for her crafts booth.

"I don't think we should go overboard with this Serendipity Green® thing," cautions D. William Aitchbone. "I really don't."

"And wait until you see the Serendipity Green® mittens the Methodist Moms are knitting for their booth," Delores Poltruski adds. "They're the cutest things."

Aitchbone knows he can't expect much out of Paula Varney, given that she's been bouncing that Serendipity Green® giraffe on her knee since the meeting began. She doesn't disappoint. "All of the merchants plan to put out their Serendipity Green® merchandise for the sidewalk sale," she says. "Randy Foxx at Kmart has already ordered five thousand Serendipity Green® coffee mugs. He's going to stack them up like Indian teepees. What he doesn't sell at Squaw Days he's going to stack up like Christmas trees."

"Neat idea," new member Paul Kreplach says.

"Well Donald," D. William Aitchbone says, his grimace now beyond maniacal, "I suppose we'll be spitting Serendipity Green® tobacco juice this year."

"Wouldn't that be a hoot," the former mayor says.

"How about Serendipity Green® fireworks?" the current mayor offers, as if a Serendipity Green® light bulb was hovering over his head.

"Oh, that would be a hoot, too!" Delores Poltruski says.

Everyone has reported now but Katherine Hardihood. She has sat quietly. Offering no suggestions. Rendering no support. Making not a single plea for historic accuracy. Flinging not a single cynical remark. D. William Aitchbone folds his arms across his chest, certain now that it's her turn, a great river of Serendipity Green® ideas will pour from her librarian's mouth. "What you got cooked up for the Re-Enactment?" he asks.

"Same old same old," Katherine says.

As the meeting winds down, Paul Kreplach is given his marching orders. "If the Happy Landing Ride Company shows up this year with the small Ferris wheel, we're hanging you from it," the Squaw Days chairman attempts to joke.

The committee members file out into the horizontal snow. D. William Aitchbone is almost to his car when Woodrow Wilson Sadlebyrne catches up to him and clamps his cheap Democratic glove on the epauletted shoulder of his Burberry.

"Sorry to keep you from your warm bed, Bill," Woodrow Wilson Sadlebyrne says, spinning his nemesis around so the snow can pour into his nostrils. "I just wanted you to know that this Serendipity Green® nightmare of yours is just beginning."

"It's your nightmare," says D. William Aitchbone, jerking his epaulet free.

Woodrow Wilson Sadlebyrne smiles at his hollow bravado. "There's going to be a representative from the Bison-Prickert Paint Company at Thursday's council meeting. And do you know what he's going to do, Bill? He's going to offer to paint our gazebo Serendipity Green®, so they can use it to film a TV commercial to introduce their new Serendipity Green® house paint."

D. William Aitchbone blows the snow from his nostrils. "Council would never sit still for that kind of corporate exploitation."

For a few seconds Woodrow Wilson Sadlebyrne's Democratic brain is as numb as his February toes. Had super-Republican Bill Aitchbone actually said that? Corporate exploitation? The same man who rammed through the tax abatement bill that cut the property taxes of all those discount stores and fast-food restaurants that rushed to West Wooseman after the I-491 extension was built? The same man who had his ancestors' bones hauled away? "They'll do more than sit still for it, Bill. They'll do handstands and backflips and grunt like a liter of hungry piggies. Rumor has it the Bison-Prickert people will be arriving at the meeting in a brand new pumper, just like the one you promised the fire department before you went off on your privatization jag."

"Sweet Jesus."

"Rumor also has it the new pumper will be painted—you guessed it, Bill—Serendipity Green®. Bison-Prickert it seems has just added our favorite color to its line of rust-resistant commercial and industrial enamels."

And so D. William Aitchbone flees the mayor and drives out South Mill. He slides up his driveway and slides into bed. He does not kiss Karen's cold ear. Her cold ear was sired by war hero Artie Brown, who, in a spurt of patriotic fervor, sired the ears of Howie Dornick, sire of the god-awful color called Serendipity Green®.

"How'd your meeting go?" Karen Aitchbone asks.

"That bastard brother of yours is fucking up everything we've worked for. Absolutely fucking it up!"

Karen Aitchbone has never heard her husband refer to Howie Dornick as her brother before. She has never referred to him as her brother herself. She begins to breathe like a little girl who's just knocked the wind out of herself riding her tricycle off the end of the porch. "You slept with Vicki Bonobo, didn't you?"

"Who?"

Karen Aitchbone slips out of bed and stalks to her closet. From one of the purses she no longer uses, she pulls a letter. She stalks back to the bed and hands it to her husband. It is a short, cold letter. A February letter:

> Karen,
> Do you know what your husband and Vicki Bonobo did in Washington DC?

She watches her husband read the letter and crumple it into a snowball and throw it against the kittens-playing-in-a basket-of-yarn wallpaper.

It is unseasonably warm for more than a week. Then the temperature tumbles and it snows. The first day the flakes are wet and fat. They pile a foot high. The second day the flakes are as fine as donut sugar. Driven by a ferocious

Canadian wind, they form great drifts that close half the roads in the county and force cancellation of the Friday night basketball game between the West Wyssock Wildcats and the Orville Red Riders. On Saturday morning Howie Dornick and Katherine Hardihood drive to Wooster anyway.

Except for a few unflagging fools on snowmobiles, the streets of Wooster are empty. Store windows are frozen white. Drifts are as high as the coin slots on the parking meters.

The two visitors from Tuttwyler are worried that the Bittinger boy won't show up. But when they approach the hardware store they find a wedge of parking spaces shoveled out of the drifts. They park and carry their cardboard box inside.

Howie Dornick points to the young man standing behind the counter drinking a can of Mountain Dew. "That's the Bone Head there," he whispers to his woman. Like brides with cold feet, they march slowly up the plumbing supply aisle.

"We were afraid you wouldn't be open," Katherine Hardihood says when they reach the young man with the Mountain Dew. "That was quite a storm last night."

The Bittinger boy swallows the mouthful of Mountain Dew he's been sloshing. "In the hardware business, the only thing better that good weather is bad weather," he says. He tells them he's already sold six aluminum snow shovels, seven plastic ones, nine pairs of thermal gloves, half a pallet of ice melting pellets, and two kerosene space heaters. He tells them how the blizzard of '77 paid off the second mortgage on his parent's house and how they sold forty-eight electric fans over one blistering July weekend in '86. He also tells them that in September his father, driving home from the big hardware show in Chicago, fell asleep at the wheel and drove into the path of a tractor-trailer hauling made-in-China Christmas toys, not only killing himself, but killing his son's dream of working alongside Donald Johanson at the Institute of Human Origins. "I'm the head hardware honcho now," he says.

Katherine Hardihood compassionately folds her arms over her noisy caramel-brown coat. "There's no one else who could run the store?"

"Except for my brother Bob, I'm an only child," the Bittinger boy says. "And Bob, well, Bob is a little different."

"Retarded or something?" Howie asks.

"Creative or something," answers the Bittinger boy, smile gone. "He's working on his masters in poetry and playing sackbut in a medieval quintet."

"Sackbut?" Howie Dornick asks.

"Something like a trombone," Katherine answers.

The Bittinger boy is astonished. "You're the only person I've ever met who knew what a sackbut was."

"She's a librarian," Howie Dornick says.

And so the small talk winds down and after the Bittinger boy sells a plastic snow shovel and pair of thermal socks to a man wearing a spring jacket and tennis shoes, they get down to the contents in the cardboard box.

"Well, they're human bones, that's for sure," the Bittinger boy says. "And one's an adult—a woman by the shape of the pelvic bone here—and the other's clearly a child."

Katherine Hardihood is not impressed. "We could see that ourselves."

Her man is neither impressed nor unimpressed. He is simply cold and frightened. "We think that maybe—"

The Bittinger boy stops him. "No-no, Mr. Dornick. A forensic anthropologist has to go into an investigation without prejudice. What you think is immaterial. What I think is immaterial. I'll find what I find."

The store is filling up with customers and Katherine Hardihood can see that his attention is waning out of financial necessity. "How soon?"

The Bittinger boy pushes the box of bones aside, making room for the three twenty-pound bags of de-icing pellets being lugged up the electrical supply aisle by a red-faced man with a Pop-tart wedged between his chapped lips.

"Hard to say," the Bittinger boy says. "If mom's up to watching the store next weekend I'm driving down to OU to get drunk. Still got my key to the lab. So maybe week after next."

The red-face man with the three bags of de-icing pellets looks closely at Howie Dornick and grins through his Pop-tart. TV right? Guy with the ugly green house."

"That's him," Katherine Hardihood says.

"I sold him the paint," the Bittinger boy says.

Pellet bags finally resting on the counter, the red-faced man is free to take a bite out of his portable breakfast. "That was the weirdest damn story since Morley Safer inter-viewed that hundred-year-old Mormon with the sixteen wives. And who was that artsy-fartsy guy with the little dog?"

Howie and Katherine start their drive back to Tuttwyler. Highway department trucks are at work, pushing and scraping and spraying rock salt. The sky is purple-brown. Northern Ohioans know what that means: Several more inches of the white stuff are coming.

"We shouldn't have done this," Howie Dornick says.

"The weather won't be any better tomorrow," Katherine says. She is trying to defrost the door window with the palm of her librarian's hand.

"I meant this whole thing with the bones."

"We've got to know the truth, Howard."

"Take it from the illegitimate son of Artie Brown, Katherine, the truth is not always such a good thing."

"The truth is always a good thing," Katherine Hardihood says. She smiles victoriously. She has melted a small circle in the glass and can now see the endless acres of broken corn stalks that comprise Wayne County in winter. "If those are the bones of Princess Pogawedka and little Kapusta, or whatever their real names were, that would be a good thing, wouldn't it? We could honor them like the real people they were. Stop this Squaw Days circus. Have I ever told you what Pogawedka and Kapusta mean in Polish?"

"Many times. Nonsense and cabbage."

Katherine playfully grinds her frozen palm into her man's worried cheek. He howls like a branded calf. She laughs as only a woman in love can laugh. "And I've also told you many times that my plan will work. Haven't I, Howard dear?"

"That you have." He rubs his fingers on his door window until they are icy cold, then he playfully grabs Katherine Hardihood by her librarian's nose. She squeals. They laugh and they laugh.

Howie Dornick knows that his woman's plan is a good one: if the Bittinger boy finds that the bones are indeed those of an Indian woman and child, then in the middle of the night like some black-and-white movie ghoul he will re-bury them. Then his woman will tell Bill Aitchbone, in front of the other Squaw Days Committee members, of course, that Howie Dornick has just told her something that might be very important. When Howie was moving the old Aitchbone cemetery last fall, she'll say, he found the skeletons of a woman and child right on top of one Seth Aitchbone, and that given their smashed skulls and their proximity to Three Fish Creek, they just might be the bones of Princess Pogawedka and Kapusta. And if they are their bones, she'll say, the resulting media hoopla will make Squaw Days one of the top festivals in the state of Ohio, bigger than Buzzard Day in Hinckley, bigger than the Pumpkin Festival in Circleville, bigger than the Sauerkraut Festival in Waynesville that brought down Sheriff Norman F. Cole. And despite Bill Aitchbone's protests, the committee will vote to have the bones exhumed and examined. And, of course, the bones will be found to be Indian bones, of the proper age, with the proper smashed skulls. Podewedka and Kapusta for certain!

The delicious part of his woman's plan, of course, is the obvious question of why Princess Pogawedka and Kapusta were buried on top of Seth Aitchbone. An investigation of old county records will show that Seth is none other that Bill's Aitchbone's great-great-great-great-great uncle, the sixth and never-married son of Jobiah and Almira Aitchbone. And this can mean only one thing: Seth and Pogawedka had copulated and that poor little Kapusta is Bill Aitchbone's illegitimate great-great-great-great-great cousin; and given that someone had thought enough of Seth to place Pogawedka and Kapusta in his grave, they no doubt had copulated a lot and considered themselves a family. Such a revelation will embarrass the hell out of Bill Aitchbone. Maybe humble him. Maybe help Woodrow Wilson Sadlebyrne win re-election. Such a revelation, after all, will put two famous skeletons in Bill Aitchbone's closet—the skeleton of his wife's illegitimate brother, one Howard Allen Dornick, and the skeleton of the half-breed son of Pogawedka—and while a politician can overcome one skeleton in his closet, rarely can a politician overcome two, even a politician with Bill Aitchbone's genetic steel.

But that isn't the end of his woman's plan: producing the smashed skull of Bill Aitchbone's distant kin, she figures, will transform the Tuttwyler brothers' misdeed from a happy myth to a horrendous murder. And who today in Tuttwyler is related to these murderous brothers of yesteryear? Donald Grinspoon's thrice-afflicted wife, that's who! And so a bloody wedge will be driven between the former mayor and his political protégé, a wedge that will spit the local Republicans for decades and end all talk of privatizing village services. And best of all, Squaw Days itself will be transformed, from a carnival of lies into a somber memorial to truth. It is such a good plan.

18

Ernest Not Irish leaves his apartment on Detroit Avenue and drives his old white Pontiac with the blue fenders across the Cuyahoga River to Jacob's Field, the spectacular new stadium where the professional baseball team called the Cleveland Indians play. Other members of Cleveland's Real Indians are already keeping a vigil there, waiting for the big equipment truck with Chief Wahoo on the side to begins its annual February trek to Florida for the start of spring training.

Ernest Not Irish arrives at the ballpark just as television crews from channels 3 and 8 are pulling up. Channels 5 and 19 are already there. The reporters who will interview him are wearing earmuffs over their wind-resistant hair. The cameramen are wearing orange Cleveland Browns caps. Steam is pouring from coffee cups and nostrils.

It has been twenty-four years since Ernest Not Irish moved to Cleveland from Tennessee. His father, dead now, came north to work at the Ford Motor Company, but ended up working 1800 feet under Lake Erie, in Cleveland's famous salt mines. Ernest Not Irish's name was not Not Irish then. It was McPugh, a name perfectly respectable among the Scotch-Irish living in the shadows of the Great Smoky Mountains, but a name funny as hell on Cleveland's west side. Even the black kids thought McPugh was funny as hell.

And so young Ernest was not happy in Cleveland. Not happy at all. In the mornings when he looked south from his bedroom window, he saw filthy smoke rising from filthy steel mills. He saw highways clogged with suburbanites. He saw the identical gray roofs of ten thousand identical houses. In Tennessee when he looked south from his bedroom window, he saw the peaks of the Smokies rising like gargantuan black bears through the low wet clouds that gave the mountains their name, and the Little Pigeon River, meandering like a silver snake through ten zillion trees. So he missed the black-bear mountains and the silver-snake river and the ten zillion trees. And he missed Cora Mae Bean, his seven-eighths Cherokee grandmother; missed her chocolate eyes, and missed her face, which was the color of the sausage-grease gravy she made every Saturday for breakfast. He missed the biscuits she made to soak up that wonderful gravy, biscuits as hard as life on the outside, as soft as her heart on the inside. He missed her smile and her breath, both as sweat as the okra she battered and fried every Sunday. He missed her always busy fingers, always busy kneading dough for biscuits, embroidering flowers on pillowcases, busy on the warped keys of her old piano, scratching the top of his always itchy head, as she told him of his Cherokee ancestors, their dream for a nation of their own, their trail of tears as soldiers marched them off to death and Oklahoma. She'd scratch his head and tell him of the stubbornness of those, who despite the greed and trickery of the whites, clung to the holy mountains like the low wet clouds that gave them their name, tell him how proud she was of her one-eighth Negro blood, of the runaway slave Solomon Hangbee, who fought for the north in the War Between the States, and before being butchered at Fort Pillow along with scores of other Negro soldiers who had already surrendered, had successfully mated with her great-grandmother.

No, Ernest did not like Cleveland, Ohio. And he did not like being a McPugh.

And so the year his father was knocked off a bar stool by a stray bullet, the same year he dropped out of school and went to work unloading produce trucks at the old Central Market where Jacob's Field now stands, he threw away his white blood, with the same distaste you'd pour a carton of soured milk down the kitchen sink, embracing fully his Cherokee blood. Ernest Not Irish he became. An annual pain in the ass to the professional baseball team called the Cleveland Indians.

So once again, as the big equipment truck begins to warm up for the drive south, the local television reporters ask him the same questions they've been asking him for eleven years now.

Asks the reporter from Channel 3: "Every year you demand that the Indians drop Chief Wahoo as their mascot, and every year they ignore you. Why keep it up?"

Answers Ernest Not Irish: "We demand it every year because it is wrong every year. Why they ignore us every year you'll have to ask them."

Asks the reporter from Channel 5: "Chief Wahoo is really pretty cute. What's so offensive about him?"

Answers Ernest Not Irish: "Bunny rabbits are pretty cute. Indian peoples are not bunny rabbits. We are human beings. Human beings deserve respect."

Asks the reporter from Channel 8: "The Indian's management says Chief Wahoo is one of the most recognizable team logos in the world, that they couldn't change it if they wanted to."

Answers Ernest Not Irish: "The swastika was also a very recognizable team logo."

Asks the reporter from Channel 19: "How many years do you intend to keep this protest up?"

Asks Ernest Not Irish: "How many years do you intend on being a black person?"

While Ernest Not Irish gives these answers, his fellow members of the CRI bounce their homemade signs up and down and stomp their feet to keep the cold from leaking into their shoes. The driver of the equipment truck waves until all of the cameramen focus on him, then he pulls away in a great billow of blue diesel fumes.

Ernest Not Irish drives back across the Cuyahoga for a few hours sleep. He has already worked his full shift at the Brottenschmidt's Bakery—"We never stop loafing at Brottenschmidt's"—and he has a non-stop drive to Florida in front of him, where he will protest the arrival of the equipment truck, and answer the same moronic questions from the television reporters from Miami and Orlando, Jacksonville and St. Pete.

"So, tell me, Ernest Not Irish," asks Dr. Pirooz Aram, putting his empty demitasse on the silver tray on his desk. "Did your protest go well this year? You look like you got a little sun."

"I am an Indian. The sun is always in my face."

Dr. Aram likes that. He laughs like only an old Persian can. "I must tell you, Ernest, when I saw you on the television, you did not seem to be as angry as other years. I hope you are not losing faith."

Ernest Not Irish confesses that while Chief Wahoo still bunches his shorts, his anger these days belongs to another cause. "It's that damn Squaw Days!"

Dr. Pirooz Aram knows about Squaw Days. For years he has listened to Katherine Hardihood bitch about it. Yet he is a man who loves to be entertained as much as he loves entertaining. "Squaw Days? I don't think I've heard of it."

Ernest tells him all about it. He tells him about the parade, about the cupcake who gets almost as much applause as Princess Pogawedka, about the Tuttwyler brothers and their big papier mâché clubs throwing candy to children. He tells him about the tobacco spitting and pie eating, the construction-paper feathers the women who sell big cookies wear and the wooden Indian holding the pizza. He tells him about the Re-Enactment. "And they have this white woman dressed in white buckskins rise out of a pouf of phony-baloney smoke to forgive them for bashing in her baby's skull. And to wish them well as they piss pesticides into the creeks and rivers and vomit concrete over every sacred inch of soil. No real Indian ghost would do that."

Dr. Aram plays with his beard, twisting the coarse white hairs into little ringlets. "No?

"The real ghost of Pogawedka would rise out of the fire with a quiver of arrows and put a slice of flint into every white brain she saw. 'That arrow is for bashing my head open,' she would say. 'That arrow is for bashing my baby's head. That arrow is for pissing pesticides. That one for vomiting concrete. That one for making the wooden Indian hold a pizza.' And when her arrows were gone she would wade through that crowd of white fools with a granite ax, forgiving them one by one. *Boom!* 'You are forgiven.' *Boom!* 'You are forgiven.'"

Dr. Pirooz Aram continued to make ringlets. "So this Squaw Days bothers you? So what?"

Ernest Not Irish's Cherokee blood runs wild across his weak European cheeks. "So what?"

"Yes, Ernest! So What? So this summer you are going to make some new signs and while everyone is having a good time eating cookies and cotton candy, you are going to stomp back and forth on the sidewalk."

Cherokee blood fills the whites of Ernest Not Irish's blue-green European eyes. "I'm going to let them know that they are disgracing my people."

The old Persian pulls him from his chair and hugs him like a son and a brother and a father combined. "I will come and carry a sign with you," he says. "If you think it will do any good."

Ernest does not particularly enjoy being hugged like a son and a brother and a father. "You are right, Dr. Aram. It does no good. Americans are undisgracable."

"That is because Americans are still pooping in their diapers, historically speaking," the doctor says, returning to his chair and his ringlets. "You and I, Ernest, are from old nations. Our souls are heavy with thousands of years of culture. Thousands of years of shame and pride. Victory and defeat. Great achievements and great mistakes. Great myths. But Ernest! These Americans we live among! Their souls are still as light as the paper feathers the women who sell big cookies wear. They are still inventing their culture. They are still inventing their history that someday will weigh heavy on their souls and make them disgracable."

Tears wash the blood from the whites of Ernest Not Irish's eyes and he wishes the old Persian was still hugging him. "And make them stop pissing on Indians."

"Yes, dammit!" Dr. Pirooz Aram sings out. He starts dancing. "And stop pissing on Iranians! Do you know,

185

Ernest, that when those crazy students took those Americans hostage in Tehran, I could not go out for a loaf of bread without somebody giving me the finger? My neighbor still calls me Imam the Terrible, as though I am a butcherer of innocent children, as though the word *Imam* will insult me. He doesn't even know what the word means. He only knows how to kill the dandelions that pop up on his lawn, sweet little gifts from God. Imam means leader! A divinely appointed leader! You tell me, Ernest, what is so terrible about being a divinely appointed leader? Nothing! And then when his garden hose springs a leak, he comes and borrows mine. And on Christmas he sends me a card with a manger scene on the cover, just to get my goat, not knowing that we Moslems consider Jesus one of the greatest Imams of all time. Americans!"

Ernest Not Irish reaches out and grabs Dr. Pirooz Aram and hugs him like a son and a brother and a father combined.

"Our problem, Ernest," says Dr. Pirooz Aram, kissing the top of his head, "Is that we are Westoxified."

"Westoxified?"

"Seduced by the all-things European. Seduced by their crazy inventions and their crazy ideas. The Persian word is *Gharbzadegi.* It was coined by the Iranian writer Jalal Ale-e Ahmad, just a few years before the revolution that landed those fifty-two American diplomats in the hoosegow, which, if you don't know it, is a Spanish word for jail."

"I know Hoosegow," says Ernest Not Irish. "The Cleveland police have hoosegowed me a dozen times."

"I am so Westoxified," Dr. Pirooz Aram continues, "that to escape the torturers of the American puppet Shah Pahlavi, I came to America to be tortured by six-lane highways and magazines filled with young women showing their cleavages. That's how Westoxified I am, Ernest."

"And me?"

"You are so Westoxified that you use that crazy European invention called television to practice a crazy European idea called free speech, to protest another crazy European idea called racism."

"I suppose."

"Suppose? How many times do I have to tell you, Ernest? Know! Are you listening to me?" Dr. Pirooz Aram breaks away and presses his warm forehead against the cool window and watches a crew of black Americans pour asphalt over the last open meadow in Parma. "I know this is your session, Ernest, but I must tell you, I am so ripped between East and West it isn't funny. My brain belongs to Sigmund Freud and Carl Jung, and Kierkegaard and Sartre, and Henry Ford for christsakes. But my heart, dear Ernest, my heart still belongs to Hafez and Rumi, and Omar Khayam, and Firdawsi—who was a greater poet than Homer by the way—and the spring flowers that caress the slopes above old Tehran. Is it any wonder I dance for my patients?"

"No wonder at all," says Ernest.

"There is so much about America that I hate and yet so much that I love," Dr. Pirooz Aram says. He snatches the Indian's hands and dances him around the office. "For better or worse, God has planted us here, Ernest. And while you have a duty to your ancestors to raise as much of a ruckus as you can, never forget that you also are an American! That these undisgracable people are your brothers! So be as reasonable as you can with them. Do you hear me, Ernest? As reasonable as you can! Dammit, Ernest, are you listening?"

"Reasonable," Ernest Not Irish answers reluctantly. The session ends. But before he can shuffle to the outer office to pay the receptionist, Dr. Pirooz Aram asks him a final question: "Tell me Ernest, when you were in Tuttwyler, did you happen to see a very green house?"

Ernest Not Irish heads for home in his white Pontiac with the blue fenders. He feels calm and somewhat happy. That is why he has been coming to Dr. Pirooz Aram for the past seven years. To feel calm and somewhat happy. Yet he knows that within a day or two the spirits of a million ancestors will puncture his calm with slices of flint. Bash away at his happiness with granite axes. And despite the old Persian's words, or the American pills he prescribes, these spirits will not let him forget about Princess Pogawedka or little Kapusta. Still, Dr. Pirooz Aram is right about one thing: he must remain reasonable.

Dammit, he must remain reasonable.

19

Katherine Hardihood is having a busy February. There already has been the year's first Squaw Days Committee meeting where, despite D. William Aitchbone's maniacal smile, plans were made to include Howie Dornick in the parade. And at the the village council meeting, despite D. William Aitchbone's maniacal smile, his fellow council members, Victoria Bonobo included, graciously gave the Bison-Prickert Paint Company permission to paint the gazebo and on behalf of the volunteer fire department, accepted the keys to the new Serendipity Green® pumper. There already has been her slippery drive to Wooster with Howie Dornick and that box of bones. And there is tonight's meeting of the Wyssock County Library Board.

Once again folding chairs have been brought over from Barrow Brothers Funeral Home and the Moose Club. The number of EDIT members attending the meetings had dwindled over the months, but now that their leader, the Reverend Raymond R. Biscobee, is about to be sworn in as a member of the board, they are back, en masse, to watch him crush with his righteousness the tax-supported purveyors of pornography and pedophilia, like Jesus rid the temple of moneychangers and the sellers of sacrificial doves. Once again Sam Guss of the *Gazette* finds himself sitting between reporters from the big city papers. Channels 3, 5, 8 and 19 are there to record the promised miracle as well.

Library board president D. William Aitchbone smiles as the Reverend Raymond R. Biscobee takes his oath. The Reverend rests his right hand squarely on the tattered King James Bible his father carried in the pocket of his overalls all the years he mined coal in West Virginia.

The first item on the agenda is the contract for lawncare services at the various branches. Announcing that he is all for neatly trimmed grass and healthy shrubs, the Reverend Raymond R. Biscobee votes in the affirmative. The second item on the agenda is a new three-year contract for library director Venus Willendorf. Before casting the only dissenting vote, the Reverend Raymond R. Biscobee calls her Satan's sister. Members off EDIT applaud him en masse. Item three is the long-awaited report of the Internet Committee. En mass EDIT applauds the coming debate. En masse the reporters ready their pens. En masse the cameramen from 3, 5, 8 and 19 take aim. Katherine Hardihood, sitting in the last chair in the last row, inserts a peppermint in her mouth and stares serenely at D. William Aitchbone, who is already staring at her like a rabid raccoon.

After making it clear that his presentation of the report should not be construed as an endorsement, D. William Aitchbone reads: "'After a year of study, it is the recommendation of the Internet Committee that any patron observed using the library's computer terminals to receive and/or send pornographic texts or images will be asked not to do so, and that if said patron persists, he or she will be asked to leave the library, and if said patron does not leave, he or she will be escorted to the door, and that repeated offenses will result in temporary or permanent revocation of the said patron's library privileges.' Comments anyone?"

The Reverend Raymond R. Biscobee rises slowly, Bible in his hands. "Brothers and sisters," he begins, bouncing on the balls of his feet, Sunday sermon style, "this recommendation is unquestionably the most shameful collection of words ever assembled into a paragraph! It is not a policy! It is a capitulation! For a full year the God-fearing citizens of Wyssock County have waited patiently for this board to mend its sinful ways! To drive the cyber-leviathan's electronic tentacles back into the filthy depths from which they came! Taking with them all the library's copies of *Lake Toads and Land Frogs* and all the other un-American, anti-family trash weighing down the shelves. Instead this policy empowers the branch librarians—atheists and idolaters and liberals all—to stand over the shoulders of our little lambs and show them where the good stuff is!"

With cheers and applause, the members of EDIT vociferously agree.

"Any more comments?" asks D. William Aitchbone.

The next comment comes from Satan's sister herself, Venus Willendorf. As she rises and exposes her ostrich-egg breasts and high hips members of EDIT hiss and hold over their heads downloaded photographs of naked children. No one hisses louder or waves his downloaded photographs more enthusiastically than Darren Frost.

Venus Willendorf begins: "I think I speak for all of the branch librarians when I say that we do not mind asking patrons to stop what they're doing—we've been throwing out unruly patrons since day one—but it does concern us what we're supposed to consider pornographic."

Members of EDIT boo. Some make airplanes of their dirty pictures and try to deflate her dangerous body.

"For example," Venus Willendorf continues, "do we nail someone for looking at ancient pictures from India or China or Greece or Rome showing people in sexual congress? What if we see a boy spending a little too much time looking at a picture of Michelangelo's David? Or that photo of Marilyn Monroe with her dress blown up over her head? What if we catch someone E-mailing their gynecologist? Or reading Chapter 19 of Genesis, verses 30 through 38?"

The Reverend Raymond R. Biscobee rises to defend the book he now presses against his heart. "Lot was drunk when he slept with his daughters. They seduced him on behalf of God."

Members of EDIT shout *Amen!*

Venus Willendorf now turns toward the newest board member, the power of her breasts and hips nearly causing him to tumble backwards over his folding chair. "That's the rub, isn't it, Reverend Biscobee? Librarians are not gods. It's hard for us to judge whether a patron's intentions are prurient or pure."

"Hogwash," bellows the Reverend Raymond R. Biscobee. "You can see it in their eyes. How they're breathing. Whether they're, uh, uh, uh—"

"Aroused?" asks Venus Willendorf. "Instead of checking out books my librarians should spend their day checking crotches?"

"If necessary," says the Reverend Raymond R. Biscobee. his voice suddenly squeaky.

EDIT is embarrassed for him.

Venus Willendorf now pulls her folded arms up under her breasts, making them even more bountiful. "That might work for our male patrons. But what of our female patrons?"

The reverend's voice is squeakier still. "I don't think females are a problem."

"Females don't get aroused, reverend?"

The creator of heaven and earth abandons the Reverend Raymond R. Biscobee's larynx completely. "Not in public they don't."

"Really?" asks Venus Willendorf. "How do you know that I and half of the women in this room are not aroused right now?"

Even some members of EDIT giggle.

Reporters write. Cameras roll. The Reverend Raymond R. Biscobee summons his last whit of masculinity. "This debate is not about who is aroused or who isn't, Ms Willendorf. This debate is about our children. I move we adopt the recommended policy."

En masse EDIT applauds in relief. D. William Aitchbone quickly seconds the motion and calls for a vote. The recommendation is unanimously accepted. Member of EDIT applaud and cheer and turn their dirty pictures into confetti. The library board moves on to items four, having the well water at the Hardyville branch tested for coliform bacteria.

Katherine Hardihood can't believe what's just happened here. She wonders how long it will be before EDIT realizes en masse that Satan's sister has just reached between their leader's quivering Christian legs and tore away his brains? Realizes she tricked him into demanding passage of the very policy he rose to oppose?

Katherine Hardihood now looks over at Darren Frost and knows from the way he is tearing at his kneecaps that he already realizes these things. She looks up at D. William Aitchbone and knows from his raccoon stare that he, too, realizes these things; that he likely realized them a full year ago when he first proposed putting the Reverend Raymond R. Biscobee on the library board. Katherine understands as she has always understood, though never with such clarity, that D. William Aitchbone is the real serpent in this room; that Tuttwyler, Ohio, is his tree; that the egos and the conceits and the boundless biological urges of its hapless denizens are his shiny apples.

Katherine Hardihood drives home to Oak Street, scrubs down the curio cabinet and crawls into bed. On Cleveland's only big band radio station Dean Martin is singing a song she first heard when she went to live with her aunt and uncle and her world stopped being a safe and beautiful place: *"When the moon hits your eye like a big pizza pie, that's amore . . . ."*

In the morning she walks to the library and Scotchtapes a copy of the new Internet policy on wall. She does not like the new policy. She did not become a librarian to keep facts from people, but to help them find facts, even if they were dirty and worthless facts. She did not become a librarian to judge, but to help people judge for themselves, even if their judgments were irrational and dangerous. She is not, however, the atheist nor the idolater nor the liberal the Reverend Raymond R. Biscobee thinks she is. In fact she is angered by pornography, sickened by pornography, frightened by pornography. Her uncle kept a box of pornography in his garage. Yet she knows to the roots of her librarian's soul that the great global flow of facts must not be dammed or diverted by that which angers or sickens or frightens. And that is why she is willing to Scotchtape this new policy to the wall, and if necessary enforce it, to compromise a little, in order to keep the facts flowing.

She goes about her day's work, helping people find the facts they want and need. Howie Dornick calls during lunch. The Bittinger boy wants to see them.

At six she drives to South Mill and picks up her man. Before heading south they circle through the drive-thru at McDonald's and buy a quick sack of fish sandwiches and fries. They both get a small coffee. The road to Wooster seems clear enough, but Katherine drives slowly, knowing as all Ohioans know, that in February icy spots are as abundant and as sudden as land mines in the demilitarized zone separating North and South Korea.

"You're taking the new Internet policy well," Howie says, tartar sauce oozing from the corner of his mouth. "I figured you'd scream about Bill Aitchbone all the way to Wooster."

"Sometimes you have to compromise."

Howie laughs through his mouthful of fish. "Right."

Katherine hands him a napkin. "Compromise is a noble result, Howard."

"Even if it's engineered by Bill Aitchbone?"

"Don't mistake my serenity for surrender. I know why Bill Aitchbone put Ray Biscobee on the library board."

"Because Bill Aitchbone's a bastard?"

"Because he's a brilliant bastard, Howard. This month a compromise on Internet policy. Next month a compromise on *Lake Toads and Land Frogs*. Month after that *Catcher In the Rye* and Judy Blume and Donald Duck. Compromises that will get unanimous votes no matter how far Venus Willendorf sticks out her tits or how many times Ray Biscobee thumps his Bible. Little compromises that will let the air out of EDIT's tires and drive the branch librarians nuts. Little compromises the public will think reasonable. Little compromises that will get Bill Aitchbone elected mayor, that will punish me for the color you painted your house."

Howie Dornick, appetite gone, sinks into his scarf. "I've ruined your life."

Katherine Hardihood pounds his leg, sending a spurt of near-boiling coffee into his lap. "Don't ever say that, Howard. You've un-ruined my life."

They show each other their watery eyes.

"And you've un-ruined mine," Howie says.

Katherine's serenity metamorphoses into wickedness. "And together with the Bittinger boy and the facts in that box of bones, you and I are going to ruin Bill Aitchbone's life."

Howie Dornick's appetite is back. Fish and fries fill his mouth. "If anybody deserves to have his life ruined it's Bill Aitchbone. I just wish we didn't have to be the ones to do it."

"I'm glad we're the ones."

"Maybe with all this money I'm getting from Hugh, we should just move to Florida and spend the next thirty years collecting shells and eating oranges, and maybe—"

It is the first time her man has ever spoken of a future together. Before he can complete the *and maybe,* she angrily pushes his sandwich into his mouth. "We are not running away from this, Howard."

"All I'm saying is that we have options."

"No we don't. No options at all."

With no major snowstorm imminent, Bittinger's Hardware is empty. They find the Bittinger boy hunkered over the counter. There's a stack of unruly blueprints in front of him. "Hey!" he calls out when the bell on the door dingles. "Serendipity man!"

"Bone Head!" Howie Dornick answers as he and his woman make their way up the garden tool aisle. "Blueprints? You expanding?"

"Diversifying," says the Bittinger boy. "Two national home improvements chains are going in north of town. Opening just in time to steal half of our spring business. In the hardware game spring is like Christmas. Hence, diversification."

"To what?" asks Katherine Hardihood.

"Anything but hardware," the Bittinger boy says. He shows them the plans. "We're going to divide the building into three separate stores. Put walls in here and here. The hardware business will be here on the left—luckily there are still a few old-timers left who wouldn't be caught dead in one of those chain stores—and this space in the middle is going to be a gift shop."

"The world sure needs another one of those," Howie Dornick says.

"Not just any gift shop," the Bittinger boy says. "A year-round Christmas shop with all handmade imported ornaments. Imported chocolates, too."

Katherine Hardihood lowers her librarian's finger to the blueprint. "And this shop on the end?"

"Espresso bar," says the Bittinger boy. "Muffins. Bagels. The markup on that stuff is incredible. I figure we can draw students and professors from the college." He pulls another blueprint from the bottom of the stack. "I took dad's life insurance and bought the old A&P store next door. Been empty for about ten years. If I can swing a loan from the bank—which is unlikely given that *two* home improvement chains are opening—I'm going to open a gourmet grocery. All organically grown fruits and vegetables. Range-fed beef. Imported beers. Herbal medicines. A grocery is a big risk, though. One of the Bittinger family rules is never stock perishables. Nails and screws have one helluva lot longer shelf life than tangerines imported from Spain. But we'll see what the bank says."

"Well, good luck on the diversification," Howie Dornick says. "Now, what about our bones?"

The Bittinger boy puts his blueprints away and lifts the box of bones to the countertop. "This is going to knock your socks off," he says. In a few minutes of silent work he has the two skeletons laid out, every bone in its proper place. He begins his analysis, exuding the confidence of a real forensic anthropologist, of a real hardware man: "First, it's a shame I couldn't have examined the skeletons *in situ*—at the grave site. The environment around a skeleton often tells you as much as the bones themselves. But not to worry, the bones tell us plenty. First, we can say with certainty that the larger skeleton is that of an adult woman. See the skull here? And the jaw? Adult female bones remain smooth after puberty. Males skulls are much rougher where the muscles insert. And look at the chin. A pointed chin like this usually implies a female, too But that's not all. See the pubis bone down here? Male pubis bones are triangular. Female pubis bones are more rectangular, like this one, to accommodate a larger pelvic inlet—see here—for childbearing. And see this scarring on the pubis? Evidence she gave birth. As to her age, I'd guess late teens, early twenties. No signs of wear or disease. Healthy teeth, too. All in all, what we've got here is a young adult woman, five foot-two, hundred and ten pounds, gave birth to at least one child."

Katherine Hardihood loves all these facts. She is also anxious. "But is it our Pogawedka?"

The Bittinger boy ignores her: "Now the little skeleton. Given the development of the skull—see how these frontal bones are still separated and how these teeth haven't erupted yet—it's safe to say we've got an infant here. Not a newborn, mind you, but a child of, say, twenty-eight, thirty months."

"Boy?" asks Katherine Hardihood.

"No way to tell. Simply too young for gender identification. Or racial identification."

"Coulda been a girl then," says Howie Dornick.

"And half white," says Katherine Hardihood.

The Bittinger boy ignores them. "So what we have is a young adult woman and an infant who both died of severe head trauma."

"A clubbing?" asks Katherine Hardihood.

The Bittinger boy runs his fingers over the skulls. "Certainly something big and blunt and swung with great force. Not just once but several times. Look at all these fractures. Lots of missing pieces. These weren't pretty murders." He now runs his finger along the adult female's arm bones. "And look at these fractures. She fought like hell. For a long time. Not pretty murders at all."

The Bittinger boy starts putting the bones back in the box. "Now you told me, Mr. Dornick, that you found these skeletons buried on top of another grave."

Katherine Hardihood answers for her man. "On top of Seth Aitchbone's grave. Seth was the son of Jobiah and

Almira Aitchbone. He died in 1807 at age 22. Apparently unmarried."

"And how far down did you find them?" asks the Bittinger boy.

"About four feet," Howie Dornick answers for himself.

"And was there any sign of a coffin? Old nails? Fragments of rotted wood? Discolored soil?"

"Don't know about discolored soil," Howie Dornick answers, "but there weren't any nails or old wood or anything."

The Bittinger boy plays with his inherited hardware man's chin. "Just the fact that these skeletons were buried two feet above ol' Seth implies they were buried after he was. Still, there's also evidence they died first."

Katherine Hardihood is flabbergasted by this fact. "First?"

"Maybe a year or more," says the Bittinger boy. "Before these two were buried they laid out in the open for quite a while. He pokes at the dirt clinging to the inside of the woman's skull. "See that? Petrified beetle pupa. Insects don't burrow more than an inch or two below ground. These bodies decomposed above ground. There are signs of insect infestation everywhere. And tooth marks where rodents gnawed. And look here, half of the infant's left foot is missing. More than likely carried away by a fox or some-thing." He holds up the woman's femur to the light. "Most interesting of all is this. See that? On the dirt there? That's the impression of cloth. Rough Cloth. Burlap I'd say. These bones not only laid out in the open for a long time. They also laid in a sack for a long time. Meaning—"

Katherine Hardihood understands the meaning: "Meaning that Seth Aitchbone found and kept the bones of the woman and child he loved, and when he died, some member of his family, somebody who knew how much he loved them, buried them with him."

This unprofessional conclusion makes the Bittinger boy squirm. "Well, I can't say it means all that, of course. But it does mean they were gathered up sometime after their deaths and kept in a sack and then buried on top of ol' Seth."

Katherine Hardihood is not finished drawing conclusions: "So the Tuttwyler brothers clubbed Pogawedka and Kapusta, or whatever their real names were, and Seth Aitchbone after a long agonizing search finds their bones and keeps them hidden away in a sack, under his bed maybe, or up in the rafters. And when he dies of a broken heart, his mother, or maybe one of his five brothers—though it's hard to imagine any Aitchbone man having that kind of compassion—secretly buries the bones in his grave, in the middle of the night, so no one else knows. And there Seth and Pogawedka and little Kapusta lie together in eternal peace, until Bill Aitchbone sells the family farm to developers."

"And sends me like some lackey ghoul to re-plant them," says Howie Dornick.

"I wish you hadn't re-planted ol' Seth," says the Bittinger boy. After the surprise on Katherine Hardihood's face fades he explains. "If this scenario of yours is true, then it might also be important how he died—other than from a broken heart."

Katherine Hardihood splays her librarian's fingers across her bony librarian's chest. "You mean the Tuttwyler brothers might have murdered Seth, too?"

"Didn't say that," says the Bittinger boy. "Maybe he murdered himself."

"Of course! Suicide!" says Katherine Hardihood. "That would prove everything, wouldn't it."

"Like what?" asks Howie Dornick.

"That he loved this woman and her child," his woman says. "That he couldn't bear living next to the evil brothers who killed them, who weren't brought to justice just because their victims were Indians. Jiminy Cricket, Howard, we've got to dig Seth back up and prove he killed himself."

"Oh no!" says Howie Dornick.

"Oh yes!" says Katherine Hardihood.

"Sorry, Mr. Dornick, but I think we should, too," says the Bittinger boy. "We're already breaking a zillion state laws. We might as well go whole hog for the truth."

"Of course whole hog," repeats Katherine Hardihood.

The Bittinger boy holds up Pogawedka's skull. "If it's the truth you're after—the real truth and not just all those conclusions you're jumping to—then hold onto your underwear. See these recessive cheekbones? And the length of this face? And the nasal passage? And this overbite here? This is not the skull of an Indian woman. This is the skull of a white woman. With 93% certainty at least."

Katherine reaches out for something to hang onto other than her underwear, finding only a revolving rack of flower seeds, which spins to the floor, packets of zinnias and marigolds flying. "White woman? The Tuttwyler brothers killed a white woman?"

The Bittinger boy is nodding proudly. "With 93% certainty they did. So, when do we exhume ol' Seth, folks?"

Howie Dornick drops Katherine Hardihood off at her two-bedroom ranch on Oak Street, then drives home to his two-story frame on South Mill. There is no moon. No stars. No passing cars. No lights in his neighbors' windows. Only February clouds and the dirty glow of the streetlight.

As he grinds up the driveway he sees someone on the porch. He hopes it is Hugh Harbinger. He fears it is Bill Aitchbone. It turns out to be Charles Pasquinade, American correspondent for the French arts magazine, *Fiel.* "It gets cold in Ohio, does it not?" says Charles Pasquinade.

Pasquinade, of course, wants an interview. All of Paris has lost its senses over Serendipity Green®. Even the nuns are wearing it, he says. Howie Dornick leads him to the kitchen table and pours him a glass of grapefruit juice.

"So tell me," Pasquinade begins, tiny tape recorder pointed at Howie's tired face, "did you paint your house this color out of your love for mankind or your hate for it? Or merely out of your ambivalence?"

After Pasquinade leaves Howie takes his checkbook out of the refrigerator freezer, where it is hidden behind a huge bag of frozen waffles, and writes the Bittinger boy a check for $100,000. He puts it in an envelope with a note:

Dear Bone Head,
    You're as much to blame for Serendipity Green® as me. Good luck with the gourmet grocery.

Howie

"You know I believe in the truth more than anything," Katherine Hardihood says. She has just settled into the huge chair and the leather is still cold.

Dr. Pirooz Aram is chasing the last drop of espresso in his demitasse with his little finger. "That is what I like about you more than anything else, Katherine."

"I'm a fraud, " she confesses.

There is a sweetness in the doctor's eyes as he walks toward her on his knees. "Boool-shit! I suppose you also want me to believe that the world is not round? By the way, did you know that the great Persian physicist Abu ar-Rayham al-Biruni calculated the diameter of the earth a thousand years before John Glenn learned to ride his bicycle?"

She lets him take her hands. She tells him about her skullduggery with Howie Dornick and the Bittinger boy; how they found not the bones of an Indian woman and an Indian baby, but the bones of a white woman and a white baby; how this unexpected discovery has upset her apple-cart but good.

"A little applecart upsetting is good for the soul," says Dr. Aram.

"But the truth I was sure I'd find was not the truth I found," she says. "And now if I tell that truth, Squaw Days will be kaput. Everybody in Tuttwyler will hate me."

"What is so wrong about being hated for telling the truth? It will put you in some very exclusive company."

As Katherine laughs, Dr. Aram pulls her from the chair, and humming "Yankee Doodle," he dances her around the office. "Dammit, Katherine! Listen to me! If you found a truth other than the one you were looking for, then the one you were looking for was not the truth at all. Was it? And if you had told anyone that un-true truth, it would have been a lie! Are you following this? I find that sometimes American minds cannot keep up with a first-class Persian mind."

"I'm keeping up."

"Good! Now keep up some more! If you had told this lie that you thought was the truth, people might have been happy for a while. But sooner or later they would realize your lie *was* a lie. And they would be very angry. And they would hate you anyway! So, Katherine! Tell them the true truth you have found, and then to hell with them."

"I guess you're right."

"All these years I have been taking your money and you *guess* I'm right? Katherine! Know it! Know it! Now tell me, are you and this Howie Dornick still having fun in bed? Yes?"

20

D. William Aitchbone drives north as fast as he can, to catch the last flight of the night to Washington. Victoria Bonobo is next to him, her seductive face sideways on the headrest, her fingers playing with the epaulet of his Burberry. He does not know whether he will copulate with her tonight or not. If he does, the VP will come to Squaw Days and make it a big success, and ensure his election as mayor, an office from which he can launch a successful campaign for Congress. If he doesn't, Squaw Days will be stuck with the secretary of some worthless department. And that won't be the end of it. Vicki will vote against every bill he wants the village council to pass, making him look weak and out of touch with voters. Copulating with the wife of Bud Weideman didn't ruin Donald Grinspoon's marriage. He sold enough Weideman boots to buy a condo in Florida! And Karen already thinks he's copulating with Victoria Bonobo, anyway! So he might as well! But can he? He loves Karen to bits.

They reach the gate just as the flight begins to board. Victoria hugs him with relief and they penguin-walk with their luggage to their seats in coach. An hour and twenty minutes later they are back on the ground, in a cab listening to the driver's tape of Yobisch Podka's lively *Insipientia.* "I love this piece," Aitchbone says, certain the driver is a Middle Eastern terrorist waiting for orders to blow the tip off the Washington Monument.

"When I was a boy I studied composition with Yobisch in Leningrad," the driver says. "We still send each other birthday cards."

"You're a musician?" D. William Aitchbone asks, certain that this tale about studying with the great Yobisch Podka is just a cover for his bomb making.

"I am a very good musician," the driver says. "I have a tryout with the Cleveland Orchestra next month."

The skeptical lawyer from just south of Cleveland hopes to trip him up. "What instrument?" he quickly asks him.

The driver answers effortlessly: "Violin. In Cairo I was first chair. In Cleveland I will be honored to sit in the last chair. It is the finest orchestra in the world."

D. William Aitchbone is suddenly proud. "We're from Cleveland."

The driver smiles into his mirror. "How about those Indians?"

D. William Aitchbone gives him two thumbs up. "This year the whole enchilada."

"You are a nice couple," the driver says. "Most of my fares think I am a terrorist."

"No kidding?" says D. William Aitchbone.

And so the cab reaches the Hyatt and D. William Aitchbone tips the driver a five, which he is sure will go into a fund to buy *plastique* explosives. "Violin my American ass," he says to Victoria Bonobo as the cab drives off.

They check in and tell the disappointed terrorist bellhop they'll carry their own bags. Inside the glass elevator D. William Aitchbone presses 18. He lets Victoria Bonobo play with his Adam's apple, even when the elevator stops at 12 for a terrorist carrying a stack of room service trays.

Bing! Ka-boomp. Eighteenth floor. Victoria's room is first and D. William Aitchbone lets her kiss him on the lips, with all the suction she can muster. But he does not let her drag him inside. "I want you as bad as you want me," he says, panting real pants. "But we've got breakfast with the VP at seven-thirty, and if we make love all night—and Sweet Jesus, it would be all night—we wouldn't be worth a damn. We'd end up with the Interior secretary again. Or worse."

Victoria Bonobo is not disappointed. She is aroused even more by his manly insistence on business first. And so early in the morning another cab-driving terrorist whisks them to the White House for a breakfast of huevos rancheros and refried beans. The VP wears a Serendipity Green® tie in honor of their little village, and after his eyes drink in the sister of his old college roommate, he promises to attend Squaw Days no matter what. "I don't care if the prime minister of England gets blown up in his Bentley," he says, "I'll be there for you. I'm really anxious to meet that Howie Dornick fellow."

Yet another terrorist whisks them back to the Hyatt and they ride the glass elevator pawing and rubbing each other from floor to floor. They have two hours and twenty minutes until check out. *Bing! Ka-boomp.* Into D. William Aitchbone's room they rush. The PLEASE DO NOT DISTURB sign goes on the door. Into the bathroom goes Victoria Bonobo to undress and insert her diaphram. She steps out and finds the manly man she has been waiting a year for, still in his blue suit, standing in a pool of eggs and chili sauce and refried beans. "Sorry," he says, his voice rippling like the belly of bullfrog. "I'm really sorry." He starts to gag, but he doesn't vomit, inasmuch as this time his finger isn't down his throat. "At least the VP is coming this time for sure," he says.

So now D. William Aitchbone knows he cannot be unfaithful to Karen Aitchbone. And from the frost in Victoria Bonobo's eyes, he knows she knows it, too. And the flight home is a miserable one. He drops her off at the end of her driveway and drives as fast as he can to his soapy white Queen Anne. He will wrap his arms around Karen and tell her over and over that he never slept with Victoria Bonobo, that he never could, nor would, nor will he ever, even if it means he will never be anything more impressive than president of the Tuttwyler village council.

He drives past Howie Dornick's Serendipity Green® house as fast as he can, pretending he doesn't see the television crew or the little crowd of daytrippers. He hurries into his own house ready for his hug. He finds a letter on his perfectly puffed pillow:

Bill,

Hope you and Vicki enjoyed Washington. I've taken Amy and Cannon to the farm. Not for a visit, Bill—for good!!!!

p.s. Penny Grinspoon died last night. Try to be civil at the funeral.

Of course D. William Aitchbone will be civil at Penny Grinspoon's funeral. It will be the political event of the year. The governor will be there. Half a dozen state legislators will be there. Buddy Bowfin, the 22nd District's fourteen-term congressman will be there. Every businessman who needs a friendly vote from the Tuttwyler Village Council, or the Wyssock County Commissioners, or the Ohio General Assembly, or the U.S. Congress will be there. Hundreds of run-of-the-mill voters will be there. Of course D. William Aitchbone will be civil at Penny Grinspoon's funeral.

On the morning of the funeral God purifies Tuttwyler with below-zero temperatures and a torrent of snow. But the cold and snow stop no one from venturing forth to pay their respects. The red-brick Methodist church on the east side of the square hasn't been this full since Artie Brown's funeral eleven years earlier.

Though surrounded by his children and grandchildren, Donald Grinspoon sits painfully alone in the front pew, snow dripping off his old pair of Weideman boots. Surrounded by Karen and Amy and Cannon, D. William Aitchbone also sits painfully alone, nodding politically at every set of eyes that find him.

There are several eulogies. Donald and Penny's eldest daughter, Donna, who looks so much like her mother, remembers the warm peach pies and vanilla ice cream, and how her mother lead them all in singing "Jingle Bells" at 6:30 every Christmas morning. Younger daughter Jeanie, with her father's eyes and smile, remembers the potato salad and the marshmallow fights and how her mother decorated the living room at their Key Largo condo exactly like their living room on South Mill, so her family and her many friends would always feel at home. The governor remembers the selfless days and nights dear Penny put in manning the Republican Party booth at the Wyssock County Fair, making sure everybody who walked by got a campaign button for their lapel, a bumper sticker for their car, and a warm Republican smile for their hearts. Finally, D. William Aitchbone speaks of Penny's unflagging loyalty to her husband, and of Donald's unflagging love for her. "Penny Grinspoon was simply the best," he says. "We will all miss her so."

The church empties. The procession to the village cemetery begins. Penelope nee Tuttwyler Grinspoon gets a good-bye swing around the square and a final look at her soapy white Victorian on South Mill. "I have never been unfaithful to you," D. William Aitchbone whispers to Karen Aitchbone as they crawl along in their American-made Japanese luxury sedan, just five car behind the hearse, just one car behind the governor's limousine. "I love you like Donald loved Penny."

"Really?" Karen Aitchbone whispers back, glancing into the back seat to make sure Amy and Cannon are occupied by their books from the library. "Does that mean you're going to buy me a condo in Key Largo?"

Her loyal husband is stunned. "You know about the Weideman Boots thing?"

"The whole town knows about the Weideman Boots thing. Penny made sure everyone knew."

"Penny knew?"

"Wives always know."

"I swear, Karen, Vicki Bonobo and I have never—"

"Save it for your lawyer, Bill," Karen Aitchbone says, in anything but a whisper. "And make sure it's a good lawyer, Bill. Because I'm going to get a great lawyer."

D. William Aitchbone isn't whispering now either. "I swear, Karen, you've got more brass than a marching band!"

At the cemetery the great herd of frozen, glove-banging mourners crowds around the grave Howie Dornick has dug. The village backhoe sits just twenty yard away, frozen Ohio clay stuck to its hydraulic claw like cake frosting stuck to a mixing bowl beater. Penelope is handed over to God with as much Christian joy as a day in February allows. The minister invites everyone to the Grinspoon house for lunch. The glove-bangers retreat to their cars. Thirty minutes after the hearse pulled in, the hearse pulls out, leaving only three living humans in the cemetery.

Two of those still-living humans are Donald Grinspoon and D. William Aitchbone. They stand by the flower-covered grave for a long while, saying nothing. Then they meander through the rows of headstones toward the Civil War memorial. The granite soldier leaning on his rifle atop the memorial watches them approach.

"I appreciate what you said about Penny at the service," Donald Grinspoon says. "She thought you were the best, too."

"Thank you, Donald."

"She was so proud when you passed the bar."

"I still have the card she sent me. She put ten dollar inside, like it was my birthday or something."

"That's Penny for you."

"I bought a couple of neckties with it."

Donald Grinspoon smiles nostalgically. "At my store?"

"Of course at your store."

The mentor gently brushes the snow off the shoulders of the protégé's Burberry. "I'm sorry about Karen leaving with the kids. Really sorry." The sudden growl of the backhoe's engine fills Donald Grinspoon's eyes with tears. "The whole thing makes me feel like crap, Bill. I told you to go ahead and diddle Vicki, after all."

"That's just it, Donald. I didn't diddle her. I went to Washington thinking I might. But I couldn't go through with it. You'd think Karen would know I couldn't, wouldn't you?" He tells him how be stuck his finger down his throat and threw up the huevos rancheros.

They are at the base of the Civil War monument now. They brush the show off the granite bench and sit. They watch the backhoe fill Penny's grave. "Karen's a good woman. She'll forgive you," Donald Grinspoon says.

D. William Aitchbone is tempted to ask if he knew that Penny knew about the Weideman Boots thing. But he lets sleeping dogs lie. "It's going to be a real tightrope, Donald. At the same time I'm convincing Karen that I didn't sleep with Vicki, I've got to keep Vicki believing that someday I will."

"That is a real tightrope," the mentor agrees.

"And I've got to stay balanced on that goddamn tightrope until the VP comes to Squaw Days. After that Vicki Bonobo can go diddle herself."

The other still living human at the cemetery is, of course, the operator of the backhoe, one Howie Dornick. Hoping to outlast the other two, he takes his time covering the grave. It is not an easy task. Graves are small holes. The claw at the end of the backhoe's scorpion tail holds a lot of dirt. But with the help of the cold and the snow, he does outlast the others, and now that he is alone and the last scoop of dirt deposited, he digs Katherine Hardihood's cellular phone from the bib pocket of his overalls and calls her. "Coast is clear," he says.

By the time Katherine and the Bittinger boy arrive at the cemetery, Howie Dornick has already positioned the backhoe's claw over the grave of one Seth Aitchbone, great-great-great-great-great uncle of one D. William Aitchbone.

They have wisely decided to exhume ol' Seth during the light of day. The growl of the backhoe after dark might raise suspicion. It might bring the law. It might bring the entire conspiracy crashing down on their heads with the force of the Tuttwyler brothers' clubs. So they will open ol' Seth's grave in the light of this gray, snow-flying day.

Howie Dornick has dug scores of graves. He knows just when to stop the big claw before it rips the lid off ol' Seth's new box. He eases the backhoe out of the way then slides into the hole with a shovel. It has only been a few months since this new eternal resting place was dug and the dirt and clay easily scoops off. Katherine Hardihood watches for cars or people walking their dogs. "The coast is clear," she says.

The lid goes up. The Bittinger boy eases into the hole. He goes straight for ol' Seth's skull. "Yessss!" he says, as if the famous Donald Johanson had just called him with a job offer. "Entry hole right through the roof of the mouth. Point-blank. Consistent with a self-inflicted wound." He pulls a camera from his parka and shoots all 36 exposures. He pulls out a tiny ruler and takes a number of measurements. He examines the rest of the skeleton, finding nothing suspicious.

Katherine Hardihood now goes to her car and returns with the box containing Seth Aitchbone's family. The Bittinger Boy shakes their bones right on top of ol' Seth's bones, mingling mother, father and child for all eternity, or at least until the next exhumation. That job completed, Howie Dornick works quickly with the backhoe.

Hugh Harbinger meets Buzzy at the Peacock and with mugs of the day's house blend in hand, they sit in the front window and watch the West Villagers dig their cars out of the tofu-hard snow that fell all night. "I hear Koko's back from Morocco," says Buzzy. "And she's brought some beautiful brown camel boy with her. Humpty humpty."

"I thought she was never stepping foot in New York again."

"You said the same thing."

"And I meant it."

New York irony never gets any better than this and they giggle at their own brilliance. "So," says Hugh Harbinger, "any dish on what Koko's got up her sleeve?"

Buzzy's voice melts like mozzarella. "Wwwwhite!"

"White?"

"Fabulous, isn't it? The world's biggest slut suddenly in love with white. I hear she's designed seventy-seven shades, everyone of them named after some virtuous woman in the Bible, the Koran or the Bhagavad Gita. I hear she and her camel boy got off the Concorde simply dripping in white. Robes and hats and scarves. All sorts of baubles. Even their shoes. White white white. The couture houses are already beating a path, I hear."

Hugh Harbinger throws his mug of house blend through the window. Although the shower of glass is loud and spectacular, no one inside nor outside the Peacock is startled. Artists and writers have been throwing mugs through the window of the Peacock for decades. "Good gravy, Hugh, chill!" says Buzzy, making sure no glass has sprinkled into his coffee, "You've had a fabulous ride with Serendipity Green®. Now it's time for Koko and her camel boy to ride fabulously for a season or two. Humpty humpty hump. No biggie, is it?"

Hugh Harbinger yanks his Serendipity Green® watch cap over his ears and disappears up Greenwich Avenue.

One waitress goes for a broom and dust pan. Another goes for the big piece of plywood in the storeroom.

21

Ernest Not Irish fastens his ponytail with a turquoise clip. He puts on the denim shirt and khaki Dockers he purchased that afternoon from the JC Penny Company. Over his head he slips his favorite bolo tie, the one with the silver wolf's head. He puts on his only sports coat. He removes the FREE CHIEF WAHOO button from one lapel, the I'M A REAL CLEVELAND INDIAN from the other. He sprints through the March rain to his Pontiac and drives south. He is on his way to be reasonable with his white brothers in Tuttwyler, Ohio, as the wise Dr. Pirooz Aram has suggested.

Ernest knows it will not be easy being reasonable. For five hundred years his ancestors have tried to be reasonable. The Arawaks tried to be reasonable with Christopher Columbus, not knowing he was under orders from the king and queen of Spain to steal their gold, riddle their bodies with European diseases, fill the wombs of their women with European sperm, and collect their souls for the European god. The Wampanoags tried to be reasonable with the Pilgrims, not knowing they were spies for a huge island of tree-chopping lunatics called the English. His own Cherokee ancestors tried to be reasonable, too. They reasonably signed a treaty with George Washington, ceding most of their lands in exchange for eternal peace. They reasonably accepted the advice of Thomas Jefferson and built good roads and sturdy cabins, cleared their forests in order to grow corn and apples and graze sheep and cattle. They reasonably built gristmills and sawmills and blacksmith shops, schools and a library with one thousand books. They reasonably created a written language, started a newspaper, adopted a constitution with an elected chief and a legislature with a house and a senate. Yes, they reasonably accepted the life their white brothers said they should. But the Cherokee land was good land, and there was so much of it, and there were rumors of gold. And so despite their reasonableness, the Cherokee were rounded up, and like a herd of cows, driven through the blinding snow to a land in the west the Choctaws called Oklahoma—"Land of red people"—where those who survived this trail of tears were promptly starved and swindled anew. Yes, so many Indian brothers had tried to be reasonable with so many white brothers, only to discover again and again that these brothers of theirs were all a bunch of gold-gouging, tree-chopping, sperm-shooting lunatics with empty souls. And now he, Ernest Not Irish, like so many before him—like Wahunsonacook of the Powhatans, like Samoset of the Pemaquid, like Tecumseh of the Shawnee, like Little Crow of the Santee, like Crazy Horse of the Oglala, like Cochise of the Apache, Manuelito of the Navaho, Tooyalaket of the Nez Percé, Wovoka of the Paiutes, Big Foot of the Hunkpapas—is on his way to Tuttwyler, Ohio, to be reason-able with a white brother named D. William Aitchbone.

By the time Earnest Not Irish reaches I-491 the rain has turned to sleet and the pavement is deadly with an invisible coating of ice. All around him cars and trucks are spinning into the median strip. But his old Pontiac—named after an Ottawa chief who once tried to be reasonable—stays on the road and soon he is cruising up West Wooseman, two cars behind a dump truck spitting out salt—salt mined from the same tunnels under Lake Erie, where his father worked before taking a stay bullet in the head.

West Wooseman takes him to the village square. He finds the village hall and parks. Someone has thoughtfully spread blue de-icing pellets on the sidewalk. Inside he sits three chairs away from an unappetizing woman with the features of a librarian. There are only a handful of others in the audience: a small pale man with a reporter's notebook in his lap; a sad old man holding a Styrofoam cup of coffee.

As he waits for the council to arrive, Ernest Not Irish reads again his most recent letter from someone in Tuttwyler:

Dear Mr. Not Irish,

Don't waste your time writing letters to Mayor Sadlebyrne about Squaw Days. The real chief cook and bottle washer in Tuttwyler is D. William Aitchbone. You'll find him lording over the village council on the first and third Thursdays of the month. Meetings start promptly at 7:30.

Like all of the previous letters he's received from Tuttwyler, it is not signed.

Finally the village council files in and sits at the long table in front. The man in the middle seat, holding a gavel and spraying the audience with a smile, stands and leads everyone in the Pledge of Allegiance. Earnest assumes this man is the chief cook and bottle washer identified in the letter. So he raises his hand and speaks loudly. "May I address the council?"

"Not yet you can't," says D. William Aitchbone.

The president of the CRI sits quietly for two hours and twelve minutes while the council debates and votes on a series of important legislative matters: whether members of the volunteer fire department should have to pay for their own subscriptions to *Ohio Firefighter;* (which passes 3 to 2); a variance allowing Clark Besserman of 651 Tocqueville to put a ten-foot fence between his house and the new Cap'n Scrubby 24-hour car wash, even though the village code says privacy fences can be no more than six feet high (which passes 3 to 2); an ordinance preventing people from having more than one garage sale a month (which passes 4 to 1); whether to give Quotidian Bolt & Screw Company a twenty-year abatement on property taxes if it vacates its crumbling 90-year-old factory in Cleveland and builds a new state-of-the-art plant in Progress Center, the 600-acre industrial park being carved out of Gordon Teaselbaum's cornfields and cow pastures (which passes unanimously.)

"And now, " asks D. William Aitchbone, "does anyone in the audience wish to address council?"

Ernest Not Irish stands and lets everyone get comfortable with his dark skin and ponytail and the silver wolf on his bolo tie. Now he speaks: "I am Ernest Not Irish, president of Cleveland's Real Indians, and —"

"We enjoyed your letters," interrupts D. William Aitchbone.

Ernest Not Irish counters the council president's mad smile with a reasonable one. "I hope they did not sound too confrontational." He talks for twelve minutes about historical accuracy and human dignity. He reminds all of his white brothers and sisters in the room that Princess Pogawedka and Little Kapusta were real people, as were the men who murdered him. "But this story about Pogawedka rising out of the stumps and forgiving those who stole her people's land and stole her baby's life is a bunch of baloney."

"I thought you people believed in spirits and stuff like that?" asks D. William Aitchbone.

You people ! The words make Ernest Not Irish tremble. He wants to scream. He wants to throw his folding chair. He wants to tell this D. William Aitchbone exactly what he told Dr. Pirooz Aram, that if Pogawedka really had risen from the stumps, it would have been with a bow and a quiver of arrows and a granite ax. But he is determined to be reasonable. "Yes, we believe in spirits. And we believe in forgiveness."

"Then what's the problem, chief?" asks D. William Aitchbone.

Chief! This word make the other members of the village council tremble.

"I am not a chief," Ernest Not Irish says.

"Well, I am a chief," says the president of the Tuttwyler village council, "and unless you've got ten thousand braves in warpaint in the parking lot, I don't think we have anything to talk about, do we? This is our town and our history. And whether you like it or not, Princess Pogawedka rose up through those stumps and forgave us. And we're real grateful for that. And we're going to go on showing our gratitude every goddamn summer, whether it ruffles your headdress or not!" D. William Aitchbone brings down his gavel like a fly swatter. "This meeting is adjourned."

As the village council gathers up its papers and flees, Ernest Not Irish feels friendly fingertips on the knuckles of his clenched fist. It is the unappetizing woman who was sitting three chairs away from him. "Don't let him get under your skin," she says, gentle eyes dancing. "He's experiencing a rather uncomfortable slide into oblivion these days."

As she walks away, zipping up her noisy coat, the pale man with the reporter's notebook asks him if Not Irish is one word or two.

"Two," he says.

Ernest Not Irish leaves the village hall and walks across the parking lot where ten thousand braves in warpaint are not waiting for a secret owl-hoot to attack. He drives north, hatred dripping off his steering wheel, a sports call-in show fading in and out on his radio, someone asking the know-it-all host if the rumors about Cleveland Indians' pitcher José Mesa being traded to Seattle are true. Ernest Not Irish wonders if the know-it-all host knows that Seattle is named after a gullible Suquamish chief who tried to be reasonable?

D. William Aitchbone waits in the men's room for twenty-three minutes, until the other members of council have surely gone home. With the big stiff collar of his Burberry pulled up around his face like the blinders milk wagon horses used to wear, he hurries down the hall toward the door. He hears hoarse laughter and peeks over his collar. In the mayor's office, sitting at the mayor's desk, is the current mayor, Woodrow Wilson Sadlebyrne, stroking his throat. Victoria Bonobo is standing behind him, one hand on his shoulder, the other dabbing her wet eyes with a Kleenex. In front of them is an open *Cleveland Plain Dealer.* He ducks back inside his collar and hurries out.

He drives up West Wooseman to Burger King and buys the last *Plain Dealer* in the box by the door. Inside he buys a coffee and he sits alone by the cold front window. He finds the story that made Woody Sadelbyrne hoarse and Victoria Bonobo cry. As he reads he slowly crushes the plastic container of non-dairy creamer in his hand. "Doesn't this just take the cake," he says.

What takes the cake, of course, is the story running across the bottom of page five. It is a story about the Vice President of the United States and his alleged complicity in a scheme to register illegal Mexican aliens to vote. The story takes place in the VP's home state of Texas where a twister—an F-5 with winds topping 285 miles per hour— flattened a little Panhandle town named Tilly. Two weeks after the twister flattened Tilly, an emu farmer in Kingfisher County, Oklahoma—some 180 miles away—spotted his big birds eating envelopes. Fearing they'd choke, he jumped the fence and gathered up more than two hundred envelopes, some half-eaten, some still bundled together with rubber bands. Texas twisters being the ferocious and finicky beasts they are, all of the envelopes were addressed to the same person, a Mrs. Margaret Cumberworth of Tilly, Texas. Most envelopes contained nothing more interesting than old tele- phone and electric bills. But one intrigued the emu farmer to no end. It had been mailed from 1600 Pennsylvania Avenue. To the emu farmer's disappointment, the letter inside was not from the President of the United States, but from the Vice President. Said the letter:

> Congratulations on your retirement, Margaret. Your years of flawless service to Texas and the nation makes us all proud. And thanks again on all you did to make Montezuma's Revenge the big success it was.

The emu farmer did what any good citizen does when finding the private correspondence of a famous person. He went immediately to the nearest newspaper, the *Jeromesville Messenger*, which dutifully printed it on page one. VP'S LETTER BLOWS IN FROM TILLY, the head- line read. It was not long before this particular issue of the

Messenger made its way to the library in Tulsa, where the librarian in charge of periodicals wondered just what Montezuma's Revenge was—other than a bad case of diarrhea from drinking water south of the border—and just what this Margaret Cumberworth did to make it a big success. So the librarian sent the story on to her old college roommate in Austin, who was now the personal assistant to the famous muckraking columnist, Moxie Givens.

And so Moxie Givens investigated and blew the lid off of Montezuma's Revenge, the secret and successful Republican Party plan to register just enough illegal Mexican aliens in rural Texas Counties to counteract the big voter turnout expected in Dallas and Houston by blacks and all those liberal northerners who moved there back in eighties when, as Moxie Givens wrote in her always colorful way, "the buckle on the Sunbelt was still as shiny as fresh jackrabbit poop." It seems that Margaret Cumberland, before retiring that past June, was the director of the Sparks County board of elections. With her help, and the help of more than a dozen other directors of local boards of elections, Republicans carried Texas by 1654 votes, enabling the President and his ever-loyal VP to win re-election by the slimmest of margins.

And now, though he denies any part in it, it appears that the VP is up to his neck in Montezuma's Revenge and Democrats in the House of Representatives are demanding day and night on C-SPAN that a special prosecutor be named.

D. William Aitchbone sips his coffee slowly, calculating how this scandal might affect his own fortunes. His political fortunes. His marital fortunes. Clearly he does not want to ride in the Squaw Days parade with a VP about to be impeached and imprisoned. Had he succumbed to Victoria Bonobo in that Washington hotel room, he would have been forced to do just that! So at first glance his faithfulness to Karen looks like a godsend. No sex with Vicki, no VP at Squaw Days. Same deal as last year. But he knows only too well that Victoria Bonobo is as ruthless as he is, and what at first glance looks like a godsend may at second, third or fourth glance prove to be a god-awful mess. So he sips his coffee even more slowly.

He thinks about that scene in the mayor's office. It's clear why Woody Sadlebyrne was laughing at the VP's misfortune. He's a Democrat. And an asshole. But why was Victoria Bonobo laughing? Pretty soon it's as clear as the nose on his face: She knows he puked those huevos rancheros on purpose. She knows he has no intention of copulating with her, that despite his obvious lust for her, he is a loyal and loving husband. And because of that fatal flaw, she will make him pay, see to it that the VP comes to Squaw Days no matter what. And he, the ever-loyal Republican, will have to ride with him in the parade no matter what, politically humiliated, tainted with scandal, no more likely to win the next election for mayor than Katherine Hardihood is likely to win the next Miss Universe pageant.

And so with no other choice—no other choice at all— D. William Aitchbone drives to Woodchuck Ridge, to Victoria Bonobo's wide concrete driveway. He runs to the porch and rings the bell and when she opens the door he takes her by her wonderful shoulders and squeezes her wonderful breasts against his pounding heart. "Vicki," he says, his thin lips all over her smooth neck, "I've got to have you! Right now, Vicki!"

As she giggles in his ear, he looks into the kitchen and sees Woodrow Wilson Sadlebyrne drinking a tall glass of milk, wearing nothing but a skimpy pair of Serendipity Green® jockey shorts.

22

It is April again. Howie Dornick has never liked April. It is the month the storm sewers back up and send him underground to claw out clumps of leaves and mud and the rotting carcasses of rats and cats, the month potholes appear, like sores on a leper, sending him into the wet village streets with shovelsful of asphalt patch. It is the month when the traffic lights short out, sending him up ladders, a zillion volts of electricity just that far from his runny nose.

And so here he is, with rain in his face, rain about to turn into BBs of ice any second now, balancing atop a ladder, minivans and sport utility vehicles circling him like hyenas, rewiring the traffic light at Tocqueville and South Mill. "Hey!" someone in a fine black Lincoln yells up at him. "Where's that green house?"

Howie Dornick points his electrical pliers down South Mill. It is the fifth time he's pointed his pliers that morning. It is also the fifth time he's wondered just why in *thee hell* is he standing atop this ladder—still working like an old unappreciated dog for the village—when he has enough money in the bank now to buy half the damn village? There are plenty of deep and dark psychological reasons he supposes. Self-hatred maybe. Or low-esteem? Or atonement for the sins of his war-hero father? Fear maybe, or some convoluted sense of duty. Perhaps the pleasure of being a pain in the ass. Who knows why he stays in this worthless job? Maybe it's just that you can't teach an old unappreciated dog new tricks. Maybe that's all there is to it.

A final dangerous twist and snip and the traffic light is fixed. He puts the ladder in the village pickup. "Where's that syrupy green house?" an old woman in a red Oldsmobile asks him. Her hair is dyed nearly the same shade of red as her car, as is the hair of the five or six other women wedged inside. He points down South Mill.

"Do you suppose the man who owns the syrupy house is at home?" the woman with Oldsmobile red hair then asks him. "We baked him some cookies."

"I think he's on a Caribbean cruise," He answers sympathetically. "But I suppose you can leave the cookies on the porch." The women drive off and he hurries to the control box on the corner and resets the traffic light.

Red.

Yellow.

Green.

Order is restored. The cars on South Mill dutifully stop. The cars on Tocqueville dutifully go.

Howie Dornick spends the rest of morning looking for the leak in the village hall roof that's turning the newly carpeted fire chief's office into a federally protected wetland, or so the fire chief has complained. He spends the afternoon replacing the shingles and copper flashing around the hall's decorative cupola. The cupola was added to the village hall the same year the gazebo was built, two extremely high-maintenance and totally unnecessary gewgaws erected at great expense to make all those new people moving into the new housing developments feel like they're living in a real honest-to-gosh country town, with a handy shopping mall, handy interstate exit, and handy summer festival. Before going home for the day, he Shop-vacs the water out of the fire chief's carpet. No threat of heron or ducks building nests there now.

Thankfully there is only one car of daytrippers parked in front of his two-story frame. Eyes straight ahead he walks past them, pretending he doesn't hear their pleas for autographs. He picks up the tin of cookies left on the porch and goes inside. He doesn't turn on any lights. In these months since he and his house became famous, Howie Dornick has learned that a light in the window is an open invitation to strangers. So he sits in the dark and sups on Thermos coffee and—what a surprise—green cookies.

The cookies are not exactly Serendipity Green®, but Howie Dornick knows it is only a matter of time before

Serendipity Green® food coloring will be on the market and he'll up to his ears in Serendipity Green® bakery. Hugh Harbinger has already sent him a case of Serendipity Green® Easter egg dye.

At eight Katherine Hardihood call him. "Can you come over?"

"I was just there last night."

"Can't we can see each other two nights in a row?"

"We never have before."

"Then you're coming over?"

"Of course."

"Just don't expect anything," she says. "I'm in no mood."

"Me neither," he assures her.

Howie Dornick chooses the most masculine of the five Serendipity Green® umbrellas Hugh sent him and walks briskly through the BB-gun ice shower to Oak Street. "I brought you some cookies," he says to his woman when she opens the door and pulls him inside. The living room smells of Pine Sol. Rhubarb is perched on top of the couch wearing one of the two dozen Serendipity Green® flea collars Hugh Harbinger sent a while ago.

Katherine Hardihood fills a pair of Serendipity Green® mugs with boiling water and shakes an envelope of instant cocoa into each. She opens a bag of miniature marshmallows with her librarian's teeth.

Howie knows from the mound of marshmallows she floats in her cocoa that his woman is out of kilter about something. She has been out of kilter a lot lately. They head for the sofa. "Good day at the library?" he asks.

It's the question she has been waiting for. She thanks him with a kiss right between the eyes. "Darren Frost came in this afternoon."

"Surfing the Net for porn?" Howie Dornick knows nothing of computers or the Internet, but like everyone in the world today, he knows how to say "Surfing the Net."

"Of course," says Katherine Hardihood, marshmallow clogging the corners of her mouth. "But under the new rules

I can't let him look at it, let alone print it out and wave the pictures around like he's just found definitive proof that the Constitution of the United States was a communist plot."

"So you had to ask him to stop. Beautiful."

"But he wouldn't stop, Howard. He started shouting about his First Amendment rights. Threatening to call the ACLU."

"Darren Frost believes in the First Amendment?"

"He was being sarcastic, Howard."

"Oh."

"I had to call the police."

"All right!"

"By the time they got there that goofball had thrown two computers through the window and ripped the covers off fifty-seven children's books."

"*Lake Toads and Land Toads*?"

"It was out. It's always out." Katherine Hardihood eats a green cookie. Now there are green crumbs stuck to the marshmallow on her lips. "It's all Bill Aitchbone's fault, of course."

Howie wets his thumb and tidies his woman's mouth. "Now, Katherine. He's not to blame for everything."

"The hell he isn't. He put Ray Biscobee on the library board knowing very well Venus Willendorf would wrap him right around her big nipples."

Howie Dornick fears his woman is slipping more out of kilter by the minute. "I think you mean around her little finger."

"I said big nipples and I meant big nipples."

"Sorry."

"Bill Aitchbone knew from the get-go Ray Biscobee would crumble," she explains, "and he knew that would only make Darren Frost, or one of EDIT's other crazies, all the crazier. 'Satan got the reverend, but he won't get me.' That sort of thing."

"Good God, Katherine, do you really think—"

"You bet I think."

"You want to watch some TV?"

It was the wrong thing to say. "Watching some TV is your answer to everything."

"Sorry."

Katherine Hardihood puts her empty cocoa mug on the coffee table and curls up next to her man. "Did I tell you that Ray Biscobee wants all the librarians to take a loyalty oath."

"Loyalty to what?"

"To Community Standards. I'm not taking any oaths, Howard. I'm not."

"What about Venus Willendorf's big nipples? Won't they come riding to the rescue?"

"Oh, sure. But Bill Aitchbone will see to it there's some kind of compromise. A compromise I'll have to live with until Darren Frost comes in with an Uzi. That's why I wanted you to come over tonight, Howard."

"I see," he says, not seeing anything.

"I think Bill Aitchbone is too much for us."

Now he does see. "We're not going public with the bones, are we?"

"He'll grind us finer than table salt."

"What about the facts? What about the truth?"

"He's too much for us, Howard."

Howie Dornick picks up the TV remote. But he knows enough not to use it. He plays with it like a string of worry beads. "I'll get my own Uzi. And guard you day and night."

Katherine takes the remote from his hands and wraps her librarian's arms around his maintenance engineer's neck and fills her lungs with enough oxygen to last through an hour of lovemaking. "You'd do that for me?"

"I thought you were in no mood."

"I love you, Howard."

He pushes her back on the cushions and then falls on her like the trunk of a rotted redwood. The marshmallow on their lips cements them together like Crazy Glue.

"We're going through with it," Howie Dornick says with masculine certitude as they kiss and kiss and kiss. "Even if I have to point my Uzi at you."

"You can point your Uzi-woozie at me anytime you want."

"We're going through with it," Howie Dornick says again, unbuttoning her librarian's blouse with the speed of a farm wife podding spring peas. "No matter how crazy Bill Aitchbone or Darren Frost or anybody else gets."

Katherine Hardihood twists and unhooks her bra for him. Rhubarb heads for his Serendipity Green® food bowl in the kitchen.

An hour later Howie and Katherine are stretched out in bed. Rhubarb is curled up between them, enjoying the exotic smells. Rain is banging on the roof like a bus load of Kentucky clog dancers. The April wind is pruning the trees. "So when we gonna do this?" he asks.

"It's going to cause such a stink," she says.

"We won't be making any friends."

"We've done pretty well without any so far."

They giggle at the total truth of that sad reality. When his woman sits up to turn on the radio, Howie Dornick watches the glow from the streetlight walk down her vertebrae. "I love you, Katherine."

She smiles and rests her cheek on his wiry chest hair. "Do you think we should tell him first?"

"Bill Aitchbone?" He can feel her nodding yes. "Why on earth would we want to do that?"

"Because we're decent people," she says. "Because if someone was about to go public with some horrible secret about our ancestors we'd appreciate knowing first. Because Bill Aitchbone, bastard that he is, is going through a tough time with his marriage. And he's sitting alone in his big house missing his kids."

Howie Dornick does love this woman. "When?"

"When the time is right. When he is at his absolute lowest. When we can grind him up like table salt."

God does he love her.

Dr. Pirooz Aram sucks the last drop of espresso from his demitasse and pushes the blinking button on his phone. "Hugh Harbinger! My receptionist says you have been calling every fifteen minutes like some crazy person. You are not crazy again, are you?"

"I'm afraid I'm getting there."

"I keep reading about how rich and famous you are again. America is some amazing place, isn't it? You can be rich and famous as many times as you want. You are still in New York?"

"Up to my neck."

"You are taking your Solhzac?" Dr. Aram asks. He does not hear his patient's answer. He is too busy thinking about how amazing America is. "I have been playing chess again, Hugh. In fact, that is why you have been calling me like a crazy person all afternoon. I've been at the mall playing chess with my friend Igor Zugzwangadze. He is not a very creative player, but like all Georgians he is a very good tactician."

"I thought everybody from Georgia was named Bobby Clyde?"

"Igor is not from our Georgia, Hugh. He is from the real Georgia. The one that hangs under Russia's big belly like an udder of sweet milk. He was an officer in the Red Navy for twenty-seven years. Now the fleet is rusting in Odessa and he is in Cleveland, Ohio, selling South Korean automobiles for some Italian millionaire and playing chess with some lazy Persian who makes his patients call and call. His wife is Malaysian, if you can believe it. Eight years ago she came to America to study podiatry and now she is getting rich and famous importing cat toys from Vietnam. They've just bought a big house in Bay Village. Six bedrooms. A Jacuzzi you could swim laps in. So tell me Hugh, why are you going crazy again?"

Dr. Pirooz Aram wedges his tongue between his front

teeth and listens as Hugh Harbinger tells him how a rival designer named Koko—the only person in New York with color instincts equal to his—is back from Morocco with a beautiful brown lover and seventy-seven shades of white named after virtuous women; how this Koko is already making deals with the manufacturers of clothes and cars and kitchen appliances; how Jean Jacques Bistrot is already writing articles; how the waiters at Zulu Lulu are already looking at him with pity and disdain; how before long Serendipity Green® only will be popular among the demographically challenged living in the Midwest and Deep South; how before long he will be depressed again and penniless again, and living again with Bob and Eleanor In Parma.

Dr. Aram twists his fingers into his beard. "Can you hear a ripping sound, Hugh? It is the sound of me ripping the hairs out of my head. Dammit! You are under no obligation to jump off a roof just because some phony-baloneys in New York City don't like your color any more."

"Intellectually I understand that better than anybody," says Hugh. "I'm one of the biggest phony-baloneys to ever set foot in this city."

The doctor chuckles. "Stop your bragging. I lived in New York for nine years. I met hundreds of bigger phony-baloneys than you."

Now Hugh Harbinger begins to cry. He does not want to be depressed again, he says. He does not want to be at the bottom of that big empty gray bowl again, unable to see out, unable to scale its slippery walls.

Dr. Pirooz Aram presses his phone tight against his ear and visualizes the tears trickling down his patient's face. "Let me talk not as your psychiatrist, but merely as someone much smarter than you. May I do that?"

"Shoot."

"Good. Now listen. God has been watching you like a hawk since the day you were born. And for some reason he likes you. He likes you so much that one day he followed you all the way to Tuttwyler, putting up with your parents' jibber-jabber mile after mile on the Interstate. And he showed you a wonderful color. A color that awakened you and transformed you. A color you could take to the world. And now someone whom God likes just as much comes along with seventy-five shades of white—"

"Seventy-seven," corrects Hugh Harbinger.

"And you are ready to crumble like a muffin. As if this Serendipity Green® actually belonged to you! Hugh! Are you listening? God shows me the moon every night but that does not mean I own the moon. If one night a big cloud fills the sky and I can't see the moon, it does not mean God wants me to stop looking at it. It only means that once in a while they sky gets cloudy."

"I know all that," says Hugh.

"Boool-shit! If you knew all that you wouldn't be calling my office every fifteen minutes while I'm sitting in the mall playing chess! "

"I don't want to be depressed again."

"I will double your prescription."

"Double my prescription? That's the best you can do?"

"That is quite a lot, don't you think?" Dr. Aram looks at his watch. He must meet his sweet wife Sitareh at Foon Choon's in only nine minutes. If he is late she will order without him and that means the pepper steak and he will be farting all night. "You must not confuse your fear of getting depressed with actually being depressed. Your Solhzac will keep your chemicals under control until the clouds blow away and you can see the moon again. Go to church and light a candle and thank God for showing you this wonderful color. Ask him to show you more wonderful colors. Make love to someone you care about. Eat a pint of strawberries. Rent the *Wizard of Oz*. When you get a bill from your psychiatrist, pay it immediately. Do these things and you will be fine."

The silence on the other end tells Dr. Pirooz Aram that his patient has surrendered. "Good-bye my good prince of Serendip!"

He hurries to the parking lot and drives his red sports car as fast as he dares toward Foon Choon's. As he drives he worries about Hugh Harbinger. He worries about Katherine Hardihood. He worries about Ernest Not Irish. He worries about the Americans who come to him by the hundreds, demanding prescriptions for magical medicines, demanding permission to follow their hearts. Who is he, he wonders, to hand out either? He knows he is a terrible psychiatrist. He knows he should have become a dentist as his mother wished. Instead he went to Paris and then to New York and then to hell filling Americans full of drugs and full of dangerous ideas about self-realization. "Damn you, Pirooz," he growls at himself.

23

It is the rainiest May in memory. And so far the coldest. And for several days now the denizens of Tuttwyler, Ohio have been debating just why the weather has been so foul. The cappuccino drinkers at the Day Dream Beanery tend to blame it on corporate polluters. The beer drinkers at the VFW are certain Moammar Khadafy and Saddam Hussein are to blame. But neither the rain nor cold, nor the uncertainty over their causes, can stop Chiselworth & Tubb Advertising from flying in a crew to film the new Serendipity Green® gazebo commercial for the Bison-Prickert Paint Company. The crew has big nasty lights to burn the rain and cold away. The crew has hot coffee to drink and Serendipity Green® ponchos to wear. Most importantly the crew has a deadline. It must get this 30-second Serendipity Green® commercial shot and edited and on the air by game one of the National Basketball Association's championship finals.

And so the village square is a beehive of activity. There are not only the cameras and crew brought in to film the commercial, there are the cameras and crews from channels 3, 5 ,8 and 19 sent to record this historic event for the six-, ten- and eleven-o'clock news. There is a perimeter of yellow crime scene tape and sheriff's deputies parading in SWAT gear. There are two- maybe three-hundred umbrella-wielding local folk who have never seen a commercial being shot before and twelve or so actors flown in from New York and LA to portray the local folk. There are wardrobe people and makeup people and food-service people, and serious-looking people in Burberry raincoats who, when not yapping into their cell phones, are scowling at their big-as-bagel wristwatches. All in all, this cold and rainy day in May is nearly as festive as Squaw Days itself.

The plot of the commercial is simple enough: The happy people of Tuttwyler, Ohio, gather on a beautiful summer day to paint their old white gazebo Serendipity

Green®. The actors flown in to portray these happy Tuttwylerites will not actually paint the gazebo, of course. The real painting of the gazebo was accomplished two weeks before by a team of union painters flown in from Chicago. Today is just for pretend, for close-ups of actors brushing and grinning and drinking lemonade and joyfully wiping splatters of Serendipity Green® paint off the nose of a firehouse Dalmatian flown in from LA.

And so the filming begins. The rain comes and goes. The crowd ebbs and flows. Finally there is just one more scene to shoot: A silver-haired actor, who has appeared in several national ads for pain relievers and sinus medicines, will wrap his plaid-shirted arm around Howie Dornick's shoulder and warmly say, "Looks great Howie!" Howie will beam back at the actor and say, "I think I like it!" The real Howie Dornick, being the unappetizing man he is, will not appear in the commercial. He is being portrayed by an actor who has appeared in national ads for cholesterol-free cooking oil, instant gravy and life insurance.

The director, fashionable ponytail sticking from the back of his bald head like the tail of a tadpole, picks up a megaphone. "We've got audio in this shot people," he says. "That means quiet, quiet, quiet! Am I understood?"

He is understood.

And there is quiet.

There is quiet for exactly five seconds.

Then there is a communal shriek.

The crowd divides like the Red Sea.

Deputies in SWAT gear spin like a tabletop of Hanukkah dreidels into the yellow crime scene tape.

A pewter-colored American-made Japanese luxury sedan, Yobisch Podka's *Insipientia* blaring from its open windows, bulls into the Serendipity Green® gazebo. Splinters fly.

24

Howie Dornick is high on his ladder painting the ceiling of the gazebo when he sees Dick Mueller and Delores walk hand-in-hand across the north end of the village square. He does not care much for Dick and Delores as individuals—they are both a little holier-than-thou when it comes to religion and patriotism, and Dick always treats him like he's a little bit retarded—but he sure admires them as a couple. For years he admired the way they kept their love affair private and now he admires how they flaunt it, holding hands and kissing and patting each other's behinds. He hopes the day will come when he and Katherine Hardihood can be a public couple, shopping together for groceries, eating together in restaurants, walking together across the square, laughing and touching no matter how unappetizing everybody thinks they are.

And Howie Dornick can see that this day is coming. Coming soon. Their collective courage is growing by leaps and bounds. Already they've been a couple in Wooster, unashamedly conspiring with the Bittinger boy. Already they have been a couple in the cemetery, exhuming ol' Seth Aitchbone in broad daylight. How long can it be before they stroll bravely into the Daydream Beanery and sit at one of the window tables and sip their hazelnut coffees and wipe muffin crumbs off each other's chins? Any week now that could happen.

Tonight they will be taking a big step in that direction. They will be going as a couple to Bill Aitchbone's house.

He makes sure he is finished painting exactly at 4:15. He makes sure it takes exactly forty-five minutes to take his ladder and empty paint cans back to the village maintenance garage and to clean his brushes and scrub the specks of Serendipity Green® paint off his face and hands. At exactly five he starts for home. As he walks his stomach feel like it's full of sparrows. He does not want to confront D. William Aitchbone tonight or any night. Still, he wants to get it over with. He passes the freshly repaired and freshly painted gazebo. It looks good as new. He passes the newly painted Serendipity Green® houses on South Mill. No matter how hard he squints, these impressive giants are not the same Serendipity Green® as the Serendipity Green® on his humble two-story frame. How can they be? How possibly can the Bison-Prickert Paint Company mix his life-time of misery into their paint?

When he reaches his driveway he signs the Serendipity Green® tee shirts of two old women with humped backs and bowling pin breasts. Their tee shirts are not really Serendipity Green®. But the Indonesian sweatshop that made them has come pretty close. He does not sign the tee shirts across the front as the old women ask, but across their humped backs. He picks up a half dozen boxes and tins of Serendipity Green® cookies and cupcakes left on the porch by various pilgrims. When he reaches the kitchen he throws them into the Serendipity Green® garbage can Hugh Harbinger sent him.

His kitchen table and counters are covered with the various Serendipity Green® appliances Hugh sent, none of them truly Serendipity Green®.

He showers and and then sits down on his Serendipity Green® toilet seat and dries off with a fluffy Serendipity Green® towel. He hears Katherine Hardihood's librarian's knuckles banging on his back door.

They are both too nervous to eat anything substantial, so they nibble on oyster crackers and sip a little ginger ale, as if they had the flu. They watch the Cleveland news: an east-side fire has claimed the lives of two babies; a hidden camera has caught the assistant city finance director drinking beer at an east side strip club when he should have been working; a teacher at a suburban high school has been indicted for having sex with eighteen former students, possible many more. Then they watch the national news: Israel is balking at the President's latest Mideast peace proposals; Russian generals are suspected of selling biolog-ical weapons to North African terrorists; the attorney general of the United States may or may not appoint a special prosecutor to investigate the Vice President's alleged role in the Montezuma's Revenge affair—or as Dan Rather calls it, Revengegate.

At seven they kiss and hug and head for Bill Aitchbone's soapy white Queen Anne. "You know we've got to do this," Katherine Hardihood says to him as they force their way up the sidewalk like Columbia River salmon.

"I know," Howie Dornick answers.

South Mill is never more impressive than in June. The maples and oaks are in full leaf. Men are not yet sick of mowing and fertilizing, and every lawn is as trim and smooth as a golf course green. Many thousands of dollars worth of petunias and pansies and impatiens have been planted. Most impressively, the spring rains have scrubbed the soapy white Victorians and Greek Revivals of their winter filth. They sparkle under the afternoon sun like movie star teeth.

But South Mill is a nervous street this June. A metamorphosis is underway. A number of homeowners have already slathered their soapy white houses with glistening coats of the Serendipity Green® latex paint now being featured at all Bison-Prickert stores. A number of others are busy scraping their clapboards. Soon Tuttwyler won't just be famous for Squaw Days, it also will be famous for its street after street of Serendipity Green® houses.

Howie Dornick and Katherine Hardihood reach the Grabbenstelter's flat-roofed Italianate. Ken and Kelley Grabbenstelter have just painted it a ripe persimmon red, not as an act of rebellion against the copy-cat Serendipity Green® houses, but as a beacon to draw attention to their Serendipity Green® window frames and shutters, their Serendipity Green® porch posts and Adirondack chairs, and the impressive wrought iron fence stretching from property line to property line, now transformed into a living hedge by a coat of Bison-Prickert's rust-resistant Serendipity Green® enamel.

They are standing on Bill Aitchbone's porch much too quickly. Katherine smashes the door bell button with her librarian's thumb. *Bing-bingly-bingly-bing!* "You don't have to say anything," she says to Howie. "I know exactly what to say."

He is relieved. "Whatever you say."

D. William Aitchbone does not come to the door. Not after the first *Bing-bingly-bingly-bing!* or the sixth. Their courage flags. "Maybe he's dead in there," Howie Dornick says. "Nobody's really seen him since he drove into the gazebo."

Katherine Hardihood presses her nose into the door crack and sniffs. There is no evidence of a rotting corpse. She bangs on the door with the callused meat of her librarian's fist. "Bill Aitchbone! Answer the door!"

Suddenly Howie Dornick is overcome with the need to find Bill Aitchbone dead. He hardens his shoulder and pulls in his neck, ready to ram. But first he tries the doorknob. The door is unlocked. They shuffle in.

It is a beautiful house. There are beautiful wallpapers. Beautiful chandeliers with dangling crystals, beautiful white carpets and blue carpets and all of the furniture in the living room is oak. "Bill? Bill?" Katherine Hardihood shouts sweetly between investigative sniffs. "Bill? Bill?"

They drift into the kitchen and admire the stainless steel cooktop and gray granite countertops. They frown at the pile of dirty plates in the twin sinks. Most of the plates are smeared with spaghetti sauce. There also are several cereal bowls encrusted with Cheerios. "Jiminy Cricket, Bill? Are you alive?"

An answer explodes up the basement stairs. "Down here, for christsakes."

And so Howie Dornick and Katherine Hardihood find D. William Aitchbone in his basement, playing with his electric trains.

It is a remarkable sight: D. William Aitchbone is sitting atop the vibrating clothes dryer. He is wearing nothing but boxer shorts. He badly needs a shave and a shampoo. Surprisingly, this manliest of men has very few hairs on his chest, but there is enough hair erupting from his armpits to weave a pair of good sized bird nests. His nipples are no bigger than Lincoln pennies. His hands are locked around a bottle of Miller Lite. His trains are racing around the rim of a long plywood table. Inside the maze of tracks is a miniature replica of the Tuttwyler village square.

Howie and Katherine inch forward. They study the miniature village square. Every buildings is exact. But this is not the Tuttwyler square of today. There is no Daydream Beanery. No Just Giraffes or Pizza Teepee. No art galleries or antique shops. Nosireebob. D. William Aitchbone's tiny Tuttwyler has H.W. Colby's Hardware and Borden Brother's Shoes and Porter's Western Auto and Morton's IGA and Klinger's Paint and Sylvia's Family Restaurant and Grinspoon's Department Stores. There is no tiny wooden Indian holding a pizza and none of the Matchbox cars parked around the square are newer than a '57 Chevrolet.

D. William Aitchbone's tiny Tuttwyler, however, does have one appendage that pre-Interstate 491 Tuttwyler did not. It has a gazebo; and just like the real gazebo, this tiny gazebo has been updated with a coat of Serendipity Green® paint, at least a quart of it, poured like syrup over a stack of pancakes; the gazebo also has been flattened like a pancake, as if God Almighty had angrily thrust one of his sledge-hammer-like hands down through the firmament.

"Happy now, Howie?" asks D. William Aitchbone as his uninvited guests explore the little town and watch the trains go around.

Howie Dornick can't be sure, but he thinks he knows what D. William Aitchbone means. And yes, he is happy now. Seeing Bill Aitchbone in his underwear with nothing but a vibrating dryer and bottle of beer to keep him company makes him very happy, indeed. But he says nothing. His woman wants to do all the talking. He will let her.

"We didn't come here to talk about Howie's happiness, or yours," she says. "We came to talk about Squaw Days."

D. William Aitchbone takes a mouthful of beer and grimaces it down his throat. "My favorite subject."

"Not after today," says Howie Dornick.

"Bill's being sarcastic," explains Katherine.

D. William Aitchbone grimaces another swig. "You guys want to hear my big surprise for this year's parade? I'm going to march buck naked with a big Serendipity Green® *A* painted on my white ass. Like that idea, Howie?"

Howie Dornick answers, "Really?"

"He's still being sarcastic," his woman explains. "He's referring to Nathaniel Hawthorne's 17th century novel about a woman who's convicted of adultery and forced wear a scarlet letter *A* on her dress."

"What's that got to do with his ass?" Howie Dornick wants to know.

Again his woman explains: "By painting a Serendipity Green® *A* on his ass and parading naked, Bill would be blaming his adultery on you."

"My alleged adultery," says D. William Aitchbone.

"And why is his alleged adultery my fault?" Howie Dornick asks Katherine.

"Because he's got to blame somebody besides himself."

D. William Aitchbone starts laughing. Beer dribbles down his chest and makes his Lincoln-penny nipples glisten.

Katherine Hardihood explains further: "You see, Howard, having a wife with an illegitimate half brother—correct me if I'm wrong, Bill—has been the one thing that's kept his life from being perfect. Being related to dumb old Howie Dornick."

Dumb old Howie Dornick nods his head wisely. "Ahhhh."

"And now that he's been caught putting his manhood where it doesn't belong . . ."

"Allegedly putting," says D. William Aitchbone.

". . . he has subconsciously and symbolically tied all of his misfortunes to Artie Brown's original sin of impregnating your mother. Karen leaving with the kids. Woody being mayor. Paying all those inheritance taxes on his uncle's farm. You ruining his first year as Squaw Days chairman by painting your house that god-awful color. And most importantly, I suppose, his not being man enough to control everything and everybody, the way the great Donald Grinspoon would have controlled everything and everybody."

"Wow," says Howie Dornick.

D. William Aitchbone has stopped laughing. "So what's so damn important about Squaw Days that it can't wait until I'm sober?"

Katherine walks to the wall and pulls the plug on D. William's Aitchbone's trains. She pulls the plug on his vibrating clothes dryer, too. Now that she has the silence a librarian deserves, she begins: "First let me say, Bill, that I take no pleasure in telling you any of this. . ."

To which D. William Aitchbone says, "I bet."

". . . but I have to tell you, because it is the truth and everyone has the right to know the truth . . ."

To which D. William Aitchbone says, "Nobody cares about the truth."

". . . Well, I care about the truth And you're going to care about it. You know I've never been happy about Squaw Days. The disgraceful carnival it's become . . ."

To which D. William Aitchbone says, "Never would have guessed."

". . . But I kept my mouth shut and went along. For the good of the village. Knowing the whole Pogawedka thing was a lie . . ."

To which D. William Aitchbone says, "You're the one who did the research, if you remember."

". . . And now I'm going to undo it . . ."

To which D. William Aitchbone asks, "And how do you undo research?"

". . . With more research. Bill, the irony of this is going to slay you . . ."

To which D. William Aitchbone says, "Lay it on me, Katherine. I haven't been slain with irony since Karen left with the kids."

". . . Let's start with the Tuttwyler brothers clubbing the two human beings we now call Pogawedka and Kapusta—which, by the way, are Polish words for nonsense and cabbage. Now the myth, of course, is that Pogawedka's spirit rose from the stumps to forgive her murderers and give her blessing for the rape of her ancestral lands, and presumably giving us permission to desecrate her memory with pie-eating contests, tobacco-spitting and the biggest Ferris wheel we can get . . . ."

To which D. William Aitchbone says, "It's a good myth, isn't it?"

". . . And now it seems that the real bones of our mythical Pogawedka and Kapusta have been discovered. And guess where, Bill? In the grave of Seth Aitchbone . . ."

To which D. William Aitchbone says, "Sweet Jesus."

" . . . The bones and smashed skulls of a young woman and a baby, resting atop your great-great-great-great-great uncle. Right there on that beautiful hill overlooking Three Fish Creek. And why would those bones be on top of Seth Aitchbone's if they weren't his illegitimate family?"

To which D. William Aitchbone, glowering at Howie Dornick for playing with his ancestors' bones, says, "So he had a squaw on the side. Big whoop."

"Ah! But she wasn't a squaw. Wasn't an Indian. She was white. And her baby was white. And that means those wonderful brothers who founded our little village murdered a white woman and a white baby. Not that murdering an Indian woman and an Indian baby would have been any less despicable, of course, but at least that's something you can build a nice festival around. And by the way, Bill. Guess how ol' Seth died? He shot himself in the mouth!"

To which D. William Aitchbone says, "So the irony, you think, is that because of my greed—paying lover boy here to uproot my ancestors so I could sell the farm and get rich—a dark secret has been uncovered. One that would ruin me politically if it ever got out? And so you've come to blackmail me. Make Squaw Days respectable or you'll tell the world. Is that it, Katherine?"

"This is not about blackmail, Bill. This is about telling you the truth first, out of decency."

To which D. William Aitchbone reaches into his tiny Tuttwyler and uncouples the locomotive from one of his trains. He presses it to his beer-sticky chest and pets it like a puppy. "This is a 1930 Blue Comet, considered one of Lionel's greatest achievements. If I wanted to sell it, and all the cars, I bet I could get seven, eight thousand bucks. My father gave it to me on my twelfth birthday. He would have been eighty-two this year. June fifth. My son, Cannon, was born on the sixth. I was praying he'd be born on the fifth, like my father. But he was born on the sixth." He puts the Blue Comet back, carefully coupling it to the coal car. "So, you're going to set the world straight, are you, Katherine?"

Katherine Hardihood nods.

To which D. William Aitchbone asks, "When?"

"Not until this year's festival is over. Everybody's already done at lot of work. But when it's over. Maybe in the fall. I'm not a beast, Bill. I just believe in the truth."

To which D. William Aitchbone begins laughing like a flock of southbound Canada geese. "You're not going to tell the world the truth, Katherine. You don't have the balls. You love Tuttwyler more than anybody. More than Donald Grinspoon. You went along with Squaw Days in the first place because you love it, and you'll keep on going along because you love it. I appreciate all your research. But who on God's green earth are you kidding? No balls, Katherine. No balls at all. You just make sure this year's Re-Enactment is the best ever. And you, Howie, you make sure the portable toilets are clean."

"I don't blame you for being bitter," Katherine Hardihood says, "but I am going to go public with this."

To which D. William Aitchbone throws his Miller Lite bottle against the wall. "I've got a great idea, Howie. Why don't you paint those portable toilets that shitty green of yours? And the streets and the sidewalks and all the goddamn tree trunks. Paint goddamn everything. I'll even let you paint that green *A* on my goddamn ass!" Now he bends over and comes up with a gallon can of Bison-Prickert Serendipity Green® Latex. He pries off the loose lid with his fingernails. "Come on, Howie, you can't paint my ass right now!" He starts pouring the paint over his tiny Tuttwyler, even over his precious Blue Comet. "Much much much better," he says between goose laughs.

Katherine Hardihood takes Howie Dornick by the arm and starts up the stairs. "We just wanted to tell you first," she says. At the top of the stairs she breaks away from him and goes back down. D. William Aitchbone is still pouring paint. She takes her wallet from her purse and takes out a business card, and not knowing quite where to put it, she slips it inside the elastic of his boxer shorts. She trots up the stairs.

D. William Aitchbone has emptied the can of Serendipity Green® paint.

He swings the can like a hammer now, smashing the scale model balsawood buildings he's spent his entire married life making. He smashes his trains. He pulls the card from his boxers. He reads it:

DR. PIROOZ ARAM
Psychiatrist

The house at the end of Petunia Court was still heated with coal when Darren Frost bought it in 1968. Every September, Sparky Shingleholtz would back his dump truck up to the small iron chute on the driveway side of the house and let five tons of filthy Ohio bituminous rumble into the basement coal bin, a windowless chamber maybe ten by ten.

In 1978, Darren Frost put in natural gas and turned the coal bin into his den. And tonight he is sitting in that little windowless cell, surrounded by hundreds of pornographic pictures taped to the walls, the stench of coal still lingering after all these years. He is sitting in front of the new computer he bought with his son's college savings bonds, right after that unfortunate incident at the library. He is downloading information on how to make pipe bombs. His cupcake costume is hanging from a big brass hook screwed into the ceiling. His can of orange soda is resting atop his Bible. His once-prized photograph of the Reverend Raymond R. Biscobee is in the wastebasket, ripped into pieces the size of postage stamps. His wife is working her evening shift at the new Red Lobster on West Wooseman. His kids are upstairs watching God-knows-what on the TV.

25

"I can't believe you've never been in PA," Buzzy says to Zee Levant as they zip along the top of a long Pennsylvania mountain in the Serendipity Green® Volvo station wagon the dealer in Great Neck, Long Island gave Hugh Harbinger. Hugh, stretched out on the back seat, hasn't made a peep since they crossed the Hudson. Neither has Matisse, who's curled up in wicker laundry basket in the wagon part of the station wagon.

Zee is not the least bit ashamed of never being in Pennsylvania before. But she counterattacks anyway. "I can't believe you have."

Buzzy loves her counterattack. "How many states have you actually been in, Zee? Not flown over. Actually been in?"

She thinks. "New York. Connecticut. Massachusetts. California. Colorado. Hawaii. And now New Jersey and Pennsylvania."

Buzzy loves it. "That's it? Eight states? You are some American, Zee."

"And how many have you been in?" she asks.

"Forty-two. Forty-three when we get to Ohio."

Zee Levant is stunned. "Why?"

Buzzy loves her snobbery. "OK. How many countries?"

She doesn't have to think about this one. "All the ones everybody's been to, of course: France. England. Ireland. Belgium. Luxembourg. Monaco. Germany. Denmark. Sweden. Czechoslovakia. Austria. Morocco. Italy and Greece. Israel. Egypt. Turkey. Spain and Portugal. India. Mexico. Cuba. Brazil. Japan. Thailand. Singapore. New Zealand. How many is that?"

"I'm not counting."

"And, let's see: Belize. Mali. Zimbabwe. Tonga. Togo. Poland. Latvia. Hungry. Lebanon. China. Mongolia. Figi. Uganda. Kenya—Buzzy, Buzzy, Buzzy! This is so boring! I've never been in the front seat of a car this long in my life. How long until Cleveland?"

"Another eight hours, I think."

"We could fly to Prague in eight hours."

It's cloudy up here on the mountain top. In the valley the sunlight is brilliant, though there's nothing worth a damn down there worth illuminating. "Do we dare stop for lunch?" Buzzy asks.

"Yes we do," answers Zee. 'I'm absolutely hollow. What's the next city?"

Buzzy fumbles for the map folded over his crotch like a loin cloth and hands it to his co-pilot. Having once driven a Land Rover across Kazakhstan, she has no trouble finding their exact location. "Bloomsburg? There wouldn't be anything remotely Mediterranean in a town called Bloomsburg."

Buzzy loves it. They drive on.

Buzzy, Zee Levant and Hugh Harbinger are speeding west in the Serendipity Green® Volvo because last night, during a book launch for famous South Carolina novelist Kwame Oyo at Café Ru Ru, Hugh, sucking woozily on a fifty-dollar contraband Cuban cigar, all of a sudden decided to give the Gangrene Velveeta, as he's been calling the big boxy wagon since it was delivered on Monday, to Bob and Eleanor Hbracek. He'd drive it to Ohio himself, he decided. And Buzzy and Zee Levant, afraid it was just a ruse for him to commit suicide in the middle-of-nowhere, decided they'd better come along. And so now Buzzy is driving and Zee Levant is running her fingers along the map, and the color genius responsible for this lunacy is flat on his back in the back seat.

Buzzy and Zee have every reason to believe that Hugh Harbinger might take his life. He's been skidding since Koko returned from Morocco with seventy-seven shades of white. For weeks now he's had no interest in restaurants or sex or art galleries or deriding the middle class. For weeks now he's been sitting at Zee's Bjorn Dahlstrom breakfast table, feet up on her Sori Yanagi chairs, Matisse asleep in his lap, a can of warm Pepsi in his hand, looking down at the little people in Central Park.

They have tried everything to get his mind off things: They've brought him bakery from Mousey's. They've brought him soup from Watty's. Buzzy has performed his Senator D'Amato impression. Zee has danced naked to Armenian folk songs. One night they even brought Jean Jacques Bistrot over to play Trivial Pursuit. None of it has worked.

They even have tried to make him deal with his funk head on, reminding him that every color fades in popularity and that Serendipity Green® is, after all is said and done, just another color. They have assured him that there are still plenty of colors out there to be discovered. They have put his stack of un-cashed royalty checks next to his stack of J. Peterman catalogs, to show him what a lucky bastard he really is. Buzzy has shaken him by the shirt collar. Zee has reached under his Serendipity Green® bathrobe and shaken him by the testicles. They have even reminded him of Dr. Pirooz Aram's admonishment that he not confuse his fear of getting depressed with actually being depressed. None of this has worked.

And so they are racing along the back of a Pennsylvania mountain.

Frightened by the prospect of Pennsylvania food, Zee Levant and Buzzy decide to go hungry until they reach Cleveland. Food depravation has a certain Zenness to it, they decide. But is Cleveland food likely to be any more edible than Pennsylvania food? Not likely. They will set a good example for Hugh and confront their fears. They choose a truck stop called Spunky's. It takes five minutes to coax Hugh Harbinger out of the back seat. It is mid-afternoon but there are still breakfast menus on the sticky table. Zee decides she'll order the Belgian waffles and maybe some hot tea. Buzzy thinks he'll get the French toast and a tomato juice. "I bet they don't make the TJ fresh," he says. Hugh Harbinger doesn't open his menu. Or his mouth. And his eyes are barely open. At least he's inside where they don't have to worry about him wedging his head under the tire of some monstrous truck.

Eventually the waitress gravitates toward their booth. Hugh's mouth falls open. His eyes fall open. By the look on his face, his heart has fallen open, too. "Oh Momma!" he says.

This is a truck stop. The waitress has heard worse. She gravitates closer. "Ready to order?"

Before Zee can ask about the Belgian waffles, before Buzzy can inquire about the TJ's freshness, Hugh rises and gently takes the waitress by the elbows. She is short, and slightly wide, and given her high cheekbones and her brownness and the flute-tone of her little voice, not likely a native Pennsylvanian. "What exactly are you?" he asks.

"Your waitress if you'll let me," she says.

"I mean where are you from?"

"Peru. Why?"

"I've been there a dozen times," says Zee Levant.

"You're Incan?" Hugh Harbinger asks.

The waitress warms. It is the first time a customer has not figured her for a Filipino or a Pakistani. "I am Incan, yes."

"Your skin is fabulous," he says. "Are all Incans your color?"

The waitress laughs. "They wish." She tells him that she is from a village one hundred and forty-eight miles east of Cuzco. Iqicucho it is called, on the Rio Madre de Dios, too close to Bolivia for comfort. "Everyone in Iqicucho is this shade of brown," she says. "Except for children whose mammas got too close to a Bolivian. It is said the people of Iqicucho are direct descendants of the great Incan emperor Pachacuti. Who knows if that is true. But it is true that no one in my family has a single drop of Spanish blood in them. Not a drop."

"I've white-watered in Bolivia," Zee Levant says.

"I pray nobody raped you," the waitress says to her.

"You are the most incredible color," Hugh Harbinger says. "Absolutely fabulous. I mean it."

"The people in Puerto Maldonado call us potato skins because of our color," the waitress says. "But they are all jealous assholes."

Hugh must know her name.

"María Vilca Quechua Ayavilli," she says. "I'm majoring in computer science at Penn State."

Zee orders the Belgian waffles and hot tea.

Buzzy orders the French toast and TJ.

Hugh orders a cheeseburger, onion rings and a Pepsi with lots of ice. He writes the waitress's name on a napkin. And the name of her village, he writes that, too.

Dr. Pirooz Aram finishes his espresso in a few joyless swallows. His first patient of the day, a new patient, has showed up forty-five minutes early and his fidgety pacing and magazine flipping is driving him crazy. He ushers him in.

"Why are you so early?" Dr. Pirooz Aram asks in the same bewildered voice the great Persian king Xerxes might have used to berate the Greek general Themistocles after the horrendous naval debacle at Salamis: *("Why did you sink all my boats?")*

"Sorry," D. William Aitchbone says.

"So am I," answers Xerxes's descendant.

William Aitchbone sits rigidly in one of the huge leather chairs. He is smiling like a madman—which Dr. Pirooz Aram notes on his pad—and his fingers are drumming even faster than his eyes are blinking.

"I am surprised that you would come to me," Dr. Aram begins, "considering that someone you despise recommended me." The doctor is, of course, talking about Katherine Hardihood.

"I'm a lawyer," Aitchbone explains. "I have plenty of clients who despise each other. But they know I won't betray their confidence. I gather you're a professional, too. Otherwise Katherine Hardihood wouldn't come to you. She may have more brass than a marching band, but she's nobody's fool."

Dr. Pirooz Aram is flattered by his new patient's compliment, though he is glad his new patient does not

247

know about his weakness for dancing and poetry. "So, why does such a cool cucumber as yourself need my help?" he asks, knowing from his sessions with Katherine that D. William Aitchbone is anything but a cool cucumber, that in fact he has gotten himself into quite a pickle in recent weeks.

For a half hour D. William Aitchbone talks proudly about his rise to prominence and power in Tuttwyler: about his successful law practice and his political apprenticeship under Donald Grinspoon; about his impressive Queen Anne on South Mill; about his marriage to Karen Brown, daughter of the local war hero Artie Brown, and the two great kids their union has produced; about his ascendancy to chairman of the Squaw Days Committee. Then in just thirty angry seconds he tells the doctor about his wife's illegitimate half-brother, Howie Dornick; how everything was banging along fine until Howie painted his ugly-ass little house Serendipity Green®, that ugly-ass color the entire world has mysteriously gone ga-ga over; how, for some unfathomable reason, his entire life has gone to hell-in-a hand-basket since Howie defiantly slathered his clapboards that color; how his wife has left him over an affair he is not having; how, because of that same affair he is not having, the wicked Victoria Bonobo is foisting the sure-to-be-impeached Vice President of the United States on him, ending any chance he has of becoming mayor; how the Bison-Prickert Paint Company bribed the village council with a fire engine so they could paint the gazebo Serendipity Green®; how, as the cameras were rolling, he snapped like a stale cookie and drove his car into that gazebo; how he got drunk on Miller Lite and smashed the Lionel Blue Comet his father gave him on his twelfth birthday; how some goofball Indian from Cleveland is on the warpath; how Katherine Hardihood plans to tell the world that Squaw Days is a sham. After he is finished telling the doctor all this, he staggers to the window and wraps his head in the doctor's expensive Persian drapes. "Why couldn't that bastard just paint his house white like everybody else? Such an easy fucking thing."

Dr. Aram hurries over and pulls his patient's head out of the drapes, as delicately as a Girl Scout would remove a butterfly from the webbing of a net. "Perhaps you are taking things too personally. Maybe this Howie Dornick simply doesn't like white."

"What he doesn't like is me."

The doctor leads him back to the big leather chair. "You are what we in my native Iran call a *keer-khar.* A big man in town. A big cheese. Am I right?" He does not tell his patient that the term also refers to the impressive size of a donkey's penis, though he is tempted.

"There is nothing wrong with ambition," Aitchbone says.

"Of course not. I am an ambitious man myself. But big cheeses get used to having their way. They rely on it. Plan on it. Then suddenly—boom! Somebody does something unexpected and all the roses you are sniffing turn to dogshit."

"Amen to that, brother."

Dr. Aram likes the unexpected religious reference. "Now you are blaming God for your misfortunes? I thought everything was Howie Dornick's fault?"

Aitchbone's head begins to bob. "Oh, it is."

"Not even a little bit your fault?"

D. William Aitchbone calms instantly. His fingers stop drumming. His eyelids stop blinking. He smiles. It is not a maniacal smile, but a sheepish smile. "Of course it's my fault. Why would I come to you if it wasn't? You charge more than I do for christsakes."

Once again Dr. Pirooz Aram is as astonished as Xerxes. "So, already you and I are making progress."

Aitchbone folds his hands under his nose. "I've miscalculated somewhere along the line, that's for sure."

Dr. Aram erupts. "Miscalculated? I am a psychiatrist not a professor of mathematics! You want me to figure out where you miscalculated? That is why you come to me? Not to repent? Not for self-realization? Not for transcendence? Not to get your head on straight? You are a *keer-*

khar all right, Mr. D. William Aitchbone. A very big one. And I'm not talking cheese."

Aitchbone checks his watch. "I thought maybe you could prescribe some pills."

Now it is Dr. Pirooz Aram who staggers to the window and wraps his head in the expensive drapery. "Pills? All you Americans ever want are goddamn pills!"

D. William Aitchbone reaches for his checkbook. "How many sessions do you think this will take? Three? Four? Squaw Days is in five weeks. If I'm not on top of my game by then, I'm toast politically."

When the Greeks sank the Persian fleet at Salamis, Xerxes impetuously had his own officers beheaded. It was a big mistake, a mistake that prevented Persia from civilizing the world, as God had intended. Instead that honor went to the Greeks, and then to successive empires of barbaric Europeans: To the Romans. To the Christian Crusaders. To the English. To the French. To the Spaniards. To the Americans. So Dr. Pirooz Aram knows that if he is to civilize the civilizers, he must not be impetuous like Xerxes was. He is, as the *keer-khar* has pointed out, a professional. So, while he wants to throw the *keer-khar* out on his donkey ears, he pulls his head from the drapes and playfully musses the *keer-khar's* hair. "Perhaps a lawyer like yourself can undo somebody's mistakes in three or four sessions, but your mistakes are not legal mistakes, my friend. They are mistakes of the soul. Who knows? Squaw Days might come and go a half-dozen times before that terrible soul of yours is mended. In the meantime I will prescribe some pills for you, as you wish."

D. William Aitchbone is relieved. "Thank you."

The doctor scribbles on his pad. "I must confess that I have heard a great deal about this Serendipity Green® house. From Katherine and others. And most of what I have heard has been wonderful! It has awakened and transformed so many people! Unfortunately it has not awakened and transformed you. Apparently Serendipity Green® is not an equal opportunity transformer, eh? So, these pills I prescribe are not for you, Mr. D. William Aitchbone, they are for your enemies. You swallow the pills, and they will feel better."

"Whatever floats your boat."

Dr. Pirooz Aram hands him the prescription and walks him out. "Did you know that the word *serendipity* is from a very old Persian fairy tale, The Three Princes of Serendip?"

"No, I didn't."

"You know it now."

26

It is August. For the first time in thirty years the Cleveland Indians have a chance of winning their division. If they do win it—and the Chicago White Sox are fading fast—they will go on to the playoffs, where they will try to beat the Boston Red Sox and then the New York Yankees. And if they beat the Red Sox and the Yankees, they will go on to the World Series and try to beat the Atlanta Braves.

It is the dream season Cleveland's Real Indians have been waiting for. Each round of the playoffs gives CRI a chance to parade before *national* television cameras to demand that Chief Wahoo be dropped as the baseball Indians' mascot. And if it is Cleveland and the Atlanta Braves in the World Series! Well, what an opportunity to make white America feel ashamed that will be! But the CRI's president, Ernest Not Irish, is strangely blasé about this opportunity. He has put all matters concerning baseball into the capable hands of Angel Guerra Smith, a no-nonsense Apache woman whose great-grandfather once hid out with Geronimo in the Sierra Madres.

Yes, despite the baseball Indians' rare winning season, despite the rare opportunities for national exposure it offers, Ernest Not Irish is instead focusing like a flashlight on Squaw Days.

On the morning of the Squaw Day parade and Re-Enactment, Ernest Not Irish takes the .22 revolver he bought from the Slovenian who owns Paddy's 25th Street Pub, and heads for Tuttwyler. As he drives his blue-fendered white Pontiac south on Interstate 71, he thinks of the two old shibboleths that so perfectly sum up Native American History since Christopher Columbus stumbled ashore with his greed, muskets, Bibles, and diseases:

"The only good Indian is a dead Indian."
"It is a good day to die."

The first is a white man's shibboleth. The second an Indian shibboleth. It has always amazed him how well the symbiotic relationship between these two shibboleths have served the cause of White American History.

The farther south he drives, the heavier the traffic gets. Apparently lots of people are going to Tuttwyler today, the twin attractions of Howie Dornick's Serendipity Green® house and Princess Pogawedka rising from stumps making a visit irresistible. Won't they be surprised by the third attraction Ernest Not Irish has in store for them.

It will be a hot day. D. William Aitchbone showers and gives his armpits a double rub of Right Guard. He has orange juice and a tablet of Solhzac for breakfast. He polishes his shoes and trims the wiry middle-aged hairs erupting from his nostrils and ears. He tears his best blue suit out of the dry cleaning bag and makes sure to remove all the tags. He puts on the Serendipity Green® tie he forced himself to buy at the mall. Surely the VP will be wearing one. Donald Grinspoon, too, probably.

D. William Aitchbone knows today will be the worst day of his life. But he will look his best. Doesn't a good solider always makes sure every button of his tunic is buttoned before he faces the firing squad? Yessireebob he does.

Ernest Not Irish realizes too late that he should have started for Tuttwyler earlier. He is forced to park at the Wal-mart on West Wooseman and take a shuttle bus to the village square. Apparently the bus has just been painted Serendipity Green® and the fumes of not-quite-dry enamel are making him woozy. Also it is not easy to sit on a bus seat with a .22 revolver in your pants.

Katherine Hardihood has not left the house yet and Rhubarb has pissed the curio cabinet already. His mistress' nervous rushing about has made him nervous. And so to put a little order and certainty into his always vulnerable, low-to-the-floor life, he backed up to the curio cabinet and let it squirt. And now Katherine, dressed in her pioneer woman bonnet and dress, has to get out the Pine Sol and scrub like a pioneer woman.

Before leaving for the old Tuttwyler Mills snake cake plant, where the parade units are assembling, she snaps Rhubarb into his clothesline leash and stakes him in the backyard. "Don't kill any squirrels," she tells him. Rhubarb rushes to the porch to make sure that the food and water bowls are full. Relieved, he heads for the rhubarb and curls up for the exhausting day ahead.

The shuttle bus stops in front of the Daydream Beanery. Ernest Not Irish shuffles off. The sidewalks are packed with people, all white and most of them overweight. Many of them are wearing something Serendipity Green®, tee shirts or baseball caps, walking shorts or socks. Though the crowd is huge, he can see the Serendipity Green® gazebo. It looks less impressive than it did in the Bison-Prickert commercial he saw during the NBA finals.

The parade will be starting soon. But he is not much interested in the parade. It is tonight's Re-Enactment of Princess Pogawedka rising through the stumps that has his Cherokee heart bumping. Still the parade offers him an opportunity to make as many whites as he can feel uncomfortable. So he squeezes through the crowd until he reaches the Pizza Teepee and stands next to the wooden Indian with the pepperoni pizza in its hand. He waits for people to notice him, to be struck by the irony of seeing a real Indian standing next to a wooden Indian, to be so guilt-ridden they won't ever attend another Indians game, or even watch one on TV.

D. William Aitchbone arrives at the snack cake plant just as the Vice President's helicopter is setting down. He was right about the Serendipity Green® neckties. Donald Grinspoon has one on. So does Mayor Woodrow Wilson Sadlebyrne. So does that old sonofabitch congressman Buddy Bowfin, and his worthless son, county commissioner Buddy Bowfin Jr., and that over-sexed banshee Victoria Bonobo, and so does the Vice President.

"Hello, Tuttwyler!" the VP sings out in his trademark Texan as he trots down the helicopter steps and then rushes forward to glad-hand the locals, his legs and back bent so the big bird's still-spinning blades won't slice the top off his huge Texas head. If the VP is worried about impeachment, he isn't showing it.

Howie Dornick is watching from the window when the Gangrene Velveeta pulls in his driveway. It seems that Hugh Harbinger has brought somebody with him. He watches Hugh get out, wearing a Serendipity Green® tuxedo—the fancy kind with tails—and a Serendipity Green® top hat. Now the somebody gets out. He has unruly white hair and an unruly white heard. He is wearing a Serendipity Green® beret.

Howie Dornick watches Hugh Harbinger and the someone as they stand in the yard and grin up at the house. Finally they climb up on the porch. He opens the door for them. "Howie," says Hugh Harbinger, "this is Dr. Pirooz Aram, my psychiatrist."

"You don't mind that I have tagged along?" this Dr. Pirooz Aram asks.

"The more the merrier," says Howie Dornick.

All three of them now hurry into the Gangrene Velveeta and with Howie Dornick giving directions, hurry toward the old snack cake plant. "I have heard so much about you, Howie," Dr. Pirooz Aram says. "How is it again that your father had only one foot?"

Katherine Hardihood takes her place on Princess Pogawedka's float, next to the pair of ceramic lawn deer. She is relieved when she sees Howie Dornick crawl from the back seat of a boxy Serendipity Green® station wagon. She also is disappointed. Her man has not worn the pair of Serendipity Green® overalls the people at Oshkosh B'gosh sent him. He is wearing his navy blue dress pants and of all things a pink polo shirt. She watches as he and Hugh and somebody with a Serendipity Green® beret climb into the Serendipity Green® Mustang convertible provided by Bill Blazek Ford.

The first parade unit to reach the square is a black sheriff's car. Its blue lights are blinking. Its siren is blaring. The crowd applauds. The deputy driving the car waves like he's the queen of England.

The next parade unit is the VFW color guard. Two of the veterans carry a long canvas sign between them. ARTIE BROWN POST, the sign reads. The crowd applauds.

Next comes the school bus fitted with a hydraulic lift for handicapped students. A long sign on the side reads: SCHOOL STARTS IN 16 DAYS. The adults in the crowd cheer. The kids in the crowd jeer. Then everyone laughs as if they are extras in an old movie directed by Frank Capra. Behind the bus are the unicyclists in their chipmunk suits.

Next come clumps of Cub Scouts and Brownies and clumps of 4-H kids, some of them pulling goats, some carrying chickens and rabbits, some just waving and waving. Every clump gets a heartfelt round of applause.

The next parade unit is the Serendipity Green® Mustang carrying the famous Howie Dornick and the famous Hugh Harbinger and some man in a Serendipity Green® beret. A boom box blares Kermit the Frog's "It's Not Easy Being Green." The crowd sings along.

Next comes Darren Frost in his cupcake costume. The handle of the plywood butcher's knife sticking from the cupcake's back is painted Serendipity Green®. The crowd applauds defiantly.

Now there is the *clicky-clacky-click* of drumsticks on metal and the *threet-threet-threet* of a drum major's whistle The Marching Wildcat Band of West Wyssock High kicks into "Louie-Louie." *Bomp-bomp-bomp. Bomp-bomp. Bomp-bomp. Bomp-bomp. Bomp-bomp-bomp.* The band does have one surprise this year, however, Their old red and gold uniforms have been replaced by new Serendipity Green® uniforms. The band director, dressed like Davy Crockett, urges the crowd to sing along: *"Lou-eeeea, Loooo-i, Ohhhh no! I godda go."*

Many more parade units pass by: Boy Scouts and Girl Scouts. Clowns. Little League baseball teams dangling their legs over flatbed trucks. Former Mayor Donald Grinspoon, wearing his scarf and goggles, waving from his oil-farting old Harley. Waving sheriff's deputies on prancing appaloosas. The Senior Squares square-dancing club do-si-doing through the horse biscuits.

Ernest Not Irish's eyes are watching the parade, his mind on tonight's Re-Enactment. He is going to give these white fools a Squaw Days to remember. Tonight when that white woman with the stained butterscotch pudding skin rises above the stumps, a real Indian will rise with her. This real Indian will rip the wig off the fake Indian's head and shake it at the crowd. This real Indian will pull a .22 revolver from his pants. Then this real Indian will say this: "Like to worship dead Indians, do you? Worship this, you unreasonable white bastards!" Then the real Indian will put the .22 to his real Indian temple and put a real bullet through his real Indian brains.

Now there is the familiar *DOOM-doom-doom-doom* of Indian drums. The enthusiastic crowd grows ecstatic. Everybody stretches their neck to see. A cheer rattles up the street. Then there she is, Princess Pogawedka, standing high on the back of a farm trailer, pulled along by a huge Serendipity Green® tractor. This year little Kapusta is nestled in a Serendipity Green® backpack.

Then: *Booooooo!* Here comes John and Amos Tuttwyler with their papier-mâché clubs and fistfuls of candy for the kids.

Were this any other Squaw Days, the next parade unit would be The West Wyssock Junior High School Band, wearing their construction paper feathers, squeaking and honking their way through "America the Beautiful." But this is not any other Squaw Days. This year the Vice President has come.

Katherine Hardihood holds onto the neck of a ceramic deer so she doesn't fall off the bouncing trailer. She does not feel as ashamed as she usually does. She knows this will be the last year for this nonsense. Sometime this fall she is gong to call a press conference and tell the truth about Princess Pogawedka. It won't be pleasant. Her friends and neighbors will hate her and shun her and more than likely force the library board to fire her. Certainly Bill Aitchbone will enact some cruel revenge on her. But, Jiminy Cricket, facts are facts, and the truth is the truth. And isn't that what really counts?

Given the VP's troubles over Montezuma's Revenge, he is welcomed with an even bigger *Boooooooooooo!* than the Tuttwyler brothers.

The VP is riding atop the village's new Serendipity Green® pumper, the one the Bison-Prickert Paint Company bribed the village council with. He is not alone up there. Mayor Woodrow Wilson Sadlebyrne is on his left and Council President D. William Aitchbone is on his right. Councilwoman Victoria Bonobo is just behind him, as are the two Buddy Bowfins. Assistant Fire Chief Dick Mueller is driving the pumper. Like his passengers, he is smiling and waving and wearing a Serendipity Green® tie. Secret Service men are squishing right through those horse biscuits the Senior Squares so artfully do-si-doed around.

D. William Aitchbone listens to the boos and knows they are the howling winds of his own political demise. He wants to reach back and push Victoria Bonobo off the pumper. He wants to see the wide tires of this great machine smash her like a cockroach under the heels of a flamingo dancer. "They're booing me," he says to the VP, "not you. They love you, sir. Absolutely love you."

Ernest Not Irish is still thinking about how he will jump through the smoking stumps when he spots D. William Aitchbone atop the Serendipity Green® pumper. He remembers how this white devil humiliated him the night he came to be reasonable.

Those two old shibboleths he has dwelt on—*The only good Indian is a dead Indian* and *It is a good day to die*—are suddenly replaced by the words of Little Crow, chief of Mdewkanton Sioux. Little Crow had angered the young warriors of his tribe by signing a treaty. These warriors did not want to live peaceably with the whites. They wanted to go to war against the whites and in the dead of night they came to confront Little Crow in his bed, to demand war. They called him a coward. But Little Crow told them he was not a coward and said to them: "You are like dogs in the Hot Moon when they run mad and snap at their own shadows." Recalling these words Ernest Not Irish realizes that he is behaving like a dog in the Hot Moon. Little Crow had counseled against war with the whites because there were so many whites. War against the whites would be suicidal, he said. "You will die like the rabbits when the hungry wolves hunt them in the Hard Moon of January," he said.

But the Mdewkanton warriors would not listen. They went to war and died like rabbits. Ernest Not Irish realizes that enough Indians have died like rabbits. He realizes that it is not such a good day to die after all. At least not for him to die. So he pulls the .22 revolver from his pants and he lays his arm across the wooden Indian's wooden pizza and he takes aim at D. William Aitchbone, who is just now passing by. Just as he squeezes the trigger a white woman wearing a construction paper headdress bumps into him with her big wad of Serendipity Green® cotton candy. The bullet meant for D. William Aitchbone goes astray. In desperation Ernest Not Irish fires every bullet in his gun. *Pop pop pop pop pop.*

Trying to jump off the pumper, D. William Aitchbone has knocked the VP on his Texas ass. So a bullet that surely would have gone through the VP's Texas head, instead has buried itself in Aitchbone's Ohio elbow. One bullet has sailed all the way to the gazebo, ricocheted off the copper roof, and harmlessly burrowed itself into the big bubbling crock of sloppy joe mix in the Knights of Columbus food tent. One bullet has harmlessly struck the square's only remaining box elder tree. One bullet has killed one of the giraffes in Paula Varney's window. One bullet has shattered one of the ceramic deer on Princess Pogawedka's float. One bullet has found its way into Katherine Hardihood.

Darren Frost had big plans for this Squaw Days. Hidden in his cupcake costume were three pipe bombs. He made them in his converted coal bin with instructions he found on the Internet. Tonight he planned to place them at equal intervals around the library and right when Princess Pogawedka was rising above the stumps, they were going to explode and accomplish for America what the big-talking Reverend Raymond R. Biscobee had not accomplished.

But now there have been gunshots. There is panic everywhere. And blood is running out of Katherine Hardihood's chest. So Darren Frost's big plans will have to wait. Someone has beaten him to the punch.

27

"Don't be surprised if she dies," the Reverend Raymond R. Biscobee says to Howie Dornick. "God is good and angry at Tuttwyler."

It is the Reverend Raymond R. Biscobee's first visit to the hospital. It is Howie Dornick's tenth. One visit a day since Ernest Not Irish attacked the Squaw Days parade. Visits that last from six-thirty in the morning to nine-thirty at night.

"The nurses say she's doing as good as can be expected," Howie answers. They are not in Katherine Hardihood's room with the tangling tubes and the quiet smells and the eyes that don't open and the *beep beep beeps*. They are in the visitor's lounge just down the hall, watching the blue and yellow tropical fish in the huge wall tank. The lounge walls are painted Serendipity Green®.

As the Reverend Raymond R. Biscobee searches his Bible for an appropriate verse, a great pot of vulva-pink calla lilies enters the lounge, in the arms of Wyssock County Library Director Venus Willendorf. She leans over her flowers, and her ostrich-egg breasts, and kisses Howie on the cheek. She tries to kiss Ray Biscobee's cheek, too, but he shrivels and flees, mentioning other patients he needs to see. "He is such a dung beetle, isn't he?" Venus Willendorf hisses before she laughs.

Venus stays just ten minutes. She is followed by Delores Poltruski who stays a half hour. Karen Brown Aitchbone stays an hour—she and Howie are brother and sister, after all—and Woody Sadlebyrne stays a half hour, assuring Howie he can miss as much work as he wants.

Yes, people come to see how Katherine Hardihood is faring, but mostly it is just Howie and the television set, Howie and the old magazines, Howie and the Mr. Coffee with its half-inch of stale brew, Howie and the stack of Styrofoam cups.

Then at seven a flamingo-pink beret wobbles into the visitor's room like an errant Frisbee. The man beneath the beret is Dr. Pirooz Aram. "Howie Dornick! How are you?"

The old Persian dances to the Mr. Coffee and turns it off. "I hope you have not been drinking this slop."

"Most of it."

"And you are still alive?"

Howie Dornick begins to cry.

Dr. Aram takes him in his arms, and unlike American-born men, who can only give another man a few quick stiff pats on the back, he squeezes him and holds him close, until their hearts are *thu-bumping* in unison. "You have not eaten yet, have you?"

The answer is no. And so Dr. Pirooz Aram takes him down the elevator to the cafeteria. "Madam," he says to the woman behind the stainless steel counter with a hair net on her head and plastic bags on her hands, "don't you have any fish or fresh vegetables? No rice? Only these poor mashed potatoes? And what is this meat supposed to be?"

They both get the tuna and noodles. Take their trays to the table by the plastic flower garden. The flowers are dusty.

When the tuna and noodles are finished, the old Persian dances to the dessert shelf and returns with a single walnut brownie. He cut it precisely down the middle with a plastic knife. "It is not because I'm a cheap sonofabitch that I've bought only one brownie. Small amounts of things are more enjoyable than large amounts of things. This is something Americans haven't learned yet."

Then he says this: "I know that you are filled with questions, Howie. What was that crazy Indian thinking? What was God thinking? Is your sweet Katherine going to live or is she going to die? I don't have a single answer for you. But I do want you to listen to me—not pretend to listen, but really listen! If Katherine lives you will be very happy and very grateful. But if she dies, Howie, you must also feel happy and grateful. And why is that? Because once upon a time you and this wonderful woman achieved the most wonderful thing two people can achieve—you achieved *vasal!* I know you do not know this word, Howie. It is a word given immortality by the great Sufi poets, Hafez and Rumi and others. It means to consummate your love, both

263

sexually and spiritually, to succeed in unity. The only thing more beautiful than achieving *vasal* with a lover is achieving *vasal* with God. Melting back into God when you die. Fruition. That is what *vasal* means.

"And so, Howie, if Katherine dies it will be okay for you to be sad for a while. Okay for you to hate God and that crazy Indian for a while. It will be okay for you to miss Katherine forever. But while you are missing her, you must remember that you were awakened and transformed by this woman. Remember that Katherine has melted back into God, where both she and God are awaiting your fruition. Your melting. So you see! You are a lucky bastard no matter which way it goes. I'm not boool-shitting you, Howie. Did you hear anything I said?"

Howie Dornick nods.

"Good. Now eat your half of the brownie before I do."

28

Green.

Yellow.

Red.

The cars on South Mill stop. The cars on Tocqueville go.

Howie Dornick, the leash in his left hand attached to Matisse, crosses the street and heads into the cemetery. Katherine Hardihood is right behind him, pulling Rhubarb along on his clothesline. "Jiminy Cricket cat," she huffs, "how hard is it to put one paw in front of the other?" Above the black treetops they can see the Ferris wheel's blurry lights. It is the big Ferris wheel. D. William Aitchbone finally has found someone with the grit to demand the big Ferris wheel.

As they meander through the gravestones they begin to hear the *DOOM-doom-doom-doom* of Indian drums. The Re-Enactment is beginning.

It has been some year.

A month after Katherine was released from the hospital, she and Howie drove to the state penitentiary at Lucasville, to tell Ernest Not Irish the truth about Pogawedka and Kapusta. He was just finishing the first week of his eight-year sentence. "Now you tell me," he said.

Then Katherine sent out notices for a press conference. Only two reporters showed up, Sam Guss of the *Gazette* and Weezie Wetzel, Wyssock County correspondent for the Wooster paper. Despite all the empty chairs in the library community room, Katherine went right ahead and told the truth: The woman and baby clubbed to death by the Tuttwyler brothers were not Indians, but white; the baby was fathered by Seth Aitchbone, who shot himself in the head when he could mourn no longer; all the proof anyone would need was waiting under Seth's gravestone in the village cemetery; Pogawedka means nonsense in Polish; Kapusta means cabbage; it is a good thing to celebrate the past, but only if the past really happened. Finally, she apologized to the village for participating in such a fraud and resigned from the Squaw Days Committee.

Sam Guss and Weezie Wetzel reported everything Katherine Hardihood said. And it changed nothing.

"Who cares what really happened," D. William Aitchbone told the two reporters at a press conference of his own. "What's important is that we honor our ancestors, and have a good time."

And so a year has passed. And it is time for Squaw Days again. It's a perfect August night. The worst heat of summer has passed and the nights already feel like autumn. Matisse and Rhubarb are enjoying the walk. Enjoying each other's company. Both are happily pissing every stationary object they can find, tree trunks and bushes and park benches. They would be pissing the gravestones if Howie and Katherine would let them.

Howie Dornick has grown very fond of Matisse. Wishes he could keep him forever. But any day now Hugh Harbinger will come to claim him. Hugh is in Peru, with Zee Levant, high in the Andes, in the little village of Iqicucho, studying the brown faces of the descendants of the great Incan emperor Pachacuti. Hugh's letters continue to be void of any depression. He says when he gets back he will make every human on earth want the fabulous brown skin of the truckstop waitress María Vilca Quechua Ayavilli. He says he is thinking of a line of skin dyes. Meanwhile Matisse is staying at Howie Dornick's Serendipity Green® house on South Mill, the last house on South Mill still painted that god-awful color.

Howie Dornick and Katherine Hardihood leave the cemetery and walk past the Catholic Church, which has been minus one member since Delores Poltruski moved to Indiana with Dick Mueller. The marriage of Dick and Delores came quite unexpectedly during jury selection for Ernest Not Irish's trial. With Delores's help, Dick was able to sell his auto parts store, his house, and all of his rental properties in less than a month. The town they've moved to did not have an auto parts store. According to Delores's letter to Katherine, the town has a wonderful festival celebrating the seven-and-a-quarter-inch left thumb of Ruby Courgette. It seems that Ruby, normal in every other way, had this gargantuan left thumb. The biggest thumb on record, not only in Ohio but the entire United States. Two years after she died at age ninety-three, the town starting holding Thumb Day. Howie Dornick thinks Delores is just pulling Katherine's leg about this festival. Someday they're going to drive over to that town in Indiana and see if Thumb Day is for real.

There have been so many changes this past year. Paula Varney closed her Just Giraffes shop right after Christmas, marking every stuffed giraffe down sixty percent. But the storefront didn't stay empty for long. In April, Candyce Zarnik opened EEK, A MOUSE!, a shop selling nothing but mouse bric-a-brac: stuffed mice and ceramic mice and books about mice and mice plates and mice paintings and expensive denim blouses with mice embroidered on the pockets. Howie Dornick actually went in there once and bought a rubber squeak-toy mouse for Rhubarb. Matisse ate it.

They walk down the west side of Tocqueville and start up South Mill. All of the impressive Victorians and Greek Revivals are painted soapy white again. The fervid repainting began shortly after Oprah Whinfrey did a show with the famous color designer Koko. The Serendipity Green® craze is over, Oprah proclaimed. Now everything is white white white. White clothes. White shoes. White fingernails and white lips and white cars and white sheets and white houses. But, as Koko pointed out, and Oprah agreed, this new world of whiteness does not mean a bland and colorless world. Koko has, after all, designed seventy-seven shades of white, each named after a different virtuous woman. Howie Dornick finds the current white craze a hoot. He knows that any day now Hugh Harbinger will be back from Peru and before long the world will be brown brown brown.

They let Matisse and Rhubarb piss the hedge in front of Donald Grinspoon's impressive gothic. The house is for sale. Just ten weeks ago Donald Grinspoon took a rope with him to the empty snack cake plant. It was his protégé D. William Aitchbone who found him dangling over the rusting cupcake wrapping machine, suicide note safety-pinned to his sweater. Now Donald is in the cemetery with his Penelope, the date of his death freshly chiseled on the stone. Donald loved Penelope more than anything, and except for his necessary tryst with the wife of the Weideman Boot Company president, he was as loyal and as faithful as any man ever was. He was the salt of the earth, that's what Donald Grinspoon was.

Matisse and Rhubarb also want to piss the ornamental fence in front of D. William Aitchbone's impressive Queen Anne. The house is as soapy white as it ever was. Say what you will about Bill Aitchbone, he was never one to succumb to fashion. Yes, he had a rough row to hoe there for a while—all that business with Victoria Bonobo, Karen leaving with the kids, smashing into the gazebo—but with the help of Dr. Pirooz Aram, he's on top of his game again. Karen and the kids are back home where they belong. And he's about to be elected mayor of Tuttwyler. He's the only candidate on the ballot. Woodrow Wilson Sadlebyrne went off to live with Victoria Bonobo in Washington after the Vice President rewarded her with a job at the Department of the Interior.

D. William Aitchbone also could be in Washington if he wanted. After he took that bullet in the elbow for the Vice President he could have gone to work in any cabinet depart-ment he wanted. The attempted assassination created such sympathy for the VP that the Justice Department's report implicating him in Revenge-gate went unnoticed by both the public and the press. But D. William Aitchbone wants to be mayor for a term or two, and then a member of Congress when old Buddy Bowfin steps down. He'll be a shoe-in. His only potential rival is county commissioner Buddy Bowfin Jr. And did Buddy Bowfin Jr. take a bullet in the elbow for the Vice President of the United States? He did not.

Howie Dornick and Katherine Hardihood reach the square. Even though the food tents and craft booths are still open, the square is empty. Everyone is at the Re-Enactment. The gazebo looks nice now that it's been re-painted white. Just the other day the *Cleveland Plain Dealer* published a big story on the bath Bison-Prickert took on all that leftover Serendipity Green® paint. Myron Bison III told the paper that while the company's debt is wrecking havoc with its stock values, the relocation of its production facility to Matamoros, Mexico will return it to profitability by the third quarter. Helping, said Myron Bison III, will be its new line of white paints, an amazing seventy-seven shades offered in both latex and rust-resistant enamel.

Howie Dornick makes sure they skirt the gazebo—he did the repainting and he'll be damned if Matisse and Rhubarb are going to piss it. They head toward the library.

Katherine Hardihood had worked at the library for so many years. Helped make so many just-average kids smarter. So many smart kids smarter yet. Steered so many people toward the truth. Found them the facts they wanted and needed. But the drug test for employees pushed through by D. William Aitchbone was the last straw. She resigned and as soon as she and Howie were back from their honeymoon in the Poconos, she opened a little bookstore on the square, filling the window with every book EDIT didn't like.

Megan Burroughs is head librarian at the Tuttwyler branch now. And right now Megan's amplified voice is echoing across the village as she reads to the crowd about John and Amos Tuttwyler who, while hunting for a spot on Three Fish Creek to build their grist mill, happened across the Indian squaw Pogawedka, and perhaps thinking they were in danger of being attacked by other noble savages hiding in the trees, clubbed her and her baby to death. For many years Katherine Hardihood read this crap.

When Megan Burroughs finishes reading, The Marching Wildcat Band of West Wyssock High begins its peppy marshal version of Pachebel's "Canon in D major."

They pull Matisse and Rhubarb across the street and into the black lawn surrounding the library.

Howie Dornick could never admit this to his woman, of course, but he finds the noise of the Re-Enactment comforting. It's another sign that things are finally getting back to normal. The royalty checks have stopped coming and the Serendipity Green® paint on his clapboards is beginning to chip and fade. It has been months since daytrippers left cookies on his porch and reporters from foreign lands banged on his door.

Best of all, people are ignoring him again. Oh sure, sometimes someone waves when he's mowing the cemetery grass or cleaning out a storm sewer, and sometimes when he's shopping for food or buying socks at Kmart someone will ask, "How's it going?" But by and large things are getting back to where they were. He's nobody again. He gets up and goes to work and comes home and watches TV. At night he and Katherine walk Matisse and Rhubarb. Sometimes on a Saturday or a Sunday they drive to Hinckley Lake and watch the ducks swim in circles in the shallow bay by the boathouse. Every month or so they drive over to Wooster to see how the Bittinger boy is coming along with his new business ventures. The espresso bar and gift shop aren't doing so well, but the gourmet grocery is a big success and the Bittinger boy is talking about opening one in Tuttwyler. He's got his eyes on the empty auto parts store.

So Howie Dornick happily pulls Matisse along on his leash and Katherine Hardihood happily pulls Rhubarb along on his clothesline.

There is a dark shape moving along the back wall of the library. It is a strange dark shape. It is wide and round and flat on top. And it has two legs and two arms. And those arms are carrying something. During the festival teenagers are always lurking in the shadows, necking and smoking cigarettes, but this is a strange shape and Howie and Katherine are more than a little curious.

They advance, quietly, until they reach the azalea bushes by the rock garden. Matisse and Rhubarb want to piss the bushes, so they stop and let them. They can see the dark shape more clearly now. It is a large cupcake. Which, of course, means it is Darren Frost, the village expert on pornography. They watch as Darren Frost carefully places one of the things in his arms against the wall. It is a long and cylindrical thing. It's a pipe bomb, that's what it is. Darren Frost intends to blow up the library.

They watch as Darren Frost disappears around the corner. Matisse and Rhubarb are finished pissing and so they follow. They stop by the bomb he has already planted. They listen to it ticking. They slip to the end of the building and look around the corner. Darren Frost is hiding another bomb, this one between the Rhododendrons planted two Arbor Days ago by Jamie Vanderpike's kindergarten class.

Howie Dornick and Katherine Hardihood are not happy about this bomb thing. They frown at each other and search each other's eyes. Of course they should stop Darren Frost from doing this. Howie could tackle that cupcake and punch and kick it until the idiot inside tells him how to stop those pipes from ticking. Katherine could yell and scream and maybe throw a rock through a window so the burglar alarm goes off.

These are the things they could do. These are the things they should do. Right this second they should do these things. But they know what happens to people who stop idiots from blowing off bombs. They become the same thing soldiers who save Seabees become. They become heroes. And heroes become public property, like storm sewers and parking meters and rumors. Heroes are forced to ride on floats in parades. Their eyes agree that they do not want to be heroes.

But sneaking away is a cowardly thing. Artie Brown not only remained on the bank of the Matanikau shooting and shooting at those advancing Japanese, he advanced on them, driving that Seabee bulldozer right onto that flimsy bridge.

So it comes to this: Do they sneak forward and become heroes? Or do they sneak away and become cowards?

Finding Darren Frost hiding his pipe bombs is anything but serendipitous.

Why doesn't Matisse bark? Why doesn't Rhubarb yowl? Let them be the heroes.

The Marching Wildcat Band of West Wyssock High is playing "Turkey in the Straw" and in just a minute the Singing Doves will begin their medley of "My Country 'Tis of Thee," "She'll Be Coming Around the Mountain," the famous Shaker hymn "Tis The Gift to Be Simple," and Canned Heat's "Going Up the Country." And then there will be an explosion of fake fire and smoke and Princess Pogawedka will rise above the stumps. Some in the crowd will gasp. Others will applaud and cheer. Howie Dornick and Katherine Hardihood know that any second now they will have to decide. Let it happen or stop it from happening. Their eyes weigh the pros and cons. Their eyes test each other's conscience. Each other's soul. Either they will have to sneak forward or sneak away.

Then Katherine Hardihood whispers: "Jiminy Cricket, Howard."

And so Howie Dornick lets go of Matisse's leash and sneaks forward on all-fours, toward the huge cupcake fiddling with a bomb by the library wall.

And when he has the cupcake firmly by the ankles, and the cupcake is swearing and flopping, Katherine Hardihood starts yelling "Fire-fire-fire!"